Praise for VENGEANCE

'As with the previous books, this one is replete with all the period detail and atmospherics one could hope for in a thriller. Black is a master of presentation. The nudges and the winks, the red herrings and the wool-pullings are all consummately done. The gears of the plot mesh silently and inexorably and the whole machine moves forward to its disastrous outcome. On the way to its terminus, the book becomes more and more Banvillean and it is all the better for that . . . But Black's and Quirke's Dublin remains the gritty and deplorable place it has always been and *Vengeance* is a memorable and compelling snapshot'   *Independent*, Ireland

'This is the fifth in John Banville's magically evocative and dark mystery series set in Fifties Dublin and it's the best yet'
Daily Mail

'Superb . . . a pleasure to read'   *Irish Times*

'It's beautifully written and a scrupulously characterised portrait of mid-twentieth-century Dublin'   *Literary Review*

'There are very few writers who can write elegantly about murder, but there is no question that Benjamin Black is one of them'   *Washington Times*

Vengeance

Benjamin Black is the pen name of acclaimed author John Banville, who was born in Wexford, Ireland, in 1945. His novels have won numerous awards, including the Man Booker Prize in 2005 for *The Sea*. He lives in Dublin. *Vengeance* is the fifth book in Benjamin Black's celebrated Quirke series, which is being adapted for the BBC and will star Gabriel Byrne.

ALSO BY BENJAMIN BLACK

Quirke Mysteries

Christine Falls

The Silver Swan

Elegy for April

A Death in Summer

The Lemur

BENJAMIN BLACK

VENGEANCE

A Quirke Mystery

PICADOR

First published 2012 by Mantle

This edition published 2013 by Picador
an imprint of Pan Macmillan, a division of Macmillan Publishers Limited
Pan Macmillan, 20 New Wharf Road, London N1 9RR
Basingstoke and Oxford
Associated companies throughout the world
www.panmacmillan.com

ISBN 978-1-447-26401-9

1 3 5 7 9 8 6 4 2

A CIP catalogue record for this book is available from the British Library.

Typeset by SetSystems Ltd, Saffron Walden, Essex
Printed and bound by CPI Group (UK) Ltd, Croydon, CR0 4YY

I

1

Davy Clancy was not a good sailor, in fact he was secretly afraid of the sea, yet here he was, on this fine summer morning, about to set out on it in a boat that looked to him like a large and complicated toy. It was, they all said, a perfect day to be on the water. They did not say it was a perfect day to be in a boat, or to be out sailing. No: *a perfect day to be on the water*, as if it was their motto or something. And they were all so jolly and brisk, smiling in a smug, self-satisfied way that set his teeth on edge. Unlike him, they knew what they were doing, the wind-burned men in yachting caps and khaki shorts and shapeless jumpers playing at being old sea-dogs, and their loud-voiced, leathery wives—sea-bitches, he thought, with a twinge of bleak amusement. He did not belong here, among these sailing folk with their lazy expertise; he knew it, and they knew it, too, which meant they had to behave twice as heartily towards him, though he could see that look in their eyes, that gleam of merry contempt.

It was June, and although it had rained every day the first week of the holiday, this morning was sunny and warm with not a breath of wind. The tide was high, and the water in the bay had a sluggish, swollen look, the surface oily with streaks of sapphire and pink and petrol-blue. He tried not to think of what was below the surface, of the murk down there, the big-eyed fish nosing along, and things with claws scuttling around on the bottom, fighting in slow motion, devouring each other. Victor Delahaye had brought the jeep round to the front of the house that morning and they had rattled the ten miles over the mountain road to Slievemore Bay in silence. Going for a sail was the last thing Davy wanted to do, but it had not been possible to refuse. 'You can crew for me,' Delahaye had said the night before, in Sweeney's bar, and everyone had laughed, for some reason, everyone except Delahaye himself, and Delahaye's wife, who had looked at Davy narrow-eyed with that smile of hers and said nothing. And so here he was, about to venture out against his will on this frighteningly calm and innocent-seeming sea.

The Clancys and the Delahayes had been close for as long as anyone could remember. Samuel Delahaye and Philip Clancy had gone into partnership together at the turn of the century, running coalboats from Wales; later Samuel Delahaye had spotted the potential of the motorcar and the partners had opened one of the first big garages in the country, hiring in mechanics from England, France, Italy. The business had flourished. Although the founders were supposedly in equal partnership, everyone knew from the start that Samuel Delahaye was the boss and Phil Clancy merely his manager. Phil—poor Phil, as people were inclined to say—was not of an assertive disposition, and had quietly accepted his inferior role.

Now Samuel's son Victor was in charge of the firm, and Phil Clancy's son Jack was supposedly his partner, but it was still as it had been in the old days, with Delahaye in charge and Clancy his second-in-command. Unlike his father before him, Jack Clancy resented his subordinate position—resented it deeply, though he tried hard, and mostly with success, not to let his dissatisfaction show.

But a Clancy could not say no to a Delahaye, that was understood, which was why Davy Clancy had only smiled and shrugged when in Sweeney's the previous night Victor Delahaye, on the way to getting drunk and with a soiled look in his eye, had leaned over the table and invited him to come out for a sail in the *Quicksilver*. He knew nothing about boats, but everyone had laughed, and someone had clapped him on the shoulder, and what could he do but say, yes, thanks, sure, and bury his nose in his glass? 'Right,' Delahaye had said, smiling tightly and showing his teeth, 'I'll pick you up at nine,' and sauntered back to the bar. And that was when Delahaye's wife had looked over at Davy with that thin-lipped, mocking smile.

The two families spent their holidays together every summer; it was a tradition that went back to Phil and Samuel's time. Davy could not understand why his parents still carried it on. Old Phil was gaga now and in a nursing home, and Samuel Delahaye was in a wheelchair, and although Davy's father and Victor Delahaye kept up the pretence of friendship, it was an open secret how bad relations were between them, while Mona Delahaye, Victor's young wife—his second, the first wife having died—had barely a civil word to throw to Davy's downtrodden mother. Yet every summer the whole gang of them decamped for the month of June to Ashgrove, the Dela-hayes' big stone house halfway up the back slope of Slievemore. The place had ten or twelve bedrooms, more than enough to accommodate Victor Delahaye and his wife and their grown-up twin sons, Jonas and James, as well as Victor's unmarried sister Marguerite—Maggie—and the three Clancys. This year there was an extra guest, Jonas Delahaye's girlfriend, Tanya Somers. Tanya, a student at Trinity College, cut so provocative a figure in her one-piece black bathing suit that the men in the party, except her boyfriend and, of course, Jack Clancy, hardly dared allow themselves to look at her, a thing that added to the tension in an already tense household.

This morning the little harbour was crowded with boats, their owners' voices sounding sharp and clear across the lifeless surface of the sea amid the snap of ropes and the clink of brass fittings. Victor Delahaye was greeted warmly on all sides—he was commodore of Slievemore Sailing Club this season—but he hardly responded. He seemed preoccupied, and the flesh between his heavy black eyebrows was knotted in a fixed frown. Davy supposed he had a hangover. Delahaye wore sandals and tailored white trousers and a sailor's dark-blue cotton shirt, and the rakish blue sailor's cap that he had brought back from a business trip to Greece. He had a tanned, craggy face that wore well its forty-something years. Walking dutifully behind him, Davy felt everyone must know him for the hopeless land-lubber that he was.

The *Quicksilver* was moored at the end of the stone jetty, its sails furled. Seen close up, it did not look at all like a toy, but had the sleekly menacing lines of a giant white swordfish. Delahaye stepped nimbly down to the deck, but Davy hung back. He remembered being told once by a science teacher—Harkins it was, a Christian Brother, the one who had been sent away for interfering with the boys in the junior classes—that you could move a vessel as big as an ocean-going liner with just a push of one hand against the hull. He was supposed to be impressed, but the thought of such a huge thing being susceptible to the force of a boy's hand had filled him with dismay. Delahaye was already unwinding the mooring rope from the bollard. Sure enough, when Davy put his foot to the deck he felt the whole boat tilt a fraction, and his innards heaved. The contrast between the solid stone of the jetty underfoot and the boat's ponderous buoyancy made him giddy. He would probably be seasick, he thought gloomily, and saw himself hanging over the side, heaving and retching, while Delahaye stood above him with his fists on his hips, smiling in that cold, fierce way, showing his teeth.

Davy had wondered how the boat would be made to go, since there was no wind, but now Delahaye went to the back—the stern—and started up the outboard engine there. That there was an engine seemed to Davy a kind of cheating, and the thought bucked him up a bit. But then the boat yawed out from the jetty and swept in a tight turn on the oily water and he had to grab for the rail to keep from being thrown off his feet. Delahaye stood at the wheel, with his cap over his eyes and his jaw squarely set, looking like Gregory Peck as Captain Ahab. Once again Davy pondered the question of why he was here, aboard this boat that had seemed so large, tethered to the jetty, and that now felt as if it were made of balsawood, skimming towards the broad and desolate horizon. He thought he might know why, and hoped he was wrong.

The speed surprised him. In a few minutes they had cleared the headland and turned towards the open sea. Delahaye was all business now, shutting off the engine and unfurling the sails and pulling on cords and lashing ropes to those brass things on the deck. There was a good breeze out here, and the surface of the sea had begun pricking up everywhere in dancing white points. Davy sat on a bench at the back—the stern, the stern!—and tried to keep out of the way. He might as well not have been there, as far as Delahaye was concerned. A black bird with a long neck flew past in a straight swift line a foot above the surface of the sea—where was it going to, in such a hurry and so determinedly? The big sails shivered and rattled and then suddenly the wind filled them and at once the boat bounded forward, lifting its pointed front—the prow, he told himself, the prow was what it was called—as if it would take to the air. Davy closed his eyes but that made him feel dizzy and he opened them again and fixed his gaze miserably on the swaying horizon. Everything was straining forward now, the mast and sails tensed like a cocked crossbow and the water slapping and sucking at the boards. He supposed they were not doing more than fifteen or twenty miles an hour—knots: are knots the same as miles?—but it felt as if they were going at an impossible speed, surging over the little waves and seeming barely to hold to the surface. His hands on either side were gripping the bench so hard his fingers had begun to ache.

Delahaye, satisfied that everything was set just so, pushed past him, going towards the back of the boat, and Davy caught his smell: salt, sweat, aftershave, and something else, something sharp, sour, bitter. He sat down at the tiller and Davy turned on the seat to face him. The peak of his cap still hid Delahaye's eyes. What was he thinking? Davy was suddenly afraid of more than the sea.

What was the point of sailing? Davy did not know, and had never dared to enquire. Sailing, doing things in boats, was as natural as walking, among the Delahayes. The Delahaye twins, Jonas and James, were champion yachtsmen, and had trophies to prove it; one year they had crewed on some millionaire's boat in the America's Cup. Even their aunt Maggie was an expert sailor. Davy's father had tried to get Davy interested, and Davy had done his best, but it was no good: he could not overcome his aversion to that uncanny, treacherous realm the main aim of which, as far as he was concerned, was to drag him under and drown him.

'You all right?' Delahaye growled, startling him. He nodded, trying to smile. He still could not see Delahaye's eyes under the peak of his cap but he knew he was watching him. What, *what*, was he thinking?

Davy looked back; the land behind them now was a featureless dark line. Where were they going? The horizon in front was empty. They were headed south, there would be no land now until—what?—Spain? Surely there would be a marker, a buoy or something, to tell them where they should turn around and start back. But on they went, and with every mile—every league?—they travelled the sea deepened under them; he thought of it, the coastal shelf falling away steadily into silence and utter dark. He shut his eyes again, and again felt dizzy.

Delahaye was saying something about Davy's mother. 'Did you see her, this morning, before we left?'

Davy did not know how to reply. It sounded like a trick question, but what could the trick be? 'Yes,' he said warily, 'yes, I saw her. She made breakfast for me.' Queasily he conjured up again the rashers of bacon, the fried bread, the egg yolk leaking across the plate. His eyes closed, this time of their own accord. His mind swam.

'Good,' Delahaye said. 'That's good.'

Davy waited, but that seemed to be the end of the subject of his mother. He looked behind again at that thinning line of land. Should he suggest turning back? Should he say he had an arrangement to meet someone? It was half past ten. He could say he had an appointment, a date, at half eleven. But even as he heard himself say it in his head it sounded wholly implausible. Yet they could not just keep going like this, towards that bare horizon— could they?

'Do you talk to your father?' Delahaye asked suddenly. 'Do you and he . . . discuss things?'

Again Davy was baffled. What new line was this, and where was it headed? 'We have a pint together, now and then,' he said.

Delahaye made a dismissive grimace. 'No, I mean, do you *talk*? Do you tell him about your life, what you're doing, what your plans are, that kind of thing?'

'Not really, no.' Despite the cool breeze in his face Davy realised he had begun to sweat, and he could feel the dampness at his wrists and between his shoulder-blades. 'My old man and I, we're not . . .' He did not know how to finish.

Delahaye pondered, nodding slowly. 'No,' he said, 'fathers and sons, they don't really talk, do they? I don't talk to the boys, the twins, not much, anyway. I did when they were young, but now . . .' With the hand that was not holding the tiller he fumbled a packet of Churchman's from a pocket of his slacks and got one into his mouth but did not attempt to light it. Davy wished he could see his eyes; there was the glint of them there, under the cap's peak, but it was impossible to guess at their expression. 'My father in his day didn't talk much to me,' Delahaye went on. He chuckled grimly. 'And these days, of course, we don't talk at all.'

There were two white birds now, diving for fish; they would fly up steeply in a fluttering, corkscrew motion and then flip themselves over and draw back their wings and drop like blades, making hardly a splash as they entered the water.

Davy made a show of consulting his watch. 'I wonder—' he began, but Delahaye was not listening, and interrupted him.

'He was a great one for self-reliance, my father,' he said. 'Self-reliance and loyalty. *A man is not much if he can't depend on himself,* he used to say, *'and nothing if others can't depend on him.'* He took the unlit cigarette from his mouth and rolled it between his fingers. 'I remember one day he took me into town in the car. I was—oh, I don't know—six? Seven? Young anyway. We were living in Rathfarnham then. He drove all the way across the city, out to Phibsborough, or Cabra, somewhere like that, and stopped at a corner shop and sent me in to buy an ice cream for myself. I don't think I'd ever been in a shop on my own before.' He was leaning on the tiller now, relaxed, it seemed, and smiling thinly to himself, remembering. 'Anyway, he gave me the money and I went in and bought a wafer of ice cream—you know, a penny wafer?—and when I came out he was gone. Just—gone. No father, no car, nothing.'

He stopped, and there was silence save for the beating of the waves against the prow and the shrieking of the sea birds. Davy waited. 'What did you do?'

Again Delahaye seemed not to be listening. He tossed the cigarette backwards over his shoulder and the churning wake swallowed it. 'Funny feeling, I remember it, as if the bottom had fallen out of my stomach, my heart thumping. I must have stood there for a long time, outside the shop, rooted to the spot, because the next thing I was aware of was the ice cream dripping on the toe of my sandal. I can see it still, that corner, the kerb painted in black and white segments and a hardware shop across the road. Strange thing is, I didn't cry. I went back into the shop and told the shopkeeper my daddy had gone away and left me. The shopkeeper went out to the back and fetched his wife, big fat woman in an apron. They sat me up on the counter where they could get a good look at me, to see if I was fibbing, I suppose. The woman took what was left of the ice cream from me and wiped my hands with a damp cloth, and the shopkeeper gave me a barley-sugar sweet. I could see them looking at each other, not knowing what to do.' He shook his head and chuckled again. 'I can still taste it, that sweet.'

When Davy tried to speak, his voice did not work the first time and he had to clear his throat and start again. 'What happened?' he asked. 'I mean—did he come back for you?'

Delahaye shrugged. 'Of course. It seemed like hours to me but I suppose it was no more than ten or fifteen minutes.'

'Where had he been?—where had he gone to?'

'Just round the corner. He took the shopkeeper aside and spoke to him, and gave him a pound. The woman looked as if she was going to spit on him, and marched back in behind the shop where she had come from and slammed the door. Then we went home. Here, take the tiller, will you?'

He stood up and they exchanged places. The arm of the tiller was damply warm where Delahaye had held it. Davy's palm was wet. He was still sweating, but he was cold, too, in his shirt and wished he had brought a windbreaker. It struck him with renewed force how absurd a thing it was to be out here, skimming over God knew how many fathoms. And people sailed for fun and recreation!

Delahaye was gathering in the sails, first the smaller one at the front and then the bigger one. 'Self-reliance, you see,' he said, 'a lesson in self-reliance. *You got a sweet out of it, didn't you?* was all my father said. *And I bet the woman was all over you. And you didn't cry.* That was the most important thing—that I didn't cry.' He had folded the big sail expertly and was lashing it now to the horizontal part of the mast with salt-bleached cord. The boat faltered and seemed puzzled as it felt itself losing momentum, and dipped its nose and settled back with a sort of sigh, wallowing in the water, and for a second or two all sense of direction failed and the sea around them seemed to spin crazily on its axis. The sudden hush set up a buzz in Davy's ears. Delahaye, wiping his hands on his trousers, sat down on a big oak trunk set lengthways down the middle of the boat and leaned his back against the mast. He seemed weary suddenly, and lifted his cap to air his skull and then put it back on again, but not so low over his eyes as before. 'What I couldn't help wondering, even at the time, was: where did loyalty figure in this lesson I had been taught?' He looked directly at Davy now, with an odd, questioning candour. 'What do you think?'

Davy's fingers tightened on the tiller. 'About what?'

'Loyalty. You're a Clancy, you must know about loyalty—eh? Or the lack of it, at least.' His eyes were of a curious glittery grey colour, like chips of flint. Davy could not hold their steady gaze, and looked away. 'Come on, Davy,' Delahaye said softly, almost cajolingly. 'Let's have your thoughts on this important topic.'

'I don't know what to say,' Davy said. 'I don't know what you want me to say.'

Delahaye was silent for a long moment, then nodded, as if something had been confirmed. He stood up from the wooden trunk and lifted the heavy lid and fished about inside and brought out something wrapped loosely in an oily rag. He stood in thought for a moment, hefting the thing in his hand. 'Loyalty,' he said, 'it's not valued any more, is it? Loyalty. Honour. What used to be called common decency. All gone, that kind of thing.'

He began to unwind the rag, and as he did so Davy heard himself say something, exclaim something—*Whoa!* it sounded like—and he looked about wildly, as if, even out here, there might be a place to shelter behind. And yet at the same time he felt almost like laughing.

'Yes,' Delahaye said, as if reading his mind and sharing in his desperate amusement, 'it is an ugly bugger, isn't it? A Webley, Mark'—he brought the pistol close to his eyes and peered at the frame below the cylinder—'Mark Six. Pa got it off a fellow in the Civil War, I think it was.' He glanced sideways at Davy with a sort of smile. 'Oh, yes,' he said, 'it works. I tested it.'

He sat down again, dangling the gun in both hands between his knees. It was an absurd-looking thing, all right, big and heavy and nearly a foot long, with a chamfered barrel and a hammer at the back like a silvery tongue sticking out. There was the faintest swell now, and the boat rocked gently from side to side, the small waves making a playful chattering sound against the hull. Davy tried to get his bearings from the sky, but the sky was empty. The boat seemed not to be moving at all, as if it were at anchor, but he supposed it must be drifting, at the mercy of tide and breeze, and that it only seemed motion-less because there was nothing to measure movement against. He was amazed at how calm he felt, tranquil, almost. He might have been running in a race, a marathon that had been going on for so long he had forgotten he was running, and only now remembered, when everything had come to a sudden stop. Why was he not frightened? Why was he not terrified?

'I'd send you for an ice cream, if there were any shops,' Delahaye said, and laughed, and turned the pistol about and put the barrel to his chest and pulled the trigger.

What amazed Davy was that there was so much blood; that, and the vivid redness of it, which made him think of those spiders or insects or whatever they were, tiny scarlet specks, that used to fascinate him when he was a child, as they crawled among the rose bushes in his grandfather's garden. The blood had a faint smell, too, spicy and slightly sweet. The bullet hole in the left side of Delahaye's chest was black in the centre with a ragged rim the colour of crushed raspberries. The blood had quickly soaked the lower half of his blue cotton shirt and the lap of his white trousers, and had dripped out between his legs and made a puddle in the bottom of the boat with a single rivulet running out of it. Davy had managed to ease the packet of Churchman's out of the pocket of Delahaye's trousers—it had seemed important somehow that the cigarettes should not get blood on them. He checked his watch, as if it was important, too, to know what time it was.

The gunshot had sent Delahaye sprawling, with a look of astonishment on his face, and for the first seconds Davy had thought the boat would capsize, so violently did it yaw from side to side. He pictured the two of them sinking together feet first through the water, down through the glinting light into the shadows, and then on into the blackness of the deep.

The awful thing was that Delahaye was not dead. He would be, eventually, that was certain—Davy had never seen anyone die, yet he knew Delahaye was a goner—but for now he was still breathing, making wheezing noises, like a child when it has finished crying and is trying to catch its breath. Once he moaned, and seemed to try to say something. His eyes stayed closed, there was that to be thankful for. He had slid off the trunk and was sitting at a crooked angle. He had dropped the pistol between his legs, and the handle was in the puddle of blood in the bottom of the boat.

Davy leaned forward, holding on with one hand to the what-was-it-called, the gunwale—he *hated* boats, *hated* them—and picked up the weapon by the barrel and flung it out of the boat as far as it would go; it landed in the water with a comical plop. He sat back, and realised at once that he should not have thrown the gun away. They would not think he had shot Delahaye, would they? But what if they did? He swore, over and over, punching himself on the knee with his fist.

He looked about, scanning the sea in all directions. There was no other vessel in sight. What was he to do? Down in the middle of the boat there was a pool of water—it was there that the single thin rivulet of blood was heading for—that swayed and shivered as the little waves nudged against the sides. It was not a lot of water, but what if it was not rainwater, but seawater, coming from a leak? He remembered from films how leaks that sprang in the hulls of ships widened in a matter of seconds until the sea was cascading in, washing sailors away and floating their bunks up to the ceilings. Maybe Delahaye had bored a little hole in the bottom, a little hole that would get bigger and bigger.

Davy looked at the dying man. His face was a bluish grey, like putty, and there was a film of moisture on his forehead and on his upper lip. His breathing was slower now. He looked at his watch and was surprised to find that not quite three minutes had passed since Delahaye had fired the gun—three minutes! It seemed to Davy that he was suspended high above the boat and looking down on all this, Delahaye slumped there, and the two puddles, one of blood and one of water, and himself, huddled in the stern, his two hands out and clutching to the sides in terror. For the first time it occurred to him that he, too, would die, lost out here in a sinking boat.

A plane appeared from the south, banking to the right, headed for Dublin. He jumped up and waved his arms frantically. The boat set up an angry rocking and at once he sat down again, feeling foolish and dizzy. The plane was too high, no one would see him, and even if someone did spot him he would probably look like some half-witted fisherman waving hello to the tourists as they flew in.

He examined the outboard motor. He had no idea how to start it. Should there be a key? He turned to Delahaye, and heard himself swallow. Did he have the stomach to search in those blood-soaked trousers again? He crept forward and ran his fingers over the outsides of Delahaye's pockets. He could feel no key. Maybe Delahaye had dropped it into the sea. *A lesson in self-reliance.* He sat back once more on the bench. The sun was high now, shining directly on the crown of his head, he could feel the beads of sweat crawling on his scalp like insects. He thought again of those blood-red mites in his Grandad Clancy's garden.

Delahaye opened dazed eyes and frowned at the sky. He gave a rattly groan and struggled forward as if trying to get to his feet, spoke a string of incomprehensible words in what seemed a tone of irritation, then slumped back into silence and died.

2

MARGUERITE DELAHAYE did not like her brother's wife. She had tried to like her, had tried and tried over, but in vain. This troubled her, for Marguerite—or Maggie, as everyone called her, though she hated it—was a kindly soul and wished to think well of people. However, it was difficult to think well of Mona. Not that Mona seemed to care. There were not many things, it seemed, that Mona did care about. She was what Maggie's late mother would have called an awkward customer. Still, Maggie kept on trying. Mona was her sister-in-law, after all, and it was her duty to keep up the effort, even if in her heart she knew she would not succeed. In her heart, too, she suspected that Victor himself found it hard to like his wife. He loved her, that was certain—loved her too much, as Maggie knew to her chagrin—but she was sure it was perfectly possible to be in love with someone without liking the person. Disliking Mona meant that Maggie had to work all the harder at being nice to her. Mona took Maggie's tribute as she took all signs of kindness and regard: with indifference or at best a sort of vacant amusement.

Mrs Hartigan had put a crystal bowl of sweet peas on

the table in the hall, and their lovely scent was everywhere in the house, even in the bedrooms and the big stone kitchen off at the end of the corridor behind the green baize door. Maggie, coming down from her room, stopped on the return to admire the flowers, arrayed there in soft sunlight falling in through the transom over the front door. The leads of the transom broke up the light and reassembled it into a bright, complicated shape, like a birdcage.

Maggie loved Ashgrove. She had been coming here with her family every year for as long as she could remember. The house had been old when she was young yet she had the secret notion that it was somehow accompanying her through the years, keeping pace with her, its most favoured visitor. For the rest of the year, when she was not here, she missed the old place, as she would miss a beloved dog, or a friend, even. A pity there had to be so many people in the house. She always made sure to arrive a day or two before the others, and to leave a day or two after they were gone. That was bliss, being on her own. She loved especially to lie awake early in the morning, the newly risen sun striping the counterpane, and the house all around her stretching and creaking under the light of the new day. Solitude was her balm. She had never married. There had been offers, but she had wished to live her life in her own way, according to her own wishes and rules, without the interference of a husband.

She had spent most of the afternoon reading in her room, or trying to read, sitting by the window in the faded-green armchair, her favourite. The window looked down on a secluded corner of the garden, and now and then she would close her book—Agatha Christie; rather dull—marking her place with her thumb, and watch the blackbirds and the rabbits playing at the edge of the lawn. The rabbits, two or three of them, would venture out from the long grass under the trees, the birds would fly down quickly and the rabbits would scamper back for shelter; this little game was repeated over and over. She supposed it was not really play, but she liked to think it was.

She had delayed for as long as she could before leaving the sanctuary of her room. Her father was in one of his moods and had deliberately said something to upset Mrs Hartigan and, of course, there were ructions that would go on at least till teatime. Her father had suffered a stroke three years previously and was confined to a wheelchair and therefore was bored and prone to rancorous ill-temper, although even in his heyday he had not been exactly of a tranquil disposition. It pleased him to annoy people, to set them against each other. This afternoon it was Mrs Hartigan's turn to suffer the edge of his tongue, and having started that particular fire he had then settled down contentedly to warm his hands before it. Mrs Hartigan kept house for the weeks when the two families were here, and acted as caretaker for the remainder of the year. She was touchy, was Mrs Hartigan—Maggie suspected she considered herself too good for such menial work—and took offence easily. And of course it always fell to Maggie to smooth her ruffled feathers. Standing in the hall now, still admiring the flowers, Maggie smiled to herself; ruffled feathers, yes—Mrs Hartigan did look a bit like a plump, excitable old hen.

Samuel Delahaye was in the lounge, which was what

the main living room had always been called, listening to a programme on the wireless. He had parked his wheel-chair next to the sideboard on which the set stood, its green eye pulsing, and had his ear pressed up close to the mesh of the speaker—it was one of his amusements to pretend to be hard of hearing. He was a big man, broad-shouldered and barrel-chested, with a swept-back mane of silver hair; Maggie believed he modelled himself on William Butler Yeats—certainly he was as vain as the poet surely must have been. When she had entered the room and shut the door, and before she had spoken even a word, he flapped a hand irritably in her direction, as if she were making a commotion of some sort and interfering with his enjoyment of the programme, which seemed to be about bees. He did not look at her.

She sighed. Her sister-in-law was seated on the long beige sofa in front of the fireplace, flipping through a glossy magazine. On a low table before her stood a tall glass of gin and tonic, with ice cubes and sliced lemon; the glass was misted down the sides. The french windows at the far end of the room were wide open on to the lawn, at the far side of which was the stand of ash trees that gave the house its name.

Maggie came forward and Mona looked up from her magazine. 'We thought you must have left and gone home,' Mona said, in her languid way. 'Where have you been hiding?'

Mona's abundant hair was the colour of polished bronze, and her skin was porcelain-pale. Her eyes were violet, and tapered at the outer corners. The only flaw in her beauty, Maggie considered, was her mouth, a thin scarlet slash that gave her something of the look of a mean and sulky child.

'Oh, you know, I was just pottering,' Maggie said.

'For Christ's sake!' her father cried from across the room. 'Can't you stop that racket and let me listen?'

Neither woman paid him any heed.

'Has Mrs H. calmed down yet?' Maggie asked quietly of her sister-in-law. Mona shrugged; she was turning the pages of her magazine again, pausing only to examine the adverts with a narrowed eye.

'How should I know?' she said. 'The old bitch never speaks to me.'

Maggie sat down at the other end of the sofa. 'I do wish he wouldn't provoke her,' she said. 'If she were to leave we'd be lost.'

Mona gave a soft snort of laughter. 'No fear of that,' she said. 'She has it too easy here.'

'I think she works quite hard,' Maggie said mildly, picking a speck of fluff from the hem of her skirt. 'It's a very big house, and there's just herself and the girl she gets in at the weekends.'

Mona did not reply to this, and leaned forward and took up her glass. Maggie watched her gazing before her vague-eyed as she drank. She really was an exquisite creature—to look at, at least. She was not yet thirty, which made her—what was it?—a good sixteen years younger than her husband. It always puzzled Maggie that Mona should have consented to marry Victor. Victor was hand-some, of course, though she supposed his looks were faded a bit by now, and he was well off, and generous, but he was not the kind of man Maggie would have thought

Mona would *go for*, as she would say herself. The kind of man that Mona would go for, Maggie would have thought, would be as careless and cruel as she was herself. Thinking this, Maggie immediately felt guilty, and even blushed a little, though it had only been a thought, with no one to hear.

The dance of the drones, the voice on the wireless was saying, *is thought to be a system by which returning bees direct their fellow-workers to the richest sources of pollen in the vicinity of the hive. Bees will travel for distances of as much as—*

And then the telephone outside on the hall table began to ring.

A week of rain had left the ground in a soggy state but all the same Blue Lightning, the sprightly three-year-old from the late Dick Jewell's stables, which was supposed to like the going hard, romped home at seven to two, surprising everyone. Everyone except Jack Clancy. He collected his winnings from the bookie's in Slievemore and went round the corner to Walsh's and ordered drinks for everyone in the bar. The locals, he knew, would despise him for his largesse—*Who does your man think he is, playing the big fellow?*—but all the same they would drink his drink. Their contempt did not bother him. On the contrary, he was gratified to see the resentful looks they gave him, as they muttered behind their pints.

The publican's wife, a big redhead with green eyes—a splash of tinker blood there, surely—helped out behind the bar on race days. Jack sat in the alcove just inside the door and watched her as she worked. From here he had a view of the woman herself and also of her reflection in the fly-blown looking-glass behind the bar. She was wearing a sleeveless summer frock, and when she lifted her freckled arm to pull a pint, he glimpsed a smear of sweat-damp coppery moss in the shadowed hollow of her armpit. Her name was Sadie.

Watching the woman made him think of Jonas Delahaye's girlfriend. Not that Sadie resembled Tanya Somers even in the least degree. Just picturing Tanya in her black swimsuit gave him an ache at the root of his tongue. Not a hope there, of course. On the other hand, you could never tell. He was more than twice her age, but some young ones, he knew, had a taste for older men—look at Mona Delahaye. That would be some row, if he were to have a go at Jonas's stuck-up girlfriend and got found out. Jonas, that spoilt whelp. He knew Jonas and Tanya were sleeping together. They were in separate bedrooms, but that was only for the look of it, and not to scandalise old Ma Hartigan; every night after lights-out Jonas was in there like a shot, Jack knew it for sure. Victor Delahaye prided himself on being broad-minded and modern, now that his father was ailing and he was no longer under the old man's thumb. Victor's sister was a different matter, though: when Tanya came sashaying through the house Maggie's mouth got small and wrinkled, as if she were sucking a sour sweet.

And what about Davy? Jack was uneasily aware that his son was of an age to be his rival when it came to the ladies. Davy was a handsome young fellow—Jack had seen the looks that women gave him, even Mona Delahaye.

What if Davy were to make a play for Tanya Somers? That was a possibility Jack did not care to contemplate. A row of that scale between the two families would be disastrous, especially now, when all his plans for the future of the firm were so delicately balanced.

He thought, not for the first time, how strange it must be being a twin. The Delahaye brothers, tall, blond, blue-eyed, were like two peas in a pod. Imagine having someone around all the time who was your spitting image. Jonas and James did not seem to mind; in fact they were always together. What, he wondered, did James make of Tanya Somers? Would he resent her, would he be envious—resentful of her for coming between him and his brother, and envious of his brother for having her? And Tanya: was she able to tell the difference between the twins? What if Jonas and James were to swap places some night and James were to slip into bed with her—would she know it was him? Or what if the two of them got in with her, one on either side—would she be able to tell them apart? Those two big blond lads in bed with Tanya in the middle, that was a thought he had found himself entertaining on more than one occasion over these past weeks, with a mixture of excitement, envy and sweet regret. He was forty-seven, himself, and hated it.

He signalled to Sadie for another Jamaica red rum. He handed over a ten-shilling note, and when she brought the change she gave him a queer sort of smile, her lips pressed together and one eyebrow arched, and he did not know what to make of it. Either she was telling him she knew his type and he was not to bother trying, or the opposite, that she liked the look of him and would listen to any offer he might care to make. If it was the latter, it would be impossible, down here. He had made that mistake once before, years ago, a cattle dealer's wife over at Cross-haven—a redhead too, as it happened—and had got such a beating from the cattle dealer's three brutes of sons that there were bones in his shoulders and his back that still ached when the weather turned wet. But surely Sadie must come up to the city sometimes, to shop, or whatever. He would slip her his phone number before he left.

A fellow he knew from the sailing club came in and Jack stood him a drink and they talked boats for a while. Jack loved being in a pub at this time of a summer evening, loved the sound of slow talk and the rich reek of whiskey, loved the look of sunshine the colour of brass coming in at the open doorway and lighting up the lazy swirls of cigarette smoke in the dusky air. Being here was not being at Ashgrove, a pleasure in itself. And then there was Sadie, and the possibilities she might represent.

The sailing-club fellow's name was Grogan, a solicitor from Cork and, as Jack now belatedly remembered, a terrible bore. They had sailed together in the Slievemore regatta; Grogan in his Mermaid had taken the Commodore's Cup this year. He was saying something now about a boat with two men in it having been found adrift off Slievemore Bay—there had been a report about it on the wireless, on the six o'clock news. Jack was watching Sadie, admiring the way her frock tightened over her bust when she drew the handle of the beer tap back and down in a slow, effortful arc. Yes, he would definitely suggest a drink next time she was in Dublin. What had he to lose?

'One chap dead, it seems,' Grogan said. 'Sounds a funny business.'

Sylvia Clancy steered the big car on to the causeway below the village of Rosscarbery. She always liked to drive back from Cork along the coast road. Today, however, she had no eye for the scenery, for she was worried. This was not unusual. Being worried was Sylvia's accustomed state of mind. How could it be otherwise?—she was married to Jack Clancy and Davy Clancy was her son. Today, however, her specific concern was Mona Delahaye's party, to be held on the following Saturday night. Mona was what could be described as a party person. Three years ago she had thrown—surely the right word—the first Ashgrove Bash, as she called it, and since then it had become an annual event and the talk of the county, if not of half the country.

Most people who gave parties, Sylvia supposed, gave them in the hope that their guests would enjoy themselves and go home happy. Evidently Mona's intention was the opposite of this. She seemed to wish that everyone should have a good time, only she had a peculiar notion of what having a good time should involve. She did not want people standing about with drinks in their hands, chit-chatting: arguments, insults, challenges, fights, even fist fights, these were the kinds of things that Mona wished her parties to inspire. And if matters were not going her way—that is, if they were going peaceably and enjoyably— she was fully prepared to step in and set them awry. Mona had a genius for provocation. She stirred things up without seeming to, bestowing a smile here, a soft word there, enquiring, informing, advising. And as she progressed through the room there would spring up in her wake little conflagrations that were her doing but that yet appeared entirely unconnected with her. Then, reaching the far end of the room, she would turn and survey her handiwork with pleasure, her eyes narrowed and her thin mouth upturned at one corner.

Yet in her heart Sylvia felt sympathy for Mona. Mona was a child, really, with all a child's avidity and incurable mischievousness. Whatever was going on, Mona had to have it, and if she could not have it she would spoil it for others. It was simply her way. Sylvia suspected that Mona, like her, felt secretly that she had strayed into the wrong family. The Delahayes were a formidable clan, as were the Clancys in their different way, and to have married into them was to be devoured, or as good as. Could poor Mona be blamed for asserting herself in the only way she knew how? Mischief-making was her declaration of independence, which was why she and her father-in-law, old Samuel Delahaye, were fond of each other, if fond was a word that could be fitted to either of these wilful, reckless and malicious creatures.

Sylvia was driving the Delahayes' Mercedes—Jack was off at the races in their own old Humber—feeling nervous and at the same time faintly thrilled, for the big car frightened her, with its brutishly square front and that emblem on the bonnet that looked to her like the sight of a gun. Yet she had to admit it was exciting to be in control, however fearfully, of such a powerful machine.

She had been to Cork to see a new osteopath—they were called bone-setters, down here—whom Mrs Hartigan had recommended. Mrs Hartigan swore by him and declared him a miracle-worker, but Sylvia had consulted him only out of politeness to the housekeeper, a tiresome woman at the best of times. Sylvia had a bad back. No one had ever been able to discover why she should be suffering such awful, chronic pain, and this new man had been no wiser than the others, though he had talked a lot of mumbo-jumbo about frozen joints, and fused discs, and plates—he was very hot on plates, whatever they were supposed to be. A foolish, ignorant man, Sylvia judged. However, the evening was so lovely, with the sun flashing its burning arrows through the trees along the roadside, and the wheat and barley in the fields beyond swayed and polished by the breeze, that her heart lifted, despite the motor-car's slouching impatience and the ache in her lower spine—which, if she was not mistaken, the bone-setter had only made worse.

Sylvia was English. This seemed increasingly to be, for herself as well as for others, the most significant fact about her. Yet by now she had spent more than half of her life in Ireland. It did not matter. They would be conscious of her Englishness until her dying day. Not that they expressed resentment or showed prejudice towards her. Indeed, they seemed to admire her pluck, to think her a good sport, for being undaunted enough to make her life among them. The response in general to the fact that she was English was a sort of amused fascination; people would look at her in that half-smiling, wondering way, and say, 'And you're English, are you?' as if it were something outlandish, like being a racing driver, or a jungle explorer. She was a permanent curiosity. She could not resent this. Probably they perceived in a dim way the inner life she continued to live, which was mild, reasonable, tolerant and self-mocking—which was, in a word, English, or what she thought of as being English, Englishness as she remembered it.

Just as Sylvia knew Mona should not have married Victor Delahaye, so she knew that she should not have married Jack Clancy. Oh, she loved Jack, whatever that meant now, after all these years. At first, when they were young, certainly she had adored him. She had never met— no, she had never conceived of the possibility of there being a person such as Jack: charming, dangerous, darkly handsome, and given to a destructive gaiety that she had found immediately irresistible. These things, the charm, the danger, the satanic good looks, that impish, corrosive humour above all, these, she understood now, were the very things that should have warned her off him.

She was taller than he was, taller by a good two or three inches. He had never seemed to mind this, and only made jokes about it. She, however, was acutely aware of the disparity, not for her own sake but for his, and in their first months together had devised a way of standing beside him with her chin lowered and her left leg drawn back a little way and her right knee surreptitiously flexed, which, if it did not reduce her height in any noticeable way, at least announced that she knew she was the one who must try to right the balance, and suffer the humiliation of not being able to do so. It was not that Jack was too short, but that she was too tall.

She slowed the car and turned in at the gate of Ash-grove.

Now her mind, going its own way as always, went back to the awful prospect of Mona's party. Last year Davy had got into a scuffle with the son of some local grandee and had bitten off part of his ear. She rather thought the other boy had deserved what he had got, for obviously he was a brat, but still, getting into fights and biting people was not the kind of behaviour she would have expected of a son of hers. But then, many things in her life had turned out to be not as she had expected. Davy, she thought, was rather like this brute of a car, barely controllable, single-minded, and always eager to run ahead of himself. And now, all at once, a thought that had been lurking beneath her anxiety about the party came flashing to the surface of her mind and would not be pushed down again. It was the thought of that Somers girl. Tanya Somers had trouble written all over her. It always puzzled Sylvia that men could not see how calculating a girl like Tanya was, how all her effects were—not thought out, perhaps, but instinctive, measured and sure. What if Davy tried to take her away from Jonas Delahaye? Yes, and what if—what if someone else were to attempt—? What if—?

She had stopped on the gravel in front of the house and was sitting behind the wheel, her appalled gaze fixed unseeing on the windscreen as she contemplated the possi-bilities for mayhem that Tanya Somers represented, when she heard what seemed to be the sound of someone crying in the house. She opened the door and stepped out on to the gravel and stood to listen. Yes, definitely, someone was crying, a woman; the sound was coming from one of the open upstairs windows, jagged sobs, and in between each sob a sort of laboured mooing. Maggie. Maggie was weeping—those heaving gasps were the sounds she made when she was having an asthma attack. And why was the front door wide open like that? And what or whose was that black car, parked beside the laburnums? Something had happened—something terrible, surely. Sylvia's first thought was: *Davy*. Her second was: *Jack*.

Superintendent Wallace had thought it best that he should come out himself to Ashgrove to break the news. Not that he had much time for these folk who descended on the house for a few weeks every summer and left the place standing empty and idle for the rest of the year. It was, he considered, a queer comedown for a grand mansion such as this, the seat of gentlemen and their ladies in centuries past, that it should be reduced to the status of a holiday villa for a gang of moneyed Dublin riff-raff. The super-intendent was a mild man but, in secret, a great and unrelenting snob. Although his own origins were humble, and despite the fact that in most matters he tried to be accommodating and unjudgemental, he was implacably disapproving of the new Ireland, so-called, which had grown up in the decade since the war, and of which the Clancys, and even the Delahayes, who might have been expected to live up to their venerable name, were, in his opinion, typical representatives.

He was not surprised by what had happened this afternoon—puzzled, certainly, but not surprised. The crust of civilisation was very thin, and very brittle. In his youth he had lived through the War of Independence and the Civil War that had followed, and he had seen things done—young men slaughtered, great houses burned, the land laid waste—that flew in the face of what the priests taught and the former generations had believed in. Now there was peace in the country, yet on a sunny afternoon in the height of summer two men had gone out in a boat and one of them had been brought back dead, shot through the chest and wallowing in his own blood. It was a bad business.

Having delivered his dreadful message he was uncertain how to proceed. Everyone had rushed off to other parts of the house and had left him standing in the front hall with his cap in his hand. From upstairs he could hear Miss Delahaye crying—she was the best of the lot of them, a decent woman with a good heart—but somewhere nearby a tinny voice was delivering what seemed to be a lecture of some kind. Old man Delahaye, after a minute of slack-mouthed staring, had spun his wheelchair on the spot and bowled himself down the hall at a fast lick and disappeared into the back of the house. The dead man's wife—his widow, now—had also gone off somewhere and was not to be seen. It was as if, the superintendent thought, he had brought the plague with him, which of course in a way he had.

There was a quick step behind him and he turned to see a tall woman hurriedly bearing down on him. She was a moving silhouette against the sunlight in the doorway and at first he could not see who it was. Then she spoke and he recognised the Clancy woman. 'Tell me,' she said urgently, almost whispering, her fingers clutching at the sleeve of his uniform. '*Tell me.*'

He told her. While he was speaking she watched him intently, nodding, her eyes fixed on his lips, as if to make out there the shape of the words she did not trust her ears to absorb. 'A trawler out of Castletownbere spotted the boat adrift and brought it in,' he said. 'The poor man was long dead by then.'

'And my son,' she said, 'where is he?—how is he?'

'They have him in the Bon Secours in Cork,' the superintendent said. 'He has a touch of sunstroke, they think. He'll be all right.'

'My God—Cork,' she said, shifting her stare to one side and fixing it on nothing. 'I've just come from there.' She seemed so incredulous of this small coincidence that for a moment he thought she was going to laugh. 'I must go back,' she muttered.

She made to turn away, patting the pockets of her loose cardigan in search of the car keys, but he caught her elbow and said it was all right, that her son would be brought down from Cork in an ambulance, that he was probably on his way already. She nodded. She was frowning now. 'And Mr Delahaye is dead, you say,' she said, still unable to grasp it.

'Yes, ma'am,' he said. 'Shot.'

She stared at him again in that almost hungry fashion. 'But who shot him?'

'Well now,' he said, 'that's the question, ma'am.'

He liked her voice, the softness of it, the gentility. He had never had anything against the English, himself, though the Black and Tans had murdered an uncle of his—he was only an uncle by marriage. She turned and walked slowly to the straight-backed chair beside the hall table and sat down, folding her hands in her lap. He had been noticing something odd and now he realised what it was: she had no handbag. He had thought women never went anywhere without a handbag. Her hair was blonde, or maybe more grey than blonde, and gathered at the back in a bun that had already released a few stray straggles. That was as far as the disarray would go, he thought; this lady was not the kind to tear her hair out.

Upstairs Miss Delahaye was still crying, but with less abandon now, her sobs become hiccups.

The superintendent heard a whirring sound behind him, and turned to see old Delahaye reappear from the back of the house, wheeling himself along the black and white tiled hall with surprising speed and smoothness. He looked neither at the superintendent nor at the woman sitting by the table, but wrenched the wheelchair to the left and put out a foot in front of him and kicked open the door to the lounge and glided through. The door, sighing, swung slowly shut behind him. After a moment Sylvia Clancy stood up and followed him, and the superintendent, not knowing what else to do, followed her.

Mona Delahaye was sitting on the beige sofa, facing the fireplace. She wore a frock of dark-green silk. She was leaning forward, her clasped hands resting on her crossed knees. She held her head inclined a little to the side, as if she were listening for some faint, far-off sound. Samuel Delahaye in his wheelchair was at the open french windows, his chin sunk on his chest, glaring out at the garden.

The crazy thought came to the superintendent that perhaps these two people had not understood what he had told them, and that they were waiting for clarification, enlightenment; waiting for someone to explain it all to them again, more comprehensibly.

Sylvia Clancy went and sat down beside Mona on the sofa and tried to take her hand, but Mona kept her hands clasped, and did not look at her.

'I suppose,' Mona said, mildly, thoughtfully, 'we'll have to cancel the party, now.'

Mrs Clancy and the superintendent decided not to hear this, and to act as if it had not been said. No doubt the young woman was suffering from shock. At the window, Samuel Delahaye made a snorting sound that might have been laughter.

Was that an ambulance siren, in the distance?

'I think, ma'am,' the superintendent said softly, addressing Sylvia Clancy over the back of the sofa, 'I think I'll be on my way.'

'Yes,' the woman said, not looking at him.

Still he lingered. 'There'll be people out, after me,' he said. 'To ask questions, and the like.' He waited. No response came. He coughed delicately into his fist and turned away and walked as if on eggshells to the door. In the hall he brought out a handkerchief and took off his cap and gave the shiny peak a wipe. In the dimness at the back of the hall a white face appeared for a moment and was gone. The housekeeper—what was her name? Hennigan? No, Hartigan. He put on his cap again and went out to the car. The young guard who had driven him down here—he could not remember his name, either—hopped out from behind the wheel and scurried round to the passenger side and opened the door for him and stood to attention. The leather seat was hot where the sun had been shining on it. 'Right,' the superintendent said, with a grim sigh. 'Let's go.' The young guard started up the engine, and did something to the gears that made the rear wheels spin in the gravel.

In the lounge, Samuel Delahaye wheeled himself away from the french windows and approached the two women seated on the sofa.

'That's a fine—' he began, glaring at Sylvia, and had to stop and cough harshly and start again. 'That's a fine thing that cullion of a son of yours is after doing now.'

3

INSPECTOR HACKETT thought wistfully that he would have enjoyed a jaunt to Cork. He was fond of the city, and the coast down there was lovely, especially at this time of year—he had spent a week in Skibbereen with the missus one summer and they had both loved it and vowed to return, though they never had. But Victor Delahaye's corpse had been brought up to Dublin earlier that morning, and the two families were on their way back to town, so there was no call for him to make the journey south. He spoke on the telephone to the super down there, Wallace, that stuffed shirt, and Wallace told him that the forensics boys from Anglesea Street were examining the boat and when Wallace got the report he would send it up to him. No, no weapon had been found: the young fellow with Delahaye had said he had thrown the gun into the sea. It was not his gun, he said—he had no gun—but Delahaye's, that Delahaye had had it on board already, wrapped in a rag and hidden in a chest. 'Did you believe him?' the inspector asked. He was leaning back in his chair with his boots on his desk, picking his teeth—his dentures, rather—with a matchstick. Wallace huffed and puffed and said, yes, he did, he believed him. Hackett nodded into the mouthpiece. Wallace might be pompous and vain—and he was, he was surely—but he was not entirely a fool.

This, Hackett thought, dropping the sodden match into the ashtray on his desk, was going to be tricky. The Delahayes were a formidable clan, and would be bound to cause him heartache. First of all they would want the whole business hushed up. Their people would ring the newspapers, and the newspapers would ring him, and what would he say? If it was a suicide they would not want to know, since newspapers never reported suicides, and if it was not a suicide they would probably not want to know that, either, given who it was had been killed and who it had to have been that had done the killing. A high-society scandal would make juicy reading, but the Delahayes had clout in this town. He crossed one booted ankle on the other. What the hell had happened down there? It was not every day of the week a man took himself and the only son of his business partner off in a boat and once beyond sight of land brought out a gun and plugged himself. Or maybe the young fellow had done it, after all, despite John-Joe Wallace's best hunch? Which would be the bigger scandal?

He spent the next two hours on the telephone, talking to all the contacts he could think of and gathering from them every scrap of information that was to be had on Delahaye & Clancy Ltd, its stock-market value, its fiscal state, its standing in the business community. He was told many things that did not interest him and a few that did. There was something going on inside the company, some shift, some realignment. A management reorganisation, a power struggle, a boardroom coup? No one knew the details, but more than one of his contacts insisted that something was definitely up. Was the company in trouble? No. Were its finances sound? Yes. What about Victor Delahaye's health? As far as anyone knew he had not been sick. Hackett put down the phone and looked at the wall in front of him. A Clery's calendar from last year, a framed photo of de Valera in a top hat, a reddish smear where Hackett had swatted a bluebottle yesterday. He had a hum in his ear from being on the phone for so long. This was the part of police work that he hated, the sense at the start of a case of being purblind, of stumbling in a fog, of nothing connecting with anything. He felt like a monkey with a coconut and no stone to crack it on.

He would go and talk to Dr Quirke.

He found him in McGonagle's. Quirke was perched at the bar in his usual spot, with his back to a pillar that had a narrow mirror set into it, a glass of Jameson's at his elbow. 'I see you're having your lunch,' the inspector said drily, sliding on to a high stool beside him. It was well past two and coming up to the Holy Hour and the lunchtime drinkers were getting in a last one before closing time. Quirke was looking about him with a thoughtful eye. 'On how many occasions, would you say,' he said, 'have you and I been in this pub, Inspector?'

Hackett chuckled. 'The two of us together, do you mean, or separately?' He took off his hat and set it on his knee. 'Either road, too many times, I've no doubt.'

Quirke was looking at the detective's hat. 'I know a

man,' he said, 'a civil servant, keeps two hats, one to wear and one to leave in the office. Anyone calls when he's out at the pub, the secretary says, *Oh, he must be in the building, his hat is on the hat-stand.*'

'Civil servant, you say? That's what has the country the way it is.'

'You're right. Skivers and scrimshankers. What are you drinking?'

'A glass of water.'

'Oh, of course—you're on duty.'

This time they both chuckled.

Hackett, too, looked about him now. He was interested in the lighting. His wife had been pestering him for months to put up new fixtures in the living room and he was on the look-out for ideas. Lights were awkward. A single bulb in the middle of the ceiling, no matter what sort of shade you put on it, gave the place the look of a prison cell—'Of course, that would suit you grand,' May had said with heavy sarcasm—but standing lamps could be a curse: they had to be huddled under, like umbrellas, if they were to be of any use at all. Here the bulbs were set in two parallel rows close up to the ceiling; the dusty shades, of amber-coloured glass with frilled edges, looked like little bonnets. Maybe that was the answer for the living room, half a dozen small bulbs installed at strategic points around the ceiling—over the table, above the shelf with the wireless set, and so on. Not the glass bonnets, though: he could imagine what May would say to the glass bonnets.

'Let me guess why you're here,' Quirke said.

He was in his double-breasted black suit, as always—

he must have, the inspector thought, three or four of these suits, all identical. He was coming to look like an undertaker; it was an occupational hazard, perhaps, for a pathologist. He was putting on weight, too—the big shoulders that used to be all muscle were softening: you could see the flab compressed under the yoke of his jacket, and in the mirror behind him the back of his neck was squeezing over his shirt collar. Letting himself go; he needed a woman to smarten him up.

'Have you things to tell me?' the inspector said.

Quirke drank off the last of the Jameson's and lifted his empty glass for the barman to see. 'I take it you're referring to a certain illustrious corpse?' he said.

'Aye—one that came up this morning from Cork.'

The barman, a big, soft-faced man, brought Quirke's whiskey. 'Drink up now, Doctor,' he said softly. 'We'll be closing up shortly.'

'Thank you, Michael,' Quirke said. 'Oh, and the inspector here will take a glass of water—do you think you could manage that?'

The barman gave him a droll look and went to the sink and filled a glass at the tap and brought it back and set it down in front of Hackett with a cardboard coaster underneath it. Quirke sipped his new whiskey. They were both gazing before them towards the ranked bottles behind the bar.

'So,' Hackett said. 'What did you find?'

'Pistol, heavy duty,' Quirke said. 'Single shot. Bullet missed the heart and pierced the spleen—lot of blood— punctured the base of the left lung, causing a tension pneumothorax, leading to cardio-respiratory arrest, leading to you-know-what.' He smiled bleakly and lifted his glass in a mock toast. 'Farewell, cruel world.'

'You'd say he did it to himself? I mean, is that the way it looks?'

Quirke pondered this. 'I presume so. He was probably alive for five minutes or so after he was hit. There were just the two of them in the boat. Not a good thing to have to watch, a man lying in front of you shedding buckets of blood and the bullet hole in his chest sucking in air like a second mouth. If what's-his-name, the young fellow, did the shooting, I'd say he would have fired again, to finish him off—wouldn't you? The weapon wasn't found?'

'Clancy—the young fellow—says he threw it in the sea.'

'It's the kind of thing you'd do.'

'If it was you did the shooting. Why would he take it off the dying man and throw it away, if the man had shot himself?'

'Panic?'

The inspector was rotating the base of his glass slowly on its coaster. 'Do you ever wonder what causes it,' he said, 'that cloudiness in water? Is it the what-do-you-call-it, the chlorine, or just a whole lot of little bubbles, caused by coming through the tap?'

Quirke was smiling. 'You have an enquiring mind, Inspector,' he said.

The barman came and rapped the edge of a penny smartly on the bar in front of them. 'Time, gents; time, please.'

*

In the street the afternoon sunlight fell in angled spikes and the air was greyed with exhaust smoke and drifts of summer dust. The two men walked together in companionable silence in the direction of the Bank of Ireland in College Green. There were smells of roasting coffee beans and horse manure—a Clydesdale that was tethered outside Switzer's and harnessed to a green-sided Post Office dray had dropped a mound of steaming clods on to the road—and of scorched sugar from a candyfloss stall on the corner of Dame Street. It struck Quirke, not for the first time, that he and the detective had nothing to talk about beyond death and post-mortems, crimes and criminals, murders and motives. What did they know of each other's lives? Next to nothing. Yet by now they had years of shared history behind them. This was, for some reason, a slightly dispiriting thought.

'Do you know them, at all,' Hackett asked, '—the Delahayes, the Clancys?'

The inspector, Quirke knew, was of the belief that he enjoyed a wide circle of acquaintances and was intimate with important people at the highest levels of society, a notion that Quirke had long ago given up trying to disabuse him of. 'I suppose I might have met Delahaye,' he said.

'Has—had—a young wife. Number two.'

'What happened to number one?'

'Died, four or five years ago. Two sons, twins, grown-up now.'

They had passed the bottom of Grafton Street, and Quirke ducked into Kapp & Peterson's to buy a packet of Senior Service. When he came out Hackett was waiting for him. Quirke offered him a cigarette and they lit up and walked on. The streets were crowded, this sunny summer day. 'Mona Delahaye,' Hackett said, squinting across at the blue clock-face above the gates of Trinity College. 'That's the widow's name.' He hummed distractedly.

Quirke sighed, then laughed. 'All right,' he said, in a tone of weary resignation. 'I'll come with you.'

The inspector turned to him in feigned surprise. 'Would you do that?' It was another convention between them that Quirke had a silken tongue and could talk with ease to the gentry, while Hackett would be looked down on, laughed at and lied to. 'It might be handy, all right. Northumberland Road, big red-brick pile.'

Quirke sighed again. 'What time?'

'I said I'd be out there at five.'

'And how do we account for my presence?'

Hackett gave a snuffly laugh. 'I'll introduce you as Dr Watson,' he said.

'Very funny,' Quirke said, turning away. 'I'll see you at five.'

In the event Quirke got there early. He had taken a taxi and was waiting on the pavement in the broad canopy of shade under a beech tree when Hackett arrived. Hackett had walked from his office in Pearse Street. He liked to walk, and nowadays, thanks to his seniority on the Force, he had the time and leisure to indulge in this simple pleasure as often as he cared to. He had come all the way up the canal along the tow-path from Grand Canal Dock and turned left at Lower Mount Street on to Northumberland Road. This moneyed part of the city was spacious and handsome, but he was a countryman at heart and he missed the fields and the big skies of the midlands of his childhood. He owned a bit of land in south Roscommon and intended to build a cottage on it to retire to. This plan he had kept to himself, so far; he would have to judge carefully when to put it to May, for May was fond of the city. All these renovations and improvements she had him making to the house were, he knew, aimed at tying the two of them inseparably to the place. He, though, would want to be rid of the city when the time came for him to retire: it had too many soiled associations for him. No, he would not spend his declining years in Dublin.

Quirke was leaning against the railing, his incongruously dainty feet crossed at the ankles and his black hat tipped over his left eye. The inspector often wondered about Quirke's life, what he did in the evenings, what people he saw at the weekends. A strange and solitary man. There was that actress he used to go around with—what was her name? Galloway?—and then, of course, more recently, the Frenchwoman, who had run off to France and would not be coming back.

'The widow,' Quirke said, '—what did you say her name was?'

'Mona. Mrs Mona Delahaye.'

'Mrs Number Two.'

The red-brick house was large and plain, with tall, blank windows. They walked together along the gravelled garden path and up the stone steps to the front door. A black crêpe bow was attached to the knocker. The story was in the evening papers—'Death of Prominent Businessman', 'Mystery Death of Delahaye'—and the commissioner had been on the phone to Hackett already. Hackett had got the desk sergeant to say he was out and could not be contacted; he did not feel like talking to Commissioner Brannigan, and anyway he had nothing to tell him.

He pressed the bell.

The maid was a raw-faced girl with freckles and a mop of rust-coloured curls. When Hackett identified himself she gave them both a jaunty grin that seemed to belie the black bow on the door, and went ahead of them along the hall, her uncorseted haunches joggling. The drawing room was at the rear of the house, with a tall window at the far end of it that looked into the garden. There was a bowl of roses on a sideboard, their musky fragrance mingling with the sharper tang of an expensive perfume.

Mona Delahaye was standing to one side of the window, facing into the sunlit garden—a deliberate pose, Quirke felt sure. She wore a green silk jacket over a calf-length black skirt. She delayed a beat before turning to them with a strained expression in her lustrous Oriental eyes. Her rich dark hair, drawn back from her face, seemed to have lights like fireflies glinting in its depths. The two men stood a moment, lost in contemplation of the vision of meticulously groomed and painted beauty that she was. Then the inspector stirred, clearing his throat.

'Mrs Delahaye,' he said. 'I'm sorry for your trouble. This is Dr Quirke.'

Hackett had taken off his hat and, not knowing what to do with it, was holding it behind his back, nervously rotating the brim. His inveterate blue suit, Quirke noticed, had a higher shine than ever at the elbows and the knees; he did not care to think what the seat of the trousers would look like.

Mrs Delahaye came forward, barely glancing at the inspector but looking Quirke up and down with her cool and candid gaze. She gave him her limp pale hand to shake and let it linger in his for a moment longer than the occasion required. 'A doctor,' she said, 'I see,' though it was not clear what she thought she saw. She went to the sideboard and took a cigarette from a mother-of-pearl box there and lit it with an ornate silver lighter the size of a billiard ball. Trailing smoke she walked to a sofa opposite the window—Quirke watched her narrow shoulder-blades flexing like folded wings under the silk of her jacket—and sat down, crossing one knee on the other and detaching a flake of tobacco from her lower lip.

Did she ever do anything, he wondered, without having first calculated the effect? She did not seem a woman lost in grief. And yet he detected something in her, which was not to do with the death of her husband, something that would always be there, something worried, tentative, watchful. Spoilt children had that look, of knowing deep down that all the petting and the pampering might at any moment just stop, without the slightest warning.

On the wall behind her there was a Mainie Jellett abstract in a heavy gilt frame. She gazed up at the two men, widening her violet eyes. 'Have you found out what happened on that boat?' she said. 'I assume it was some kind of awful accident?'

They were conscious, Quirke and the inspector, of

looming awkwardly before her; under her gaze Quirke felt like a less than first-rate thoroughbred being assessed by an unconvinced buyer.

'Well, Mrs Delahaye,' the inspector said, still twirling the hat-brim behind his back, 'that's what we wanted to talk to you about.' He fetched a chair and brought it forward, his boots squeaking, and set it in front of the sofa and sat down, placing his hat primly in his lap. 'In fact,' he said, putting on his gentlest, his most winning smile, 'we were hoping you might be able to help us come to some conclusion about what exactly happened.'

The woman looked past him to Quirke, still standing in the same spot, with one hand in a side pocket of his jacket and the other holding his hat. 'You're not a police-man, though, are you?' she said, frowning.

'No,' Quirke said. 'I'm a pathologist.'

'Yes,' Mona Delahaye said, putting on again the strained frown that was surely deliberate. 'Is that like a coroner?'

Quirke smiled and shook his head. 'No, not really. I did the—em—the post-mortem, this morning, on your husband.' She waited, wide-eyed but inexpectant—in fact, giving the impression that at any moment she might close her eyes and drift off into sleep, like a cat. 'It seems he—well, it seems he shot himself,' Quirke said. 'I'm sorry.'

'Oh,' she said, 'I know that—I mean, I know he was shot. They told me all that.' She was looking about now for an ashtray. Quirke fetched one from the sideboard and she took it from him and set it on her knee and tipped an inch of ash into it. He stepped away from her and sat down, perching on the broad arm of the sofa. Although the room was large he felt disproportionate to everything in it, which gave him a giddy, toppling sensation. Mona Delahaye's loveliness seemed to pervade the room, heavy and sweet, like the smell of the roses.

Hackett tried another tack. 'Tell me, Mrs Delahaye,' he said, 'your husband's business—is everything all right in that regard?'

Mona Delahaye's eyes grew rounder still. 'What do you mean?'

'I mean,' the detective said, shifting on his chair, 'there's not any—any financial problem, is there?'

Quirke looked from the woman to the detective and back again. She was leaning forward, gazing searchingly into Hackett's face. 'I don't know,' she said simply. 'How would I know? Victor wouldn't have talked to me about things like that. You see'—she leaned still more intently forward—'Victor and I didn't really know each other, not in that way, not in a way that we would talk about his work or anything serious like that. He kept that kind of thing to himself.' She paused, and glanced at the floor, then looked up again, and now switched her gaze to Quirke where he sat on the arm of the sofa, a large man in black, watching her. 'When we got married, three years ago, Victor's wife Lisa, his first wife, had died only a couple of years before, and I don't think he realised what he was doing—marrying me, I mean.' She had the earnest air of a schoolgirl explaining that by some anomaly she had not been taught long division, or how to parse a sentence. Quirke thought he had never before encountered such a striking mixture of artlessness and calculation. 'I've been thinking about all this since yesterday,' she said, 'since the news came. I suppose it sounds very strange, to say he didn't know what he was doing when we got married, but that's how he always seemed to me. Like a sleepwalker.'

There was a pause. Far off in the house somewhere someone was whistling; that would be the redheaded maid, Quirke thought.

'Does that mean,' the inspector said, 'that he might have been neglecting the business?'

Mona Delahaye stared at him and then shook her head and gave a little laugh. 'Oh, no,' she said. 'He would never do that, he would never neglect the business. He was very good at what he did.' She gestured with her cigarette at the surrounding room, with its plush, its pictures, its padded quiet. 'He was rich, as you can see,' she said. She might have been speaking of someone she had not known personally but had only heard of, the absent proprietor of all these polished possessions.

They heard voices in the hall. Mona Delahaye stubbed out her cigarette hastily, as if she were afraid to be caught smoking. The door opened and a young man with blond hair put in his head. 'Oh, sorry,' he said, seeing Quirke and the inspector. He came in, followed by a young man who was his double. They were tall and slim, with long, slightly equine heads. Their hair was of a remarkable shade, almost silver, and very fine, and their eyes were blue. They had the look of a pair of fantastically realistic shop-window mannequins. They were dressed in white, down to their white plimsolls, and brought with them a suggestion of sun-warmed grass and willow bats and scattered applause drifting across a trimmed, flat sward.

'You must be the police,' the young man said, and advanced on Quirke with a hand extended. 'I'm Jonas Delahaye. This is my brother, James.'

Quirke took the young man's hand and introduced himself. 'He's a coroner,' Mona Delahaye said. Both her stepsons ignored her.

'Pathologist,' Quirke said to the twins. 'This is Inspector Hackett.'

Jonas Delahaye gave Hackett the merest glance then turned back to Quirke and gazed at him with frank and faintly smiling interest. 'Dr Quirke,' he said. 'I think I know your daughter.'

This put Quirke momentarily at a loss. 'Oh,' he said lamely, 'Phoebe, yes.' He had never heard his daughter mention Jonas Delahaye, or not that he could recall; but then, he was not much of a listener.

'At least, I know a friend of hers—your assistant, I believe. David Sinclair.'

'Oh,' Quirke said again, nodding. He felt acutely this young man's almost invasive presence. 'Yes, David is my assistant,' he said. 'How do you know him?' Jonas ignored this question, as if he had not heard it, and went on gazing almost dreamily into Quirke's face. His brother had wandered to the table in the middle of the room on which there was a pewter dish with apples. He took an apple and bit into it, making a crisp, cracking sound. He seemed dourly disaffected, compared to his smiling brother. Of the two it was apparent that Jonas was the dominant twin. Neither one of them had given the slightest sign of acknowledgement of their stepmother, who had turned her face away and was gazing out into the sunlit garden.

'So,' Jonas said, throwing himself down in an armchair and hooking one leg over the side of it, 'what happened to my father?' He looked from Quirke to the inspector and then at Quirke again.

'Your father died of a gunshot wound,' Hackett said. 'It seems he fired the shot himself.'

Jonas pulled a dismissive face. 'I don't believe it,' he said. 'Davy Clancy was with him on the boat. Have you spoken to him?' He was looking at Quirke. 'He should be able to tell you what happened.'

James Delahaye was watching them, leaning against the table and eating his apple. Mona Delahaye sighed, and leaned back on the sofa and closed her eyes. For a moment Quirke had a notion of the five of them, himself and the inspector, the twins, the woman on the sofa, in a scene on stage, each one placed just so by the director, and all of them waiting for their cue.

Inspector Hackett swivelled about to look at Jonas Delahaye sprawled in the armchair. 'Would you have any idea'—he glanced towards James—'either of you, why your father would kill himself?'

Jonas shrugged, lifting one shoulder and pulling down his mouth at the corners. His brother, crunching the last of the apple, looked towards his stepmother and laughed.

'I suppose,' Hackett said, 'if you were of a charitable disposition, you could say they were obviously suffering the after-effects of the great shock they've had.'

He and Quirke were walking back along Northumberland Road towards the canal. The sun was still shining but the evening shadows were lengthening; twilight was gathering itself deep in the foliage of the beeches set at intervals along the pavement. They had been discussing the Delahaye twins, their remarkable attitude to their father's death, their cool insouciance. 'Aye, they didn't seem exactly heartbroken,' Hackett went on. 'And neither did she.' He glanced sidelong at Quirke. 'What do you think?' But Quirke said nothing, only paced along in silence, frowning at his toecaps.

4

SYLVIA CLANCY was afraid of both her husband and her son. She had tried for a long time to deny to herself that this was so, but it was. She did not feel menaced by them or believe they would do her physical harm. What she most feared was their potential to harm themselves, to damage their lives, and hers; to—the word shocked her but she had to admit it—to contaminate the little world the family shared together. They were not wicked, either of them, and probably they loved her, in their way, though it would not be the same as the way she loved them. She had them, as she always thought, in her care. They were her charges. She had to protect them, from the world but, much more, from themselves. She was aware of how outlandish this would sound if her husband were to hear her say it, and she was careful never to let slip the slightest hint of how she felt, how she thought. All the same she wondered if they did know what she thought and felt, if they knew without knowing, in that way the Irish were so adept at doing.

She knew about her husband's infidelities. She was hurt, of course, each time she found out about a new one—and probably the ones she learned about represented only a fraction of the real number—but she had come to accept his affairs as a condition of her life, as unalterable as the pain she suffered constantly in her back. It was because of her back, she supposed, that Jack had strayed in the first place. It must have been hard on him, being married to a woman who flinched and drew in her breath every time he put his arms around her. She could hardly blame him for seeking comfort and release elsewhere. Yet she did blame him, she did—she accepted, but she blamed; she could not stop herself. He might have helped her to reconcile herself to his waywardness, he might at least have tried. But he was too impatient for that.

Impatience, she thought, was what drove him, was what had always driven him; impatience, and the awful resentment that went with it. She remembered the occasion, years, many years before, when she had seen these traits in him for the first time. That night, at the Delahayes' party, he had snatched the car key out of her hand and walked out into the rain with that look on his face, his mouth twisted all to one side and his eyes blazing. What was it she had said? Something about Victor and Lisa, about what a handsome couple they made, and how happy they seemed together. Had Jack been jealous of Victor? Had he wanted Lisa for himself? Perhaps he had got her—perhaps that was why he was so upset that night. Yes, perhaps Lisa and Jack had been lovers. It amazed her that she could admit this possibility with such dispassion.

Yet these speculations did weary her. Often she wished she could just walk away from everything, say nothing to anyone and just walk away. How much would they miss her, her husband and her son? She closed her eyes. If only she could empty her mind, dull her brain, kill her thoughts. That would be a kind of walking away.

How lovely the sunlight was this evening; how heartless.

She was climbing the stairs and had stopped on the landing a moment to look out of the high window there to Howth Head far off on the other side of the bay. Below, in the garden, the blossoms of the peony roses were all falling over, dragged low by their own full-blown weight. She had tried to pin them up but they had drooped anyway, as if they wanted to hang their heads like that, as if that was how they saw themselves at their best. It was strange, she thought, to be thinking of flowers at such a time. But life, ordinary life, would not stop, even for a death.

The flowers were not the only things that needed attention. The big old house, in one of Dun Laoghaire's more stately terraces, was showing the signs of years of neglect. Jack was not interested in the house. Why would he be? He was rarely there. Jack had never got used to being married—*tied down* was what he would have said, she supposed—and could always find an excuse not to be at home. But that was Jack, take him or leave him.

She went on up the last flight. She had squeezed six big Outspan oranges and poured the juice into a jug, and was carrying the jug together with a glass on a wooden tray spread with a table napkin. Davy was in bed, suffering still from the effects of being out in that boat for hours with no protection from the sun. Who would have thought the sun would be so strong, even in June? When she came into his room she caught the warmish smell of his poor scorched flesh. He lay sprawled on the bed in his pyjama bottoms, the sheet kicked aside. He was wearing the black sleep mask that she had not known the house possessed, and she could not tell if he was asleep or awake. She stood over him, listening to him breathe. The sun-blisters on his arms had broken and the skin on the bridge of his nose was beginning to peel already. She felt a twinge of embarrassment, standing in his room like this, and thought of setting the jug of orange juice down on the bedside table and tiptoeing away. But then he woke, and pulled off the mask and struggled to sit up, blinking and coughing, and drew the sheet over his knees.

The tray, she realised, was the same one on which she used to bring up his goodnight glass of milk when he was a child. How quickly the years had flown!

Davy was twenty-four but seemed younger, or seemed so to her, anyway. Maybe, she reflected, mothers always think their sons will never quite grow up. He was working for the summer as a storeman at the Delahaye & Clancy garage in Ringsend. He seemed to like the work, and was diligent, Jack said, a thing that surprised Jack, and surprised her, too. She supposed he was trying to impress them. He had confided to her his plan to train to be a mechanic and get a permanent job, but not at Delahaye & Clancy. He had not told his father, yet, and neither had she. Jack would make a fuss, but she knew there would be no point in arguing: Davy was as stubborn as his father, and would not be told, or cajoled, but would go his own sweet way. She had asked him what he wanted to work at, if he was not going to continue at college, but he would not tell her.

'I brought you some orange juice,' she said. She showed him the jug and the glass. 'It's freshly squeezed.' Looking exhausted, he sat slumped forward, with his head hanging and his arms draped over the mound of his knees. He was very fair—he had her colouring, which was why he had burned so badly under the sun. She looked down at him. A spur of hair stood up on the crown of his head, and she remembered how when he was little she used to have to wet the comb under the tap to get that same recalcitrant curl to lie flat. Was she wrong to dwell on the past like this? She should be treating him like an adult, not all the time harking back to how things were when he was still her little boy. 'How do you feel?' she asked. He shrugged, still slumped over his knees. 'Drink some of this juice,' she said. 'It will help to cool you down.'

She poured the juice and tapped the glass gently against his shoulder, and with a shuddery sigh he took it from her and drank, and had to stop to cough again, and drank again. 'That's good,' he said. 'Thanks.'

She sat down on the side of the bed. Since she had come into the room he had not once met her eye. 'How are you feeling?' she asked again.

'I can smell myself,' he said. 'I can actually smell my skin where it got burned. It's like fried pork.'

She smiled, and he smiled too, ruefully, although he still would not look at her. He finished the juice and handed her back the glass. She asked if he would like more and he shook his head, and rubbed a finger rapidly back and forth under his nose. It was no good trying not to see these little things—the way he was sitting on the bed, the way he rubbed his nose, that springy curl sticking up—that made her think of him as a child again. The boy was still there, inside the young man's body. It was the same with all of them, all the men she had ever known, in her family or outside it: they reverted to childhood when they were hurt, or sad, or in trouble.

'A policeman telephoned,' Sylvia said. 'A detective. He wants to talk to you. I said you weren't well, and that you were sleeping.' Davy did not respond to this, only sat with his head hanging, his lower lip thrust out, and picked at a loose thread in the seam of the sheet. 'What will you tell him?' she asked. 'I mean, what will you say?' Oh, that look, she remembered that, too, the brows drawn down and the lip thrust out and his neck sunk between his shoulders. 'Tell *me*, will you?' she said. 'Tell me what happened.'

'I told you already,' he said, with the hint of a whine in his voice. *That sullenness*, she thought, *that resentment, just like his father*. He tugged with miniature violence at the thread, drawing in his lip now and tightening his mouth. 'There's nothing more to say.'

'Well,' she said patiently, 'why don't you tell me again? What did—what did he say?'

'He said nothing.'

'He must have said something.'

A ship was leaving Dun Laoghaire harbour: they heard the sound of its siren shaking the stillness of the sunlit evening. Once when they were crossing to Holyhead they had been on deck when the horn went off like that, like the Last Trump, and Davy, her Davy, who was four or five at the time, was so frightened by the terrible sound he had burst into tears and clung to her legs and buried his face in her skirts. They had been so close in those days, the two of them; so close.

'He told me a story,' Davy said, 'about when he was a child and his old man took him out in the car one day and gave him money to buy an ice cream and drove off when he was in the shop.'

'Drove off?'

'And left him there. To teach him self-sufficiency, self-confidence, something like that—I can't remember.'

Sylvia pursed her lips and nodded. 'Yes, I'm afraid that would be the kind of thing old Sam Delahaye would do, all right. What else?'

'*What* what else?' That whining note again.

'Was that all Victor said? What happened then?'

'"What happened then",' Davy said with heavy sarcasm, mimicking her and waggling his head, 'was that he produced this pistol, a huge thing, like a cowboy's six-shooter, and stuck the barrel up to his chest and fired.'

Now it was she who began picking at the sheet. 'Do you think—do you think he meant to do it?—'

'Jesus, Ma!'

'—that he didn't just mean it as a joke, or something, that went wrong?'

Davy laughed grimly. 'Some joke.'

'He could be so—odd, at times. Unpredictable.'

'He meant to do it, all right,' Davy said. 'There was no mistake about it.'

'But *why*?' she almost wailed.

Her son closed his eyes and heaved a histrionic sigh of exasperation and annoyance. 'I told you. *I—don't—know.*'

And why, she wanted to ask, *why did he take you for a*

witness—why you? 'Something must have been terribly wrong with him.'

Davy snorted. 'Well, yes, I'd say so. You don't put a bullet through your heart unless there's something fairly seriously the matter.'

She did not mind the sarcasm or the mockery—she was used to it—but she wished he would look at her, look her straight in the eye, just once, and tell her again that he did not know why Victor Delahaye—Victor, of all people—should have taken him out to sea in a boat and made him watch while he killed himself. 'What shall I tell that detective,' she asked, 'if he calls again?—*when* he calls again.'

He did not answer. He was looking about and frowning. 'Give me my clothes,' he said. 'I want to get up.'

Jack Clancy was walking fast along the front at Sandycove when he heard the sound of the ship's horn behind him. It made him think of his schooldays, long ago. Why was that? There had been a bell, not a bell but more like a hooter, that went off at the end of the lunch-hour to summon the boys back to class. That sinking feeling around the diaphragm, he remembered that, and Donovan and—what was that other fellow's name?—waiting for him in the dark of the corridor where it went round by the cloakroom. They had picked on him because he was small. They would pull his hair, and pinch him. One day they had yanked his trousers down and stood back, pointing and laughing. He had got his own back on Donovan, told on him for stealing hurley sticks from the storeroom and selling them. Funny: it was years since he had thought about those days—why now? Because, he supposed, there were so many other things that he could not allow himself to think about. He was in trouble, no doubt of that.

Dun Laoghaire, formerly Kingstown, is not a harbour but a port of asylum, so called because it was designed as a refuge for merchant ships that for centuries had been lashed by easterly gales and become embayed and were unable to enter the mouth of the Liffey because sailing vessels could not climb the wind and so—and so— His mind reeled, grasping after the old lore that he used to have off by heart. His father had loved the sea and had tried to teach him the history of the port, its facts and fables. But he had been a bad learner. *A good-for-nothing and a waster,* his father would say. *Wine, women and song, that's the limit of our bold Jack's ambitions.* Now the old bastard's wits were gone and all that useless knowledge with them. The old man had spent his life crawling to the Delahayes and where had it got him? First on his belly, grovelling before that crowd, and now on his back, lost to himself and helpless and not even able to die.

Otranto Place—funny name. The evening was warm and there were bathers over at the cove still, on the sand and on the rocks, dozens of them, out from the city on the train, tenement families from Sean McDermott Street and Summerhill, the women fat and the men lean, the kids skinny and white as grubs. Above the strand stood the Martello tower. It had a comical look, he always thought, thick and squat, as if it had once been tall but the top had been blown off it by one of Napoleon's cannon balls.

He turned up Sandycove Avenue. The house looked smaller than in fact it was. One-storeyed, it, too, might have been cut off at the top, with just the front door and a window on either side and the roof sloping down. But at the back it extended a long way out, and there were steps leading down to a garden room where the sun shone in all day in summer. He knew these things because it was he who had found the house, and had even made a down-payment on it, though that had been conveniently forgotten. Women tended to take things like that for granted.

Jack rapped softly with his knuckles on the door, rat-a-tat-tat-tat, tat tat, the old signal. She might be out. Her name was Bella. That was what she called herself; her real name was—what? Anne? Angela? He could not remember. She was an artist: blue skies over poppy fields and bare-breasted hoydens lolling in the grass with flowers wreathed in their hair.

He knocked again and waited.

Dun Laoghaire, formerly called Kingstown.

Otranto Place.

Trouble.

The door opened. 'Well well,' she said, one hand on the door frame and the other on her hip. 'Hello, stranger.' She was wearing ski-pants and sandals, and a white woollen shawl, one corner of it flung over her shoulder and pinned there somehow, like a Roman senator's robe. Her dyed-blonde hair was piled on top of her head and stuck through with what looked to him like two wooden knitting needles. He noted a pair of spectacles—he had not seen them before—resting on the slope of her bosom and attached to a string that went around her neck. There was a fan of fine wrinkles at the outer corner of each eye. Yes, it had been a long time.

'Hello, Bella,' he said.

She was giving him an appraising eye, her head cocked. Had she heard what had happened in Cork?

'Come in,' she said. 'I was just about to take a bath.'

When Hackett arrived at Nelson Terrace Mrs Clancy herself let him in. She took his hat and hung it on the hat-stand and walked with him through the house to the kitchen at the back. Young Clancy was there, sitting at the table with a mug of tea in front of him. He was not small, exactly, Hackett thought, that was not the word, but compact, with a rugby player's shoulders and a neat, squarish head, his reddish hair cut short and standing upright in a flat mat of bristles, in the style of the day— Hackett could imagine some girl running the palm of her hand over that ticklish crest and wriggling inside her dress. He seemed hardly more than a boy. He certainly did not look like a killer.

Mrs Clancy offered tea; the detective declined out of politeness, then regretted it. The woman was tall, and stood in a curiously stiff way, as if someone had just said something offensive and she had drawn herself up and back in indignation.

'This is a shocking business, Inspector,' she said.

English accent, but English to look at, too, somehow, with that long bony face, and the hair tied neatly behind, and the friendly yet remote expression.

'Indeed, ma'am,' he said. 'Shocking.'

Together they turned to look at the young man sitting by the table. He did not lift his eyes. A mother's boy, Hackett thought, but with something of a boxer about him, too.

'How are you getting on?' the inspector asked him. 'You've been in the wars.'

Davy Clancy sighed impatiently. 'I'm all right,' he said. 'I got a bit of sunburn.'

'A bit!' his mother exclaimed, and seemed startled herself at the sudden vehemence of her tone. 'You should see his arms, Inspector.'

Davy plucked instinctively at the cuffs of his white shirt, as if he thought his mother might take hold of him and roll up his sleeves herself and show off his blisters.

'The sun can be a terror, all right,' Hackett said, nodding. 'Especially on the water—I believe the reflected sunlight is worse than anything.' He put his hand on the back of a chair and lifted an eyebrow in Mrs Clancy's direction.

'Of course,' she said, 'of course, please, sit.'

He sat. The chair gave a little cry as if in protest at the weight of him. He leaned forward, setting his clasped hands on the table. For some moments he said nothing, not for effect but simply because he could not think how to start, yet he felt the atmosphere in the room tightening. A person's feeling of guilt was a hard thing to measure. He had known entirely blameless people to start babbling explanations and excuses before the first question had been asked, while the hard cases, the ones who five minutes previously had been sluicing blood off their hands, could be as cool as you like, and not bat an eyelid or offer a word unless provoked to it.

'I don't suppose,' he said, looking at the whorl of hair on the crown of the young man's bent head, 'you've any idea why Mr Delahaye did what he did?' Davy Clancy shook his head without lifting it. 'No,' Hackett said, with a little sigh, 'I didn't think you would.'

Mrs Clancy, behind him, spoke. 'Tell him,' she said, sounding anxious and as if aggrieved, 'tell him what you told me.' Davy, looking up at last, frowned at her, as if not knowing what she meant. 'The story he told you,' his mother said, 'about old Mr Delahaye taking him out in the car and abandoning him.'

Davy scowled. 'It wasn't anything,' he said.

'Tell it anyway,' his mother said quickly, suddenly sharp and commanding. 'The inspector will want to know everything there is to know.'

Davy shrugged and, forced into this wearisome duty, recounted in jaded tones the story of Victor Delahaye's father and young Victor and the ice cream. Hackett listened, nodding, a pink lower lip protruding. 'And did he say,' he asked, when Davy had finished, 'what the point of the story was?' He smiled, showing his tarnished dentures. 'Was there a moral in the tale?'

Davy was peering into his mug. 'He said his father said it was to teach him to be self-reliant. And as he was putting the gun to his chest he said it again: *a lesson in self-reliance.*'

'I see.' Hackett leaned close to the table. 'And what do you think he meant by that?'

Davy rolled his shoulders. 'I don't know. Maybe he thought he was doing to me what his father had done to him.'

'And why would he do such a thing, do you think?'

'I told you—I don't know.'

The detective nodded again. 'And that was it? That was all he said? Nothing else?'

Davy, still looking into the mug, shook his head; he had, Hackett thought, the air of a schoolboy hauled on the carpet by his headmaster. He muttered something, and Hackett had to ask him to repeat it. 'What more would he have said?' the young man almost snarled, lifting his head suddenly, with a look of fury in his eyes. 'What was there to say?'

A moment of silence passed. 'How did Mr Delahaye seem?' Hackett asked. 'Was he agitated?'

'I don't know what he was. He didn't say much. He never talked much to me anyway.'

Hackett thought the boy—he kept thinking of him as a boy—was lying, if only by omission. It was clear from his evasive manner that he knew more than he was prepared to say. What exactly had happened on that boat, out on the sunlit sea? Hackett tried to picture it: the furled sails, the sudden quiet, the lapping of the water on the keel and the cries of the sea birds, the man speaking and then the shot, not loud, a sound like that of a piece of wood being snapped in two.

'My son is very upset, Inspector,' Mrs Clancy said. 'He's had a terrifying experience.'

The boy—the young man—looked at her with another flash of anger, his mouth twisting. 'Maybe he was agitated,

I don't know,' he said to Hackett. 'He must have been—he was going to shoot himself, wasn't he?'

Davy pushed the mug away and stood up and walked to the window with his hands thrust into the back pockets of his trousers and looked out at the garden.

'Would you hazard a guess,' Hackett enquired, in a conversational tone, 'as to why it was you he chose to bring with him?'

'I keep telling you,' Davy said, without turning, 'I don't know why he did any of this—why he went out in the boat, why he brought me, why he shot himself. *I don't know.*'

Hackett turned on the chair to look at Sylvia Clancy. She held his gaze for a moment, then gave a faint shrug, of distress and helplessness, and turned away.

In the garden the last of the evening sunlight was the rich soft colour of old gold. 'Isn't it wonderful,' Bella murmured, 'how long the day lasts at this time of year?' They were lying on a *chaise-longue* in the garden room, she nestling in the crook of Jack's arm and Jack asprawl with a hand behind his head. Bella had pulled her white shawl over them; the rest of her clothes she had dropped in disarray on the floor, mixed up with his. He craved a cigarette, but he did not want to move, did not want to interrupt this little interval of longed-for rest. He felt as if they were balancing something between them, he and the naked woman, some delicate structure spun out of air and light, that would collapse if he made the slightest stir. He was trying to remember where he had first met Bella.

Was it at the party in Pembroke Street that night at the solicitor's flat—what was his name?—when the two fellows who worked for the Customs and Excise had brought a crate of confiscated hooch and they had all got wildly drunk and gone out and danced in the street? He remembered Bella leaning her back against a wall with her hands behind her, swaying her front at him and smiling with those smoky eyes of hers. Or was that someone else, some other girl out for a good time?

'A penny for them,' she said now, running her fingers through the grizzled hairs on his chest.

'I was thinking of the first time I met you,' he said.

'Oh, yes—that opening in the Ritchie Hendriks Gallery. You told me I had nice earlobes.' She pinched his right nipple. 'Always the sweet-talker, pretending to appreciate things no one else would bother to notice. Earlobes, indeed—it wasn't earlobes you were after.'

Whose opening had it been? He had no memory of it—he was not even sure he had ever been into the Ritchie Hendriks Gallery. Maybe she, too, was thinking of someone else. He felt a sudden sweet pang for the lost past, all those possibilities now gone, never to be offered again. He kneaded the plump flesh of her flank just below her ribs and she twisted away from him and laughed and told him to stop, that he knew how ticklish she was. He released her and stood up, then bent to find his jacket on the floor and the cigarettes in the pocket. Lighting one, he walked to the big picture window and stood there naked, smoking, squinting out at the sunlight.

'Let me guess why you're here,' she said.

He glanced over his shoulder. She was lolling on her

back on the *chaise-longue*, the shawl covering her lap. He saw how her breasts, slacker than he remembered them, were slewed sideways, the nipples as if looking at him, endearingly cock-eyed. She was a handsome woman still, and he was sad to see the signs of how she was ageing.

'Guess away,' he said. 'Why am I here?'

'Because of what's-his-name, your partner, Delahaye.'

'Oh. You heard.'

She laughed. 'It was all over the papers!' She turned over on to her stomach, and the shawl slithered to the floor. She wriggled her behind. 'What happened? The papers said it was an accident. Was it?'

He turned back to the window and the overgrown garden. Those tangled roses looked sinister, he thought, like briars in a fairytale. 'You have convolvulus,' he said.

'I have *what*?'

'Bindweed. That creeper, with the white flower. It'll strangle everything if you don't get it dug out.'

'Jack Clancy, nurseryman,' she said, and laughed again, throatily. She rose and came and stood beside him, picking up the shawl and hitching it round her waist for a makeshift skirt. He caught her familiar smell: perfume, sweat, warmed flesh. She took the cigarette from his fingers, drew on it and gave it back, blowing smoke in the direction of the ceiling. 'Do you not want to talk about it?' she said.

'Talk about what?' He was still eyeing the convolvulus.

'All right, sulk.' She went to the pile of clothes and pulled on her knickers, her shirt, the tight black trousers. 'He killed himself, didn't he,' she said.

'How do you know?'

'When it's a suicide the papers have a certain way of reporting it. You can always tell. What was it?—was he sick?'

'Not that I know of.'

'Business in trouble?'

'On the contrary. Business'—he gave a brief laugh—'is booming.'

She stood a moment studying his back; he still had a nice bum, she thought, though it was scrawnier now than she remembered. 'You don't seem exactly heartbroken,' she said.

He turned. 'Don't I?'

She went on looking at him, slowly arranging the shawl about her shoulders and pinning it up again at one corner. 'You know why he did it, don't you,' she said; it was not a question. 'You know, but you're not saying.' She came to him and touched a fingertip to his face. He looked back at her blankly, his eyes gone dead. 'You're in trouble, aren't you?' she said softly. 'Aren't you? You can tell me, you know. I'm the wild horses' despair, I am.'

He turned from her to the garden again. 'You should get that convolvulus seen to,' he said. 'It's a killer, if you let it get established.'

She went up the steps, and he heard her in the kitchen up there, opening drawers and cupboard doors. He got dressed; he felt as if he were putting on not his clothes but his troubles, the ones that had fallen from him earlier when Bella had wound her arms round him and whispered hotly in his ear. How long was it since he had been here last? Two years? Three? Bella had always been an easy-going girl. You turned up, she opened wide her arms, you lay down together, then you got up again and left. Never once, in all the times he had walked out of here, had she asked if he would be coming back. Maybe she was the kind of woman he should have married.

She came down the steps again, carrying a straw-covered flask of Chianti and two wine glasses. She held the flask aloft in a Statue of Liberty pose. 'Have a drink,' she said, 'before you go.'

They took to the *chaise-longue* again, sitting side by side this time, facing the big window. The sunlight had gone from the garden but a bronze glow lingered, polishing the rose bushes and lending an amber tint to the white convolvulus flowers. Jack lit another cigarette. The wine tasted bitter in his mouth. He had a cavernous sensation behind his breast-bone, as if his chest had been hollowed out and emptied of every organ. It was not exactly fear that he felt, but a heavy, dull dread. Something was coming that would not be avoided.

'And how,' Bella asked, 'is the Lady Sylvia?' She put on a prissy accent. 'Spiffing form as usual, I suppose, what?'

He drank his wine and said nothing. He did not mind her mocking his wife. He supposed he should. He felt protective towards Sylvia, most of the time. She had done her best with him, for him, and he was grateful to her, in his way. Thinking this, he imagined her turning aside from him with that deliberately abstracted expression, frowning, as if she had lost something and was trying to remember what it was. *Grateful, dear? I must say, you have a funny way of showing it.* It was true. He owed her a debt, he knew that, but he knew, too, that he had no intention of settling it, not yet, anyway, not while he still had this fire in him; not while he still had Bella, and the others like her, discreet, easy, indulgent. He closed his eyes briefly. He knew in his heart that that was all over, that old, carefree life. There would be no more simple fun; from now on, everything would be complicated, knotted, insoluble. Half an hour ago, lying here in Bella's arms, he had relaxed and felt like weeping.

'I suppose you'll be the boss now?' Bella said.

'Do you think so?' He cast a crooked smile at her, and she saw that flash of mischief she remembered from the old days, that look of a boy who has got his first kiss and means to have more.

'Isn't it what you always wanted?' she said, smiling in her turn.

Her warm haunch was pressed against his leg, and there was a look of slightly unfocused merriment in her eye—she never could hold her drink; it was something that had always amused him. In a minute she would be swarming all over him again. He made to stand up but she put a hand in the crook of his elbow and held him back. 'Don't go,' she said.

'Got to,' he said. 'I'm expected.'

Yet he lingered. He did not want to go home, did not want to face Sylvia, did not want to meet that look she would give him, anxious, soulful, searching. How much did she know, how much did she guess? All this past year he had been sure she knew he was up to something. She did not trust him, never had; he could hardly have expected that she would. He did not trust himself, any more.

'How is the widow?' Bella asked. 'What's her name—
Monica?'

'Mona.'

'He was about twice her age, wasn't he?'

'She's young, yes.'

He felt a sort of ripple in her thigh, and she sat forward
and swivelled about to look closely into his face. 'Oh,
Jack,' she said softly, 'I hope you haven't been a naughty
boy, have you? Haven't been putting in your thumb there
and pulling out a plum, as you always do?'

'Oh, for God's sake,' he said.

She wagged her head at him, making a tut-tutting
sound with her tongue. 'Oh, Jackie-boy. I see now the
reason for your sudden appearance on my doorstep. It
wouldn't be the first time you came running to Bella for
shelter when the Hound of Heaven was at your heels.
Or just a husband on the warpath.'

He sighed. 'Shut up, Bella,' he said wearily. 'You have
a one-track mind.'

'Yes,' she said, and made a grab at the crotch of his
trousers, 'and you haven't, I suppose.'

He batted her hand aside and held out his glass. She
groped for the bottle on the floor and poured another go
of wine.

'I hope you're not intending to make a lamp out of
that, are you?' he said, indicating with his chin the bulbous
bottle in its straw jacket.

'Is that what you think of me?'

'Oh, yes, I forgot—you're an artist.' He had not meant
it to sound so sour.

'Dear me,' she said, 'we are on edge today.' She put the bottle on the floor again and sat back, holding her glass in both hands and nursing it against her breast. 'Were you that fond of your late partner?'

He did not respond, only drank his wine and gazed before him, frowning. 'David was on the boat with him,' he said.

'Who?'

'My son, Davy.'

She stared. 'My God. Why?'

'He asked him to go with him—Victor, that is, asked Davy. The night before, when we were all in the pub, he invited him to come out. Davy hates the sea, but he went, all the same.'

'My God,' Bella said again, more softly this time, more wonderingly. 'Did he—did he see him do it? Did he see him shoot himself?'

Jack watched one last, anxious-seeming bubble crowding at the brim of his glass. 'Yes,' he said, 'he saw it.'

'But—but why?'

'Why did he take Davy with him? I don't know. Maybe to get back at me.'

'For what?'

The wine bubble burst.

'I don't know.'

She was watching him, staring at his profile. 'I think you do know,' she said, in a voice that made her suddenly sound sober. 'I think you're lying.'

He put a hand over his eyes and massaged his temples at either side with a finger and a thumb. 'There was a— there was a problem in work. In the business.'

'What sort of problem?'

He took the hand away from his face and turned towards the window. She saw the pulse working in his jaw. He was still good-looking, with that small neat head, that strong nose, those broad lips that had a twist to them at once humorous and sly. There used to be something about him, something weak and furtively vulnerable. Now that was gone, that youthful defencelessness, but what had come in its place was not strength, only hardness. She put her glass on the floor beside the wine bottle. She should not drink so early in the evening: it always went straight to her head. It was not an occasion to be tipsy: a girl had to watch herself around Jack Clancy.

'He could never let go of anything,' he said, with a distant look now, talking to himself. 'He could never relent. Always had to be top dog, and have everyone around him acknowledge it. Got that from his father, of course, Old Ironsides himself. A pair of them in it—overbearing and ruthless yet still expecting the rest of us to treat them like proper gentlemen of the old school. And all the time they'd cut your heart out for a farthing.'

He stopped. She had an urge to put her finger to that pulse in his jaw to stop it twitching. 'Did you know?' she asked.

'What?'

'Did you know he was going to do it?'

'No. How could I? If I had, do you think I'd have let Davy go out with him? Do you think I'd have let my own son's life be put at risk?'

She picked up her glass again from the floor—what good would staying sober do? 'Tell me what was going on in the business,' she said. 'Were you fiddling the books?'

He said nothing for a moment, then laughed harshly. 'Fiddling the books? For Christ's sake, Bella.'

'Then what was this "problem" that you're so concerned about?'

He shrugged, and looked away from her again. 'Nothing,' he said. 'Forget I mentioned it.'

'Had he found out about it, your partner, Delahaye— had he found out what you were up to, whatever it was?'

He shook his head as if amused. 'What I was "up to"— as if I was an office-boy, stealing the tea money.' He lay back against the sofa, suddenly weary-seeming. 'You don't know what it's like, having something going round and round in your head, round and round. I don't sleep, I just lie there, thinking.'

She waited, but he had lapsed into silence. His eyes were closed. She could hear him breathing; he might have been in a fever, or asleep and having a bad dream. She felt sorry for him, but she was apprehensive, too. She realised that she did not want to know what it was that was going round and round in his head. Some things it was better not to know, especially when they were things that Jack Clancy knew. It had been a long time since they had seen each other but it might have been yesterday, so familiar was the sense she had of his resentment and pent-up anger. He was a dangerous person. Not violent, not menacing, even, yet in some way dangerous, all the same. That was why she had let him go before: he had been too much for her. She stood up, not looking at him. She wanted him to leave. Something had come into the house with him, the presence of which she felt only now; it was as if some animal had loped in silently behind him and hidden itself and now was getting ready to spring out at her. She felt suddenly vulnerable. It was catching, whatever it was that was tormenting him.

'I have to change,' she said. 'I'm going out.'

'Where?'

'Just out.'

'A date.'

'Yes. A date.'

It was a lie, but it did not matter, he was not listening. A dense shadowy glow had come into the window now, as it always did at this time of day. She felt like shivering. That strange light was on Jack's face, a phosphorescent sheen. *What did you do, Jack? What did you do that made your partner shoot himself?*

5

QUIRKE HAD NO BIRTHDAY. He had been an orphan—
he was an orphan still, he supposed, though it was odd to
think so—and his records, if there had been any, were
lost. Not knowing his date of birth, and therefore having
no particular day on which to celebrate the annual
crossing-over as others did, was not something that
troubled him. He knew his age, more or less accurately,
though he did not know how he knew it. Someone, at
some time, long ago, when he was a child, must have told
him, and the figure must have impressed itself on his
mind, though he could not remember being told, or having
been told. It was just there, an accumulating number, as
meaningless as any other, and as lacking in significance,
for him. Each New Year's Day he took down mentally
another used-up calendar from his inner wall, and lifted a
glass in a sardonic toast to himself. It amused him,
especially when he was in his cups, to picture his grave-
stone and the lopsided legend on it: a blank, a dash, and
then a date. Of course, they could count back, his relicts,
and put in a notional year of birth, but it would not be
certain they were right: whoever it was had told him how
old he was might have lied, or might have been mistaken.

Phoebe, of course, insisted he should have a birthday, and would pick a date each year and surprise him with it. This year she chose a random day in June, just because it was summer and the sun was shining. She and David Sinclair, Quirke's assistant and her boyfriend, took him to dinner at the Shelbourne Hotel. She had reserved his favourite table, in the corner by the window to the left that looked across the street to the trees in St Stephen's Green. The evening was overcast and muggily warm, but Quirke nevertheless was in his black suit, the jacket fastened tightly and his white shirt-cuffs on show. Phoebe wished he would let her take him over and smarten him up a bit, get him fitted for a good three-piece tweed suit in Brown Thomas and buy him a shirt or two of some shade other than white. It was not that he did not spend money on his clothes—that suit was Italian, his shoes were hand-made—but he always managed to look *dusty*, somehow. Not dirty, or unlaundered, or shabby, even, but as if he had been standing for too long in some spot where a very fine silt had settled on him, out of the air, without his noticing. Her present to him this year was a tie of shimmering green silk. She apologised for being so unimaginative, but he said, no, it was very handsome—he took it out of its cellophane wrapper and held it up to the light from the window and turned it this way and that, an emerald snake, and thought of Mona Delahaye—and besides, he said, he had been in need of a tie for ages, most of the ones he had being old and greasy by now. Sinclair had bought him a book, Yeats's *Autobiographies* in the handsome new Macmillan edition in its smart cream jacket. Quirke, to hide how touched he was, pored over it for so long, with his head bent, that Phoebe in the end had to take it away from him.

They had ordered Dover sole and a Sancerre that when it came was interesting enough though almost colourless. Quirke was fussy about his wine. Tonight he was making himself drink slowly, his daughter saw, and she wanted to tell him she appreciated it—Quirke with drink taken could be difficult, especially on occasions such as birthdays or other supposed celebrations—but she said nothing, only filled his water glass to the brim and passed him the plate of bread rolls. She felt sorry for him. He seemed slightly lost, in the awkwardness of the moment, suffering smilingly the enforced gaiety that none of the three of them could quite carry off. She supposed he found it difficult to make the adjustment between work and here, and probably David's presence made it more difficult still. But then, David too was being required to adjust. How strange it must be for both of them, dealing with the dead all day and now being here with her, marking an invented day of birth, with the elegantly crisp wine and the fragrance of the food and the glint and shimmer of that suddenly sinister-seeming tie.

'I met someone yesterday who knows you,' Quirke said to Sinclair, looking at him over the rim of his glass.

Sinclair's expression turned wary. 'Oh, yes?' he said.

'Young chap, name of Delahaye. Jonas Delahaye.'

For a moment Sinclair looked as if he would deny knowing any such person, thinking himself the victim of one of Quirke's odd jokes; Quirke had an unpredictable sense of humour. But then he nodded. 'Oh, yes,' he said again, more flatly this time.

Phoebe was looking from one of them to the other with lively interest. She enjoyed watching them together, though in a slightly guilty way. They made her think of two highly strung but excessively well-behaved prize dogs, Quirke a black boxer, say—were there black boxers?—and David one of those pure-bred terriers, aloof and watchful and not averse to showing a fang when the occasion required. David's attitude to Quirke was always circumspect, and Phoebe wondered how they managed to work together. But then, the Saddle Room in the Shelbourne was bound to be a far cry from the pathology department of the Hospital of the Holy Family. Or so she supposed, looking doubtfully at the half-eaten fish on her plate.

'Delahaye,' she said, '—why do I know that name?'

'The father . . . died,' Quirke said.

Phoebe frowned. 'Yes, of course, it was in the papers. What happened?'

'Shot himself.'

She flinched. 'The papers didn't say that.'

Quirke shrugged. 'Well, no. Our fearless purveyors of the truth in the news don't report suicides.'

Sinclair with his fork was picking over the bones of his fish with fastidious thoroughness. 'How was Jonas?' he asked.

'Very calm,' Quirke said drily. 'And the brother, the two of them—very calm and collected.' He turned to Phoebe. 'They're twins, Jonas and—what's the other one called? James? Have you met them? Replicas of each other.' He turned back to Sinclair. 'You know both of them?'

'Hard not to—they're never apart. I see them in Trinity

now and then—they play cricket. Tennis, too, championship standard. I had a match against Jonas once.' He shook his head ruefully. 'Never again.'

'Yes,' Phoebe said, 'I remember that. He did trounce you.' Sinclair looked at her dourly and she smiled and touched the back of his hand.

'They work—worked—for their father, yes?' Quirke said.

Sinclair turned to him. 'I believe so. One is in the shipping end, the other in road freight, I think. Don't ask me which does which—they probably swap around and no one notices. I doubt they actually *work*. It wouldn't be quite their style.'

Quirke was looking out of the window at the trees across the road. Their tops were touched with the last copper glints of evening sunlight. Since he had met them the Delahaye twins had been on his mind. Their manner, especially Jonas's—cool, amused, faintly insolent—had fascinated him, and unnerved him, too, a little. Theirs was not the demeanour of sons suffering from the shock of their father's sudden death, as Hackett had charitably suggested might be the case. Quirke knew about shock. In his work over the years he had dealt with many people in various distraught states. In some cases, it was true, the bereaved, especially sons, behaved in what might have seemed a callous or uncaring fashion in the immediate aftermath of a death, but that was the result of bravado mixed with helplessness. For sorrow does baffle, especially the young. The Delahaye twins, as far as he could see, were not baffled, they were not helpless.

'Is it known,' Phoebe asked, 'why their father killed

himself?' She had been watching Quirke. She knew that look, of concentration and faint vexedness, as if he were trying to scratch an inner itch and failing. 'Or do you think,' she said, 'that it wasn't suicide?'

He stirred, and turned to her. 'Why do you ask?'

Sinclair held up the wine bottle but Phoebe covered her glass and shook her head. He was lacking one of the fingers of his left hand, the result of his involvement last year with one of Quirke's more calamitous attempts to scratch an itch.

'I ask,' she said to Quirke, 'because I can see there's something in this business that interests you. What is it?'

He put down his knife and fork and leaned back in his chair and smiled. 'Ah, you know me too well,' he said.

Their history together had been fraught—for most of her life he had denied she was his daughter and had let her be brought up by his adoptive brother and his wife— and only lately had Phoebe allowed them to come to some kind of laying down of arms. She loved him, she supposed, for all his shortcomings, all his sins. She took it that he in turn loved her, in his hesitant and fumbling fashion. She would assume it to be so. It was the best she could hope for, the best she could do. Quirke was not lavish with his emotions. 'I can see you're half involved already,' she said.

He looked away, and busied himself with his food. 'I don't like to leave questions unanswered,' he said.

'It's you who ask them in the first place,' his daughter replied sharply.

David Sinclair leaned between them tactfully, like an umpire, pouring the wine. This time Phoebe did not cover her glass, and when she lifted it she realised her hand was trembling slightly. It rather appalled her, the almost in-stantaneous way in which she and her father could come to the edge of a fight. 'I'd have thought,' she said, 'your friend Inspector Hackett is the one who should be asking the questions and doing the investigating.'

Quirke said nothing to that, only went on mopping up the last of his peas and mashed potatoes. He cast a glance from under his brows at David Sinclair. Odd fellow, Sinclair, he thought. They had been working together for—what was it, five, six years?—but Quirke knew not much more about the young man now than he had at the start. He switched his glance to Phoebe. What were they to each other, he wondered, she and Sinclair? They had been going out together for more than a twelvemonth now, but what, these days, constituted going out? He looked at his daughter's long, pale hands, her dark head bent over her plate, her neat little jacket, like a toreador's, the cameo brooch, the bit of white lace she always wore at her throat. There was something irredeemably old-fashioned about her, which he liked, but which he imagined might irk a boyfriend. Not that Sinclair was exactly a rake. Perhaps they were better suited to each other than it might seem. If so, how serious was it between them? Were they—he shrank mentally from the thought—sleeping together?

He did not know what young people expected of each other nowadays. In his time the rules were rigid—a hand inside the blouse but outside the bra, a caress of the bare skin above the stocking-tops but no further, a french kiss on only the most special of occasions. What must it have been like for girls, to be constantly under siege? Had they found it flattering, funny, annoying?—had they found it humiliating? He glanced at Phoebe covertly again with a spasm of helpless affection. His feelings for her were an unpickable knot of confusion, doubt, bafflement.

'I suppose,' he said, 'he must have been in some kind of trouble.' Both of them looked at him blankly. 'Delahaye.'

Phoebe turned her gaze now to a spark of light glinting in the bottom of her wine glass. 'Yes, he must have been, surely. People don't kill themselves for nothing.'

'Sometimes they do,' Sinclair said. 'Sometimes there's no apparent reason. They just do it, on a whim. I had a cousin, when I was young, hanged himself in the stairwell one morning when my aunt was out shopping. He'd just got a place in college, was going to study medicine.'

'His poor mother,' Phoebe murmured.

'Yes,' Sinclair said, 'it was her that found him, when she came home from the shops. My aunt Lotte. It nearly killed her.'

A heavy silence fell. Quirke watched as his daughter touched Sinclair's maimed hand again in a quick gesture of sympathy.

'I don't think,' Quirke said, 'Victor Delahaye was the kind of man to do anything on a whim.'

They finished dinner soon after that. There was a wrangle over the bill, until Phoebe plucked it out of Quirke's hand and passed it to Sinclair. He produced his wallet while she delved in her purse. 'Don't worry,' she said to Quirke, 'we're going halves.'

For a second Quirke saw himself and Phoebe's mother,

at this very table, a long time ago, bickering over something—what was it? He looked out at the trees, trying to remember.

When they were leaving the hotel, and Phoebe and Sinclair had gone through the revolving door, Quirke stood back to let someone come in. It was Isabel Galloway. She wore a slim blue suit and a pillbox hat pinned at a jaunty angle to the side of her head. They both halted, staring. 'My God,' Isabel breathed, then quickly recovered herself. 'Quirke!' she said brightly, and pressed her elbows into her sides as if to shore herself up. 'You're looking well.'

Quirke smiled queasily. 'Isabel,' he said. 'How are you? You look . . .' He fumbled after words but could not find them.

Isabel's smile glittered. 'Silver-tongued as ever,' she said, then frowned, annoyed with herself, it seemed, and dropped her eyes and moved past him quickly and strode on into the lobby. He let her go, and stepped between the turning panels of the door, hearing behind him the familiar sharp clicking of her high heels on the marble floor.

Phoebe and Sinclair were waiting for him on the pavement. The last of the daylight was a greenish, crepuscular glow above the trees.

'Wasn't that—?' Phoebe began, but stopped, seeing Quirke's look.

Quirke realised he had left the Yeats book behind him, on the window-sill beside the table where they had sat. He turned back, muttering, and pushed his way through the heavy panelled door again.

*

Rose Griffin maintained a stoic view of life and the misfortunes that life piles upon what, in her best Southern-belle drawl, she would describe as *us poor lost creatures of the Lord*. Not that she believed in the Lord, or disbelieved in him, either. She rarely let her thoughts dwell on things beyond this world, this world being, as she felt, enough of a conundrum. She was intolerant of complainers, since, as she said, there was little to be gained from complaining, unless a body considered the pity of others a thing worth having. She felt pity for no one, on inclination as much as on principle. To pity people was to cheapen them, in her opinion. She realised this could make her seem hard-hearted, but she did not care. She *was* hard—what was wrong with that? Too much softness about, too much floppy, warm emotion. She had pointed it out once to Quirke, what they had in common: a cold heart and a hot soul.

She was shocked to discover that her friend Marguerite Delahaye was a blubberer. She would not have thought it of Maggie, whom she had always taken to be, underneath her spinster's genteel veneer, as tough as she was herself. It was mid-afternoon and the two women were taking tea together in the drawing room of Rose's large, gaunt house on Ailesbury Road. It was a splendid day and they were seated in a splash of sunlight at a little table in the deep bay of a window that overlooked the front garden and the quiet street. To distract herself from Maggie's sniffles Rose was admiring the undulating spiral of steam rising from the spout of the teapot, and the pink roses painted on the dainty china cups, and the rich gleam of the antique silver cutlery. She could never understand why people seemed to pay so little regard to the small but, to her, essential pleasures of life—this knife, for instance, a fine old piece of Georgian silver, the blade worn thin from use and the handle solid and weighty as an ingot in the hand. She thought of all the people who had used it over the years, all of them gone now while she was here.

'I'm sorry,' Maggie said, dabbing at her red-rimmed nose with an absurdly dainty handkerchief with a lace edging. 'It's just that I can't believe that Victor is . . . I can't *believe* he's gone!'

'Yes, dear,' Rose said soothingly. 'I understand.' Did she? She did sympathise, more or less—she had suffered her own losses—but she was not sure she understood. Maggie was behaving as if she had lost not a brother but a husband, or even a lover. Rose had siblings herself, but she rarely thought of them, and for long periods forgot about them altogether. Had she ever cared enough for her brothers that the loss of one of them would have reduced her to the kind of extravagant grief her friend was displaying? She thought it very unlikely. 'Yes, I'm sure a sudden death like that is hard to accept,' she said. She paused. 'They're certain it was—I mean, they're satisfied he was the one that pulled the trigger, yes?'

Maggie nodded, and a fresh spasm of sobbing made her shoulders shake.

When she had heard of Victor Delahaye's death Rose had first been surprised, and then not. Killing himself was just the sort of damn-fool thing that man would do, and the way he had done it—the boat, the deserted sea, the pistol, and young Clancy for a witness—was, of course, typically melodramatic and self-serving. He had entertained large notions of himself, had Victor. She had not known him well, had only met him a few times, on social occasions, but she had taken the measure of him straight off. Vain, pompous, humourless. Victor Delahaye had seen himself, preposterously, as a Renaissance figure, one of the great merchant princes, say, heir to a dynasty and father in turn to twin princelings who would carry on and embellish the grand family traditions. But inside every self-proclaimed great man there crouched in hiding a shivering boy terrified of being discovered and hauled out by the ear, wriggling and whimpering. Rose knew about these things: her first husband, the late Josh Crawford, had been one such great man.

Still, it was a puzzle. What had happened that had led Victor Delahaye to knock himself off his own pedestal? Something must have hit him where it hurt most, in his pride, or in his pocket, or maybe in both. No, his pride: he would not have killed himself over money. Something had damaged his estimate of himself. She pictured Mona Delahaye smiling, that thin scarlet mouth of hers turned up at the corners.

Maggie was talking again, between sniffs, about her brother, saying what a wonderful man he had been—a faithful husband, diligent father, loving sibling. An all-round saint, in fact. Rose suppressed an impatient sigh. The dead get so much more than their share of praise, she thought, and all just for being dead. 'Come now, Maggie dear,' she said, 'don't upset yourself so—think of your asthma.'

She wondered what would happen now to Delahaye's business. She doubted his partner, what's-his-name, would be taking over. The company might be called Delahaye & Clancy, but everyone knew who it was that ran it. Nor did she think the Delahaye twins would be picking up the reins, at least not right away, while they were still busy planting their wild oats all over town. Those boys had a reputation, oh, they certainly did.

The Delahayes were Protestant, of course, while the Clancys were Catholic. That distinction, she knew, meant everything here. She had spent a deal of time in this country, over the years; Josh Crawford had been more Irish than American, and now she was married to a man who was a hundred per cent a native son. All the same, there was an awful lot she still did not understand about life here, and probably never would understand, try though she might. The people's fear of the priests, for instance, never failed to surprise her; also, and, you might say, on the other hand, their reverence for the Protestants. The Protestants were a tiny number, yet the Catholics had only to hear one of them speak, in that drawling, cut-glass accent, to start doffing their caps and tugging their fore-locks and all the rest of such nonsense. This fascinated her, and pleased her, too, in a silly sort of way. It was as if, living here, she had gone back to an olden time, to a civilisation that was both developed and primitive—Byzantium, somewhere like that?—where the mass of the people were held in thrall and ruled over by a secret aristocratic caste, whose power was so pervasive the members of it did not even have to reveal themselves except now and then, by certain offhand yet subtle signs. Yes, that was it: she felt like an anthropologist who has been magically transported through time to an archaic world of mysteries and strange laws, strange rituals and taboos.

She heard the front door opening and, after a moment, softly closing again. That would be Malachy; her husband's quietness and diffidence of manner could be sensed even through walls. She called out to him—too shrilly, making Maggie jump—and he put his head in at the door, smiling in that vague and vaguely troubled way of his. He was tall, with a narrow head. He wore tweeds and a bow-tie. His eyes behind the dully gleaming lenses of his spectacles were pale and slightly watery.

'Oh, don't just dither there!' Rose called to him, with humorous exasperation. 'Come and sit down with us and have some of this good tea—it's that kind you like, Lapsang Souchong, that smells of old Cathay.' Mal entered and closed the door behind him and came forward creakingly, his smile congealing into a slight queasiness. Rose supposed he could not remember exactly who her guest was: new people always worried him. 'You remember Marguerite Delahaye,' she said loudly, 'my friend Maggie.'

'Ah, yes,' Mal said, relieved, his smile clearing. 'Miss Delahaye. How are you?'

He drew up a chair and sat down. Only now did he notice Maggie's red-rimmed eyes and the shine on her nose, and faint alarm spread over his face again, and he touched self-consciously the flesh-pink bulb of the hearing-aid in his left ear.

'Maggie has had a bereavement,' Rose said, pronouncing each word distinctly, so that she could not help sounding overbearing and even a little cross. 'Her brother—'

'Lord, yes, of course!' Mal said quickly, half rising from the chair but keeping his back and his long legs bent in a sitting position; what an endearingly absurd man he was, Rose thought, not by any means for the first time. 'Of course,' he said. 'Your—Mr Delahaye—your brother.' Slowly he subsided on to the chair. 'I'm very sorry for your trouble.'

It was not convention, he did seem genuinely sympathetic, and this set Maggie off again. Rose threw her eyes to the ceiling. 'It's very sad,' she said, somewhat shortly, 'very tragic, of course.'

Mal was pouring himself a cup of tea. The tea smelt of straw and smoke. Rose watched him, his elaborately slow and deliberate movements, still feeling that exasperated fondness she always felt before the spectacle of Mal's mole-like ways. Mal had been an obstetrician at the Hospital of the Holy Family, but was retired now. She often wondered what he did all day. He would leave the house in the morning, quite early sometimes, and come back in the afternoon looking, she always thought, ever so slightly shamefaced. In their early days together she used to ask him straight out what he had been up to, just for the sake of conversation, but he would take on a look of mousy alarm and say quickly that he had gone for a walk, or that he had met someone he knew. Somehow she never believed him. She had an image of him stalled on some street corner, and just standing there haplessly for hours, gazing at nothing, noticing no one and not being noticed, the passers-by stepping around him as if he were a fire hydrant, or a tree that had somehow grown up on the spot overnight. It still surprised her that she had married him.

Not that she regretted it, or was unhappy; only they were, as even she could see, a most unlikely couple, wiling away together the autumn of their lives.

He was asking Maggie if she would take another cup of tea, but she said no, and sat up on her chair and straightened her shoulders, and put the sodden hankie away in her bag and fastened the clasp with a decisive snap. She had a remarkably long neck, and now she extended it in a swanlike fashion, elevating her head and thrusting out her nose and her sharp little chin. Her already greying hair was untended, and had the look of a clump of steel wool, or an abandoned bird's nest.

'I want to ask, Dr Griffin,' she said, 'I want to ask—' She stopped, and looked at her fingers fixed on the rim of the handbag in her lap. She tried again. 'Do you think that he—do you think my brother—would he have suffered?'

Malachy frowned. Medical questions were the one thing that were sure to concentrate his attention. Yet Rose could see how torn he felt now, eager to discuss the likely details of Victor Delahaye's suicide yet hesitant in the presence of the dead man's close relative.

'It depends,' he said, 'on where he—on where the bullet entered.' He clasped his hands, moving forward to the edge of his chair. 'If the shot penetrates the heart, the person will experience first what we call a prodromal period, very short in duration, which is like the sensation before fainting, with lightheadedness and nausea, and after that there'll be a neurocardiogenic syncope. Sorry—big words, I know. Most people's blood pressure on fainting is restored by lying flat, but here, you see, this is impossible, as the pumping mechanism is destroyed. The person would have only moments after being shot before they fell over and exsanguinated—bled to death, that is. Some victims of attack say they didn't even notice they had been stabbed or shot until they saw the blood. And then—'

'What he means,' Rose said heavily, 'is that your brother would have died instantly.' She turned to her husband, signalling with her eyes. 'Isn't that the case, Malachy?'

Mal sat back on the chair, and issued a soft, sighing sound, like that of a very small balloon very quietly deflating. 'Yes,' he said meekly, 'of course that's what I mean, that he would have died instantly'—and added, faintly—'or almost.'

Maggie gazed at him unhappily, trying to believe him, Rose saw, yet not succeeding. 'It's what I keep thinking of, you see,' she said, with a tremor in her voice. 'I keep imagining him in agony, regretting what he'd done but knowing it was too late.' She was clutching the bag in her lap so tightly now that the blood had drained from the joints of her fingers. 'I suppose people don't think, when they're going to do something like that, of how it will feel, of what the pain will be like. I suppose they're so desperate they just—' She shut her eyes and two fat shiny tears squeezed out between the lids and rolled down swiftly on either side of her nose. Malachy, in alarm, looked at his wife, and Rose reached out and covered Maggie's clasped hands with one of her own.

'Oh, my dear, don't,' she said. 'You're just tormenting yourself.'

'I know,' Maggie said, nodding like a child, with her chin tucked in and her eyes clamped shut and more tears squeezing out between the lids. 'But I can't help it—I can't stop thinking of him out there in that boat, putting the gun to his chest, and—' She sobbed, her swollen lower lip shaking and the tears flowing down her face. Her breathing was becoming increasingly hoarse, and Rose hoped she was not going to suffer an asthmatic attack. Her first husband had died of emphysema, and she remembered the awful gasping and hooting he used to do at the end.

'Malachy,' she said, 'why don't you go and see if you can find something to give to Maggie?' He threw her another wild look, and she smiled patiently. 'Some *brandy*, maybe? Brandy, or something like that?'

'Oh, no!' Maggie said hastily, like a child again, threatened this time with a dose of castor oil. 'I'm all right, really.'

Mal rose silently and left the room, shutting the door so softly behind him the catch did not even click.

'When will the funeral be held?' Rose asked. She was bored now, and wished her friend would drink up her tea and go.

'Tomorrow,' Maggie said. 'I don't know how I'm going to get through it.'

'Oh, you'll manage,' Rose answered brusquely, and smiled to soften the harshness of her tone.

There was a pause and, as if to mark it, the shadow of a cloud swept across the garden outside, and in the room the daylight dimmed for a moment as though a switch had been pressed. Rose was trying to recall when it was she had last seen Victor Delahaye. Was it at that reception at the embassy last year, to do with some yacht race or other—the America's Cup?—that somehow she and

Malachy had been lured to, although Rose had never been to sea on anything much smaller than the *Queen Mary*? Quirke had been at the reception too, she recalled—what had *he* been doing there, other than soaking up the ambassador's bourbon?

Rose had found herself at one point standing by a window in a small circle of people that included Victor Delahaye and his baby-doll wife. Delahaye had been pronouncing on some point of nautical etiquette. What a donkey he had seemed to Rose, in his navy-blue blazer and grey slacks and his slip-on shoes gleaming like mahogany, standing there pontificating about tides and currents and knots and God knows what all. Good-looking, though, in a somehow artificial sort of way, with that craggy profile and his tastefully greying hair swept back from his temples. His wife, standing beside him, had looked as bored as Rose had felt. Rose guessed she must be a good fifteen years younger than her husband, maybe twenty, even. What was her name? Mona. Mona Delahaye. The name suited her. Cat eyes, a mean mouth. Was it she who had caused Delahaye to load up his pistol and take himself out to sea, never to return? Rose had known finer and more sensible men than Victor Delahaye who had been ruined by their women. Used to happen a lot, that kind of thing, where she came from; the noble code of the Southlands.

'I'm sorry, I seem to have driven Malachy away,' Maggie said, managing to sound aggrieved. Rose gave her a look. She had not realised how tedious her friend could be. How was it they had become friendly in the first place?

Rose did not make friends easily, or without due consideration. The two women had met through one of the charities Rose's late husband had supported, the Glentalbot Trust, which had its headquarters in a draughty old house in the Wicklow mountains. Rose was on the board of the Trust, and so was Marguerite Delahaye, who had taken over the seat once occupied by Victor Delahaye's first wife, now deceased. Rose had paid scant attention to Maggie, the token Protestant on the board, until that now infamous emergency meeting at which Rose had demanded the resignation of the director of Glentalbot House, a drunken incompetent. Maggie, to everyone's surprise, had supported her, and between them the two women had won the day and routed the director's party. After the meeting Rose had sent her car and driver back to town and had taken a lift in Maggie's rattly old Morris Oxford. On the way in they had stopped at a hotel in Enniskerry and drunk a bottle of wine together to celebrate their victory. That day Rose had seemed to see, piercing through Maggie's prim and proper manner, a hard cold gleam of steel. Looking at her now, sitting before her sunk in a puddle of sorrow and self-pity, Rose wondered if she had been mistaken, if what she had seen in Maggie was simply something she had wanted to see, a reflection only of her own glinting toughness.

As if she had sensed Rose's disenchanted musings, Maggie now stood up, saying she should go. She went to the mirror over the fireplace and looked at herself with a faint cry of dismay, and took a compact from her bag and dabbed powder on her cheeks and on the sides of her inflamed nose, with not much effect. Rose turned on her chair to regard her, and before she knew she was going to say it said, 'And you really don't know why he did it?'

Maggie stopped and stood very still, facing the mirror, the powder puff suspended. 'Oh, Rose,' she said, 'there are things I can't allow myself to think about, not yet.'

Rose looked at her friend's haggard face reflected in the mirror. There was something about Maggie, something faintly but definitely strange. It was as if she had an emotional squint. You felt when she looked at you that she was not seeing you straight. She had odd ways, odd tics. She was given to sudden pauses, sudden halts in the midst of things, when she would stand for five or ten seconds gazing before her with a stricken expression, as if she were seeing horrors. Then she would blink, and give herself a shake, and be quite normal again, or as near to normal as she ever got. Poor Maggie. She should have married. But then, who would have married her?

Malachy came back, bearing a dusty bottle with an inch of cherry brandy in the bottom. 'Sorry,' he said, 'this was all I could find.'

The two women looked at him.

Jack Clancy stood at the bottom of Bow Street smelling the warm, rancid stink of fermenting barley from behind the beetling walls of Jameson's distillery. He always thought it funny that old Samuel Delahaye, a teetotaller and a zealous promoter of the temperance movement, should have chosen this place, so close to the distillery, as the site for the offices of Delahaye & Clancy. Nor could he have welcomed the proximity of the Capuchin friary round the corner in Church Street. Samuel was an old-style Unionist, whose people had originated in the black hills of Antrim, and he did not take kindly to Catholics, even though he had brought in one of them, Jack's father, to be his business partner. To Jack all that seemed immensely far off now, as if it had happened hundreds of years past, and not just a generation ago.

He set off walking slowly over the cobbles. This street was strange, always had been, so hushed and secretive, with a silence all of its own, flat yet echoing. It was because of the height of the walls on either side, he supposed, and the narrowness between them; the cobbles, too, probably acted on sounds in some deadening way. As a child he was always frightened when his father brought him here, to the office, and they had walked along where he was walking now, hearing their own footsteps. Yet when had his father brought him here, and why? He would not have wanted him about the office, under his feet, and anyway he would have been afraid of what Samuel Delahaye would say, for old Samuel, the Senior Boss, certainly was not fond of children. Yet Jack saw in his mind the two of them walking along here, hand in hand, the stooping man, only in his thirties and in failing health already, and himself in short trousers and a peaked cap with a button in the crown. Was he remembering, or imagining?

He stopped at the squarish brick mansion opposite Duck Lane. It was of modest size, somewhat squat, with two windows to either side of the front door and five more above, on the first floor. The bricks were pale brown with flecks of yellow, as if butter had been mixed into them. The afternoon sun shone kindly on them. The front door, too, was squat, with a heavy black knocker and a glass fanlight above it where the name of the firm was painted in discreet gilt lettering:

Delahaye & Clancy Ltd.
Import Export

He realised, with a curious shock, how fond he was of this house, solid and four-square as it was. It seemed to him suddenly an old friend whom he had neglected for a long time but who now had stepped forward diffidently to offer him—to offer him what? Reassurance? Forgiveness? Shelter? He thought of the people inside. A few days ago he had been one of them, a man in an office, quietly working. Now it seemed to him something he had dreamed, another life, commonplace yet fantastical.

He did not suppose the twins would be at their desks. They rarely were. They dropped in once in a while, nonchalantly, to sign a few letters and collect their expenses. Such behaviour would not have been tolerated in old Samuel's day. Maverley, the head bookkeeper, had tried once or twice to discipline them but they had laughed at him. Maverley was the one Jack had always worried about, the one he knew would find him out, if anyone would, and now he had. He should have got Maverley on his side, should have brought him in on the plan, should have involved him in the grand and secret strategy he had been working on for years. But Jack had been afraid to show his hand to anyone, and that, he saw now, had been his weakness. For what he had been doing could not be done successfully by one man alone. He should have taken a partner.

Maverley would have been the obvious choice, but Jack had not considered it for a moment, and that had been his downfall. Maverley was a weasel, but weasels have sharp teeth. The bookkeeper, it turned out, had been watching him for months, watching his every move. Jack had secretly set up dummy companies, in Belfast, in Jersey, in the Isle of Man, to buy shares in Delahaye & Clancy—a daring and damn clever thing, even if he said so himself—and he had been on the brink of becoming the major shareholder when Maverley struck. Maverley had not been man enough to confront Jack directly, but had gone instead to Samuel Delahaye and told him everything. And the old bastard, of course, had told Victor.

Jack knew that Victor had never understood him, had taken him for granted. Victor treated him as he treated his twin sons, with a kind of easy, tolerant contempt. At board meetings Jack somehow always found himself at the far end of the table, with ten feet of gleaming mahogany between him and Victor up at the top, sitting in what used to be his father's chair, directing the order of business with a lordly ease. Occasionally, for the look of the thing, Victor would ask for Jack's opinion, and while Jack spoke he would sit back, with an index finger to his cheek, suppressing a smirk, or so it seemed to Jack, while the rest of the board members drummed their fingers and waited impatiently for him to finish. Victor made little jokes at Jack's expense, delivered little digs. 'Oh,' he would drawl, when some trivial topic was mentioned, 'that would be Jack's territory, not mine—isn't that right, Jack?' And Jack would have to smile and squirm and take the mockery, as if he were an office-boy brought in to be consulted on something too vulgar for Victor Delahaye to know anything about.

He looked up at the frontage of the house, at the glowing, buttery tiles, the rippled window panes, the tastefully painted sign over the door. He would never again cross the threshold here, all at once he knew it, and he turned aside quickly and walked away.

Jack wished he could forget his last meeting with Victor, but it kept returning to his mind, each time as vivid as if it were taking place all over again. Victor had called him into the boardroom. When Jack entered Victor was standing at the window with his back turned, looking out at the brick chimneys of the distillery. Fury, accusations, recriminations—all of that Jack could have coped with. But Victor had not shouted, or threatened. He had seemed more tired than angry. His shoulders were sloped and his back looked crooked somehow, like Sylvia's, as if he were in pain, like her. 'My father spoke to me,' he said. Those were his words, *My father spoke to me*. It had sounded to Jack like something out of the Bible. *Depart from me, ye cursed . . .*

Had he caused Victor to do what he had done? Would Victor have killed himself because he had learned his partner had been plotting to take control of the business? Would he? If so, it had been Victor's ultimate dismissal of him, his final gesture of disdain for Jack and his secret plans. And now it was all gone. All the months of scheming, of planning, of putting the pieces into place, of hiding and watching, of waiting, of making himself wait

—all gone. The twins, that pair of wastrels, would inherit the lot—them, and Victor's bitch of a wife. They would have it, and he would have nothing—Maverley would make sure of that.

He turned into Smithfield. A rag-and-bone man on his cart went past, his nag's hoofs clomping and the iron bands on the cartwheels harshing against the cobbles.

What now, Jack? he asked himself. *What now?*

He went out to the river and hailed a passing taxi. The driver wore a cap and did not try to make conversation, sitting in front of him sunk in his seat, his shoulders up and his big red ears sticking out. What would it be like, Jack wondered, to be him, rattling around all day in this old motor, picking up strangers and never saying a word to them? It might not be bad at all. It would require so little, just to exist. In the past Jack had rarely thought about other people's lives. Now he seemed to be on the outside of his own life, suddenly; one minute he had been safely indoors, in the thick of things, the next he had been seized on roughly and hustled out and dumped on the pavement, like a character in a cartoon, with his shirt collar standing up and stars flying in a circle round his head.

Why had Victor done it? *Why?* Was it really his fault, Jack thought, was he really to blame?

He told the driver to stop at Kenilworth Road and got out and set off walking towards the square. It was a habit he had fallen into; even when he drove himself he would stop short and park and go the rest of the way to the nursing home on foot. By that means he got an extra few minutes' delay, an interval in which something might happen, in which some accident might occur, some sudden summons be delivered, so that he could turn back and cancel that day's visit. Ridiculous, of course: nothing ever happened, and he would have to go on, at an increasingly leaden-footed pace, until despite everything he arrived at the front door and the four granite steps leading up, which might have been the steps to the gallows.

The front hall as always smelt of stewed tea and soiled mattresses. His father's room—or cell, as Jack thought of it—was on the first floor. Up here the spacious Georgian rooms had been divided by means of partition walls into smaller units that were narrow and cramped but had absurdly lofty ceilings with cut-off plaster-cast borders at an angle to each other on two sides. There was a bed, a chair, a bedside locker. A copper beech tree outside loomed in the high sash window, darkening the room within and giving it an underwater look. Jack's father inhabited this cistern-like space with the indolent furtiveness of an elongated, big-eyed, emaciated carp. Over time he had taken on protective colouring, so that always when Jack entered the room it took him a moment to make out the old man's figure against the background of drab wallpaper and the brown blanket on the bed and the rusty light in the window.

'Hello, Dad,' he said, trying to appear cheerful but sounding, as always, alarmed and querulous.

His father, standing by the window, peered upwards, frowning, and put his head to one side, as if he had heard his son's voice as a faint cry or call coming from a long way off. Jack sighed. What added to the torment of these visits was the eerie feeling he had that there was no one else here, that he was alone and talking to himself. His father seemed to feel the same thing, that he was alone yet being talked to, somehow. And so they would blunder through a painful half-hour, the son shouting himself hoarse in an effort to penetrate the fog of his father's senility, while his father grew increasingly agitated, thinking probably that spirit voices were speaking to him loudly but unintelligibly out of the ether.

As a young man Philip Clancy had been tall and thin and now he was stooped and gaunt. He had a small head with a domed forehead and a curiously pitted skull on which a few last stray hairs sprouted like strands of cobweb. His nose was huge and hooked, a primitive axe-head, and his mouth, since he had given up wearing his dentures, was thin-lipped and sunken. The Delahayes had treated him negligently all his working life and now that he was worn out there was not one of them who would come to visit him, here where he was held in captivity, vague and lost to himself and the world.

Jack walked to the window and stood with his hands in his pockets, looking out. Why would they not cut down that bloody tree, or prune it back, at least, and let in a bit of light? He had asked them often enough to do something about it and they had promised they would but of course they never had. The fellow who ran the place was an oily type, ferret-eyed behind a fawning manner, while his washed-out wife had the dazed look of someone trying in vain to understand how she had ended up like this, running a home for the old and the sick and the mad.

Jack's father was watching him with a wary surmise, running his eye all over him as if in search of a clue as to his identity. Somewhere in the house an electric alarm bell was ringing, an insistent buzzing that seemed to loop on itself slowly, over and over.

'I'm in trouble, Dad,' Jack said, still gazing out of the window. 'I tried to take over the business and I failed. Or I was beaten. Suicide you can't win against.' He paused, shaking his head slowly from side to side in bitter and angry regret. 'I did it partly for you, you know,' he said. 'To get back at them for the way they used you, all those years.' He stopped again. Was it true? It sounded fake, yet he so much wanted it to be true. He wanted to believe that there was, if not a nobler then a higher motive for what he had done, what he had tried to do. He did not care to think it had all been for himself, to satisfy his own resentment and jealousy.

His father, standing there peering at him, made a sound, a sort of questioning click at the back of his throat. What went on in his head, Jack wondered, what shards and tail-ends of thought were floating about in there, the splintered wreckage of a life? 'Ah, Dad,' Jack said, feeling suddenly worn out. Something was happening in his throat, his sinuses, behind his eyes. He put a hand to his face, and all at once the tears came, and he opened his mouth and released a sound that was half a sob and half a wail. Still covering his eyes, he reached out his other hand blindly before him, and finding his father's cold and bony arm held on to it, and wept.

6

THE NIGHT WAS TOO HOT for sleeping but they would probably not have slept anyway. Quirke sat on the side of the bed, smoking a cigarette. He was naked, yet still he was sweating. It was strange, being here again in the little house in Portobello, in this low-ceilinged bedroom with the narrow bed and the Fragonard reproduction on the wall and that little square window looking out on to the canal.

The hour was past midnight but there was still a faint glow in the sky above the rooftops. He did not like this time of year, with its slow lethargic days and eerily short nights. In summer he always felt slightly unwell, with headaches and pains in his joints and a constant faint sensation of nausea. He thought he must have an allergy, that there must be some kind of pollen or dust in the air that his system could not cope with. He should have a test. He closed his eyes briefly. There were many things he should do.

'I suppose you'll be off now,' Isabel Galloway said, 'having got what you came for.'

She was sitting up in the bed, propped against pillows, wrapped in the silk tea-gown that he remembered, with red and yellow flowers printed on it. She was smoking, too, with an ashtray in her lap. Although his back was turned to her he could feel her angry eye fixed on him.

'Do you want me to go?' he asked.

'Oho, no,' she said, with a bitter laugh, 'don't try that old trick—I'm not going to make it easy for you.'

He was squinting through the window out into the undark night. The streetlamp at the corner was casting a sulphurous sheen on the still surface of the canal. He thought of being out there, even saw himself, walking along the tow-path in the calm mild air, moving between pools of lamp-light, his long shadow shortening at his back and rising up swiftly and then the next moment falling out in front of him. To be alone, to be alone.

'I'm sorry,' he said.

'Yes, of course you are.' Isabel spoke behind him, in a tone of angry sarcasm. 'You're always sorry, aren't you?'

'I shouldn't have come here.'

'No, you shouldn't. And will you please turn around? I want to make sure you're not smirking.' He half turned towards her, showing his face to her, his expression of weary melancholy. Their love-making had felt to him more like a surgical procedure. Isabel had thrust herself angrily against him, all elbows, ribs and bared teeth. Now she sat there furious in her painted gown like an Oriental empress about to order his beheading. 'You hurt me, Quirke,' she said, with a tremor in her voice that she could not suppress. 'You broke my heart. I tried to kill myself over you.' She shook her head in rueful wonder. 'What a fool.'

He tapped his cigarette on the edge of the ashtray. 'I

should have telephoned,' he said. 'I should have kept in contact. That was unforgivable.'

Her eyes blazed, glittering with unshed angry tears. 'But of course you're asking to be forgiven, aren't you?'

He looked down. Somewhere nearby a church bell tolled once, marking the half-hour. The chime hung for a second or two in the upper air, a trembling pearl of sound. 'I thought,' he said, speaking very slowly, 'I thought we might try again, you and I.'

Isabel stared at him steadily for a long moment, then flung herself from the bed and swept out of the room, her bare feet slapping on the polished wood floor. The bathroom door down the corridor slammed shut. He listened to the faint distant tinkle of her peeing. He put out a hand and felt the warm spot in the bed where she had sat. He saw clearly, like a forking path, the two possibilities that lay before him: either stay, or get up now and hurry into his clothes and leave before she returned. He did not move.

They went downstairs, Quirke barefoot and in shirt and trousers. He sat on the sofa in the living room while she fetched glasses and a bottle from the kitchen. 'I only have gin,' she said, holding up the bottle. She smiled wryly. 'I am an actress, after all. And there's no ice, as usual. The fridge is still not working.' This was how it had been the first night he had come here, the warm gin and the flat tonic in this airless, cramped little room.

Isabel sat down sideways to face him at the opposite end of the sofa. 'Well,' she said, putting on a brisk and brittle tone, 'shall we make small-talk? You go first.'

He smiled, shrugged. 'I don't know what to tell you. Nothing notable ever happens to me.'

'Aren't you at your sleuthing? You always enjoy that—murder and mayhem, all of it happening to other people.'

He had left his cigarettes upstairs. Isabel pointed to a silver box on the mantelpiece, one that he remembered, and he stood up and fetched it and offered her a cigarette and took one himself. Passing Cloud—Phoebe used to smoke them; did she still? He did not know. He thought perhaps she had given up. He settled himself on the sofa again. The warm gin tasted like perfume, cloying and slightly viscous. 'Ever come across Victor Delahaye?' he asked.

She frowned, and shook her head. 'No. Should I?'

'He died. It was in the papers. He—' He stopped.

'He what?' Isabel asked.

'Killed himself.'

'Did he, now.' She watched him narrowly, with amusement. 'I do believe you're blushing, Quirke.'

'Sorry.'

'You don't need to be.' Her smile was as bright as steel. 'I've got used to thinking of myself as a failed suicide, so there's no reason to be embarrassed and avoid the subject. Tell me about this man—what did you say his name was?'

Quirke took a long swallow of his drink, and winced again at the glutinous texture. 'Delahaye,' he said. 'Victor Delahaye. Business family—Delahaye and Clancy, shipping, coal, timber, garages, I don't know what else.'

'And why did he kill himself?' She gave her mouth a twist. 'Not for love, I imagine.'

'No one seems to know. Or no one is saying, anyway.'

'Aha—and your little grey cells are working overtime, are they?' She sipped her drink, watching him over the edge of her glass. 'You really are a strange person, Quirke. Tell me, why did you decide to be a pathologist?'

Why? He could not recall, now. 'I don't know that I decided,' he said. 'I think I just drifted, as everyone does.'

'Your morbid streak led you on, did it?'

'That's it. My morbid streak.'

For a reason that neither of them could understand, this little exchange lightened the atmosphere between them, and Isabel extended a foot and caressed his bare ankle with her toes. 'Poor Quirke,' she said fondly, 'you're such a mess.' He was about to reply when she sat up straight suddenly. 'I know what's the matter with me,' she said. 'I'm hungry. And do you know what I want? Chips! I want a bag of chips and one of those disgusting rissoles they make out of mashed-up seagull.' She stood up, extending her hand. 'Come on, get your shoes on, we're going out.' She hurried ahead of him up the narrow stairs, singing *Put your shoes on, Lucy*.

Despite himself, he was glad he had stayed.

They had to go all the way to Ringsend to find a chip shop that was still open. Isabel had a little car now, a Fiat, bright red and glossy, like a ladybird. Quirke was touched to see how proud of it she was. He had briefly owned an Alvis, and was secretly relieved to be rid of it. They drove down by the canal, under the dark and motionless trees. The roads were empty at this hour. There was a childish excitement in the car, as if, Quirke thought, the two of them had slipped out together in the dark, hand in hand, bent on adventure.

Isabel, crouched over the steering wheel, kept shooting him sidelong glances with her eyebrows lifted and her lips mischievously pursed. 'Oh, God, Quirke,' she said, with a laughing groan, 'I have to admit it, I'm glad you're back.'

And he? Was he glad, really? He made himself smile at her. He felt as if he had been sheltering under a stone and now the stone had been lifted, exposing him to the sudden glare of the sun. He did not deserve such kindness, if kindness it was. He had let nearly a year go past without ringing Isabel even once, if only to ask how she was faring. Was he to be forgiven this easily? It seemed to him almost a scandal.

The chip shop was a box of harsh white light behind a big square plate-glass window. The metal counter was chest-high—why were chip-shop counters always high like that? Quirke wondered—and the owner, a dour fellow with a paunch and a lazy eye, had the look of a former boxer. His wife, thin as a whippet, kept to the background, tending the cauldrons of seething fat. Quirke and Isabel were the only customers. They stood at the counter waiting for their order to be prepared. Despite the late hour and the dinginess of the surroundings there was for some reason a sense of comedy in the situation, and Isabel kept giving off waves of muffled hilarity, so that Quirke, conscious of the shopman's drooping and suspicious eye, had to work hard at maintaining an expression of stern solemnity. When the food was ready they took it to eat in the car, and sat with all four windows wound fully down to let out the fatty fumes. 'My God,' Isabel said happily, 'this rissole really is revolting, isn't it?' She grinned at him. There was a smear of grease on her chin. 'You see, Quirke?' she said. 'Being happy for the odd moment now and then isn't so difficult.'

Having eaten their food they drove out to Sandymount and walked along the front to calm their queasy stomachs. The night air was still, and a vast and slightly crazy-looking moon hung at what seemed a crooked angle above the horizon, laying a thick trail of gold across the water. 'Look at that,' Isabel said, 'like a road you could walk on.' Quirke was thinking of her in her hospital bed a year ago, with her face turned to the wall, and him standing helpless in the room, not knowing what to say. 'Don't brood,' she said, as if she had read his thoughts. She linked her arm in his and pressed herself against him and shivered.

'It's chilly,' she said. 'Let's go home. I mean, let's go back.'

When they got to the house Isabel sent Quirke to sit on the sofa while she was in the kitchen preparing tea. The rissole, a glistening lozenge of greyish meat mixed with grain, had left a coating of slime on the roof of his mouth that would not be dislodged. He smoked a cigarette but even that would not take away the taste. There was what sounded like a party going on somewhere nearby— he could hear talk and laughter and the tinny wail of a record-player.

'Tell me about what's-his-name,' Isabel called from the kitchen. 'Delahaye.'

He rose and went to the kitchen doorway and stood with his hands in his pockets. He had taken off his shoes again and the floor was pleasantly cool under his stockinged feet. Isabel, who had changed into her silk tea-gown, was measuring spoonfuls of tea into a willow-pattern pot. 'What do you want me to tell you?' he asked.

'Tell me why you think there's something funny going on—because you do, I know you do. I know that look.'

He pondered, gazing at the floor. 'Well, from what I know of Victor Delahaye, he wasn't the kind of person to kill himself.'

'Is there that kind of person?'

She carried the teapot past him and set it on a cork mat on the little table in front of the sofa. He watched her, admiring the glimmer of a pale breast in the opening of her tea-gown, the full curve of her thigh pressing against the silk. She was a handsome woman, russet-haired, long-limbed and slim. He wished . . . He did not know what he wished.

'He took his partner's son with him, in the boat,' he said.

He went and sat on the sofa again. Isabel handed him his tea and offered the milk jug. 'What age is he—the son?' she asked, settling herself beside him.

'I don't know. A young twenty-five?'

'Were they close, him and Delahaye?'

'I doubt it.'

'Then why did he choose him to take with him?'

'That's what everyone wants to know.' He sipped his tea. It seemed only to add another coating of scum to his mouth. 'I suppose he wanted a witness.'

Isabel was gazing before her with narrowed eyes, holding the cup and saucer close under her chin. 'People usually don't want other people watching at a time like that,' she said quietly. She gave a faint laugh. 'A private moment, if ever there was one.'

Quirke thought it best to let this pass. He waited for a beat, watching the curl of steam above his cup. 'Delahaye was a vain man,' he said.

'And yet he shot himself. In front of his partner's son.'

'So it seems.'

They sat in silence. From where the party was there came a woman's screams of laughter, and a new song started up.

'There *is* something fishy, isn't there?' Isabel said. 'Even I can sense it.'

Quirke was lighting a cigarette. 'Yes,' he said, 'there is.'

'Did the young man do it?'

'I don't think so.'

'Then he did kill himself.'

'Yes. But what I want to know is, why. He was vain and pompous and full of his own importance. He had to have been driven to it.'

Down the street, *You ain't nothin' but a hound dog* twanged and wailed.

She took the cigarette from his fingers, drew on it, gave it back, slightly stained with lipstick. 'Sorry,' she said. 'I'm trying to give up. They're saying now they cause cancer.'

'Life causes cancer.'

She refilled his cup and her own and leaned back on the sofa, balancing the saucer against her bosom. She studied him, smiling a little. 'Well, Dr Quirke,' she said. 'What's next, for us?'

He shook his head. 'I don't know.' It was the truth.

'What about your French *amour*? Is she gone for good?'

Françoise d'Aubigny. He said the name to himself and felt a click of pain, as if a tiny bone in his breast had snapped. He had loved Françoise, despite all she had done, despite all that she had turned out to be. 'Gone, yes,' he said tonelessly. 'Gone for good.'

'And you're back.'

She was still smiling but the smile had a flaw in it, like a crack across a mirror.

'Yes,' he said. 'I'm back.'

What else could he say?

7

INSPECTOR HACKETT spotted Quirke before Quirke spotted him. They were among the crowd outside St John's, milling on the gravel in the sunshine in front of the church doors. Smell of warm dust, of hot metal from the parked cars, of the women's face powder and the men's cigarettes. Faint smell of death, too, of clay and lilies and the varnished wood of the coffin. Hackett was thinking what curious occasions they were, funerals, or this bit of them, anyway, the interval after the church service and before the burial, when no one seemed to know exactly what to do or how to behave, trying to keep a solemn demeanour yet feeling guiltily relieved, and almost light-hearted. They talked about all kinds of things, politics, the weather, who was going to win the match, but no one at this stage of the proceedings ever spoke of the person who was dead; it was as though a dispensation had been given for these few minutes, and everyone had been let off mentioning the one and only reason they were gathered here.

Hackett had arrived a minute or two before the service ended, having wanted to avoid going inside the church. When he was a lad the priests used to say that any

Catholic who went into a Protestant church was committing a sin, and although he no longer believed in such things he still instinctively obeyed. Anyhow, it was not as if he was one of the family, or even a family friend.

He took himself off to the side and lit a cigarette and eyed the crowd, in their dark suits and black frocks and black hats with veils—a regular fashion show, it looked like—picking out the ones whose faces he knew and watching how they behaved. There were the Delahaye twins, uncannily alike. Which was which? That must be James, the one staying silent, while the other one, Jonas, talked and smiled. The dead man's widow was with someone he did not recognise, a tall sleek man with ash-coloured hair brushed back like an eagle's plume—her brother, maybe, or was he too old? She wore a dark-blue two-piece costume the skirt of which was very tight and emphasised the curve of her behind. Hackett looked at the seams of her stockings, and looked away.

The Clancys, parents and son, were in the crowd and yet seemed apart from it, surrounded as it were by an invisible enclosure. Jack Clancy was dragging on a cigarette as if he was suffocating and it was a little tube of oxygen. His son, looking more than ever like a bantam-weight contender, was frowning at the sky, as if wistfully expecting something to swoop down out of it and carry him off to somewhere less grim than this balefully sunlit churchyard. Mrs Clancy—what was her name? Celia? Sylvia?—held herself in that peculiar way that she did—*standing on her dignity*, Hackett thought—with her handbag on her wrist and her gaze turned elsewhere. The three of them looked as if whatever it was that was holding them together might loose its grip at any moment and send them flying asunder.

And then there was the sister, Miss Delahaye—Margaret, was it?—raw and red-eyed and coughing steadily like a motor-car with a faulty spark plug.

Trouble on all sides, Hackett told himself, and sighed.

It cheered him, seeing Quirke, skulking as it seemed beside the church door, also lighting up a furtive cigarette, glancing swiftly about as if expecting somehow to be challenged, his black hat pulled down over his left eye. Quirke was probably the only one among all these people today who had not needed to change into a funeral suit.

'There you are,' Hackett said. He lowered his voice. 'Grand day for a planting.'

Quirke did his crooked smile.

The mourners were drifting towards the graveyard, led by the vicar in his surplice and stole and walking behind the coffin carried on the shoulders of James and Jonas Delahaye and four of what must be their friends, curt-looking young men in expensive suits. The women in their high heels stepped over the grass carefully, like wading-birds, while the men, concealing their half-smoked cigarettes inside their palms, took a last few surreptitious drags. Quirke and the inspector joined the stragglers.

'There's a sign somewhere in Glasnevin cemetery,' Quirke said quietly. '*Planting in this area restricted to dwarves*, it says.' The inspector's shoulders shook. Quirke did not look at him. 'I think,' he said mildly, 'it's trees that are meant.'

They went on, pacing slowly in the wake of the mourners.

'By God, Doctor,' Hackett said, catching his breath, 'you've the graveyard humour, all right.'

The burial was quickly over with. The vicar droned, his eye fixed dreamily on a corner of the sky above the yew trees, a hymn was raggedly sung, someone—Delahaye's sister, probably—let fall a sob that sounded like a fox's bark, the coffin was lowered, the clay was scattered. The vicar draped a silken marker over the page of his black book and shut it, and with his hands clasped at his breast led the solemn retreat from the graveside. Hackett had been admiring the two gravediggers' shapely spades—he was always interested in the tools of any trade—and now they stepped forward smartly and set to their work. Mona Delahaye, passing him by, smiled at Quirke and bit her lip. Quirke doffed his hat. Hackett watched the young woman, not looking at her nylon seams, this time. 'Mourning becomes her, eh?' he said, and cocked an eyebrow.

The cars were starting up and one or two were already creeping towards the gate. 'Have you transport, yourself?' the inspector asked. Quirke shook his head. 'Fine, so,' Hackett said. 'It's a grand day for a walk into town.'

Hackett heard a step behind them on the gravel and turned to meet a pale, middle-aged man with a dry, greyish jaw and oiled black hair brushed slickly back.

'Are you the detective?' the man asked.

'I am,' Hackett said. 'Detective Inspector Hackett.'

The man nodded. He had a curious way of blinking very slowly and comprehensively, like a bird of prey. He wore a starched high collar—who wore collars like that, any more?—his teeth were bad, and Hackett caught a whiff of his breath.

'Might I have a word?' the man said. He slid a glance in Quirke's direction.

'This is Dr Quirke,' Hackett said. 'We—we operate together.'

Quirke shot him a glance but the policeman's bland expression did not alter. Hackett did not often make a joke.

'Ah, yes,' the man said. 'Garret Quirke. I've heard of you.'

'Not Garret,' Quirke said. Why had people lately started calling him by that name?

'Sorry,' the man said, though he did not seem to be. 'Maverley—Duncan Maverley. I work—worked—for Mr Delahaye.' He glanced over his shoulder at the dispersing crowd and gestured towards the gate. 'Shall we—?'

The three men went out at the gate and turned right and walked slowly along the pavement in the shade of the plane trees. The Delahayes' car passed them by and Hackett fancied he glimpsed a flash of Mona Delahaye's eye, trained in Quirke's direction. The bold doctor, he thought to himself, had better go carefully, where that brand-new widow is concerned.

'I'm the head bookkeeper with Delahaye and Clancy,' Maverley said.

He was walking between the other two. He wore a drab black suit, slightly rusty at the collar and the cuffs, and there were speckles of dandruff on his shoulders. He was, Quirke thought, every inch what a head bookkeeper should look like.

'A very sad thing,' Hackett said, 'Mr Delahaye going the way he did.'

'Yes,' Maverley said, somewhat absently; his mind seemed elsewhere. 'I wanted to talk to you, Inspector,' he said, 'about certain—certain anomalies that I've encountered, in the affairs of Delahaye and Clancy.'

'Anomalies,' Hackett said, as if he were unfamiliar with the word.

'Yes. In the accounts. Certain movements, certain transfers, of fundings and shares. It's a complex matter, not easily grasped by the layman.'

Quirke and Hackett, the two laymen, exchanged a glance past Maverley's head. Maverley, caught up in his thoughts, appeared not to notice.

'Can you give us an idea,' Hackett said, 'an outline, of what the effect is of these—these anomalies?'

They had gone on some way before Maverley spoke again, in a voice that seemed hushed before the enormity of the matter that was being contemplated. 'The effect,' he said, 'in essence, is that Mr Delahaye—young Mr Delahaye—Mr Victor—was being . . .' He hesitated. 'What shall I say? His position was being undercut, steadily, systematically, and, I may say, very skilfully, so that in effect he is—was—no longer in the position at the head of the firm that he believed he occupied.'

'You mean he was being edged out,' Quirke said, 'without his knowing?'

'Not *being* edged out, Dr Quirke: he *was* out. Or perhaps that is too strong.' They had come to a corner and there they stopped. To the right, at the end of a short stretch of the road, the sea was suddenly visible, a sunlit blue surprise. Maverley inserted an index finger under the starched collar of his shirt and gave it an agitated tug. He cleared his throat. 'Let me put it this way,' he said. 'The balance of power within the firm has shifted—has *been* shifted, so that Mr Delahaye, Mr Victor, who was the leading partner in the firm, has become, *had* become, very much the lesser. And all this without his knowing, until I'—a soft cough—'apprised him of it.'

A silence fell. Inspector Hackett was squinting off down the road towards the sea; he took off his hat and ran his hand around the sweat-dampened inner band. Quirke watched him. There were occasions, not momentous or even especially significant, when it came to him how scant was his knowledge of this man, how little he knew of how his mind worked or what his deepest thoughts might be. The two of them, he reflected, could not have been less alike. Yet here they were, wading together into yet another morass of human cupidity and deceit.

'And who might it be,' the inspector said, turning his gaze towards Maverley again, 'that's behind this bit of clever manoeuvring?'

Maverley pursed his pale lips. 'Well now, Inspector,' he said slowly, 'I don't believe I'm in a position to say.'

Hackett pounced. 'You mean you don't know, or you're not saying?'

'I mean,' Maverley repeated, in a chill thin voice, 'that I am not in a position to say.' He brought out a handkerchief from the sleeve of his jacket and mopped a brow that to the other two seemed as dry as the handkerchief itself. 'I simply felt that in the circumstances, in these tragic circumstances, I should bring this matter to the attention of the authorities. I've now done so, and I have nothing more to add. Good day to you.'

He began to turn away but Hackett laid a hand, as if lackadaisically, on his arm. Maverley looked at the policeman's hand, and then at Quirke, as if calling him silently to witness this act of constraint.

'The thing is, Mr Maverley, I'm wondering what it is you expect me to do with this information you've passed on to me in such a public-spirited way.' He released his hold on Maverley but then, to Maverley's obvious consternation, slipped his arm through his and turned with him down the road towards the sea. Quirke followed, and Maverley looked back over his shoulder at him with an expression of outraged beseeching, as if urging him to remonstrate with the policeman. Quirke only smiled. He knew of old the inspector's playful methods of coercion.

'You see,' Hackett was saying, 'what I'm trying to discover is why you've told me this stuff in the first place, especially in the light of the fact that you're only prepared to tell me so much of it, and no more. Such as, for instance, the identity of the person who has been chicaning away at the heart of the firm of Delahaye and Clancy.' He chuckled, and waggled the arm that was still entwined with Maverley's. 'Would it be, Mr Maverley, that you expect me to guess the identity of the certain party you're unwilling to name?'

Hackett had quickened his pace, and Maverley hung back, so that it seemed the detective was dragging him along against his will. Maverley glanced back at Quirke again with a deeper look of desperation. 'Dr Quirke—' he said, his voice squeaking, but Hackett was unrelenting.

'Because,' the detective said, 'I think I can guess who

this gentleman is. Unless I'm greatly mistaken, in which case I'd be expecting you to put me right.'

At last Maverley, by a sudden violent manoeuvre, succeeded in freeing his arm from Hackett's, and stopped short on the pavement like a balking horse, indignantly hitching up the lapels of his suit jacket and smoothing down his mourner's narrow black tie. Hackett, whose momentum had sent him on a pace, stopped, too, and turned and strolled back, smiling easily. Quirke took a step back, but Hackett flapped a lazy hand at him to draw him again into the little circle of the three of them. But Maverley would have no more of it. 'I'm sorry, Inspector,' he said, lifting a hand and holding it up flat against the two men before him. 'I've said all I have to say. And now, if you don't mind, I have work to go to.'

He turned on his heel and strode away. Hackett, a hand in his pocket and his head on one side, stood with his lazy grin and watched him go. 'Do you know what it is, Dr Quirke,' he said, 'but that fellow is the spitting likeness of a tax inspector that used to come and harass my father on the bit of a farm he had when I was a child? *Mr Hackett*, he used to say, *it is my duty to inform you that if you do not fill up the forms and pay your taxes I will be compelled to set the guards on you.* Oh, I can see him still, and hear him, that pinched voice of his.' He turned to Quirke. 'Would you say no to a drink, Doctor?'

Quirke laughed. 'I would not, Inspector.'

They went to a pub on the corner of Sandymount Green. They ordered wilted cheese sandwiches—'Isn't the sliced pan a curse?' the inspector sadly observed—and a glass of Guinness each. Strong sunlight slanted in at the doorway and down from the clear top of the painted-over front window. Down the bar from them a very old man was perched on a high stool, drowsing over a copy of the *Independent*, his eyelids drooping and his head lolling. They tackled their sandwiches. 'Give me over that mustard there,' Hackett said, 'for I declare to God this yoke tastes like two wedges of cardboard with a slab of mildewed lino stuck in between.'

Quirke sipped his stout and was sorry he had not asked for whiskey. He had been careful with his drinking in recent months, and felt quietly proud of himself for it. 'So what,' he asked, 'did you make of Bartleby the Scrivener and what he had to say?'

'Maverley, you mean?' The inspector was munching bread and cheese with an expression of sour disgust. 'I kept thinking I was my father and that I should run the bugger off the property.' He took a deep draught of his drink, and wiped away a cream moustache with the back of his hand. 'It must be the partner, Clancy, that he's talking about. Who else would there be?'

'Delahaye's sons—the twins?'

'Arragh,' the inspector said, flapping his lips disdainfully, like a horse, 'they wouldn't have the wit, those two.'

'Are you sure?'

The inspector glanced at him askance. 'Are we ever sure of anything, in this vale of tears?'

Quirke pushed his quarter-eaten sandwich away and brought out a packet of Senior Service and offered it to the policeman with the flap lifted and the cigarettes ranged like a set of miniature organ-pipes. 'What if it is Clancy that's on the fiddle?' he asked.

Hackett shrugged. 'Aye—what if? Am I supposed to think what he's up to is against the law and not just the usual skulduggery that goes on in offices and boardrooms every day of the week?'

'It must be serious, for Maverley to buttonhole you like that and tell you about it.'

'Yes,' the inspector said. 'It must be serious.' He took another judicious drink of his stout. When he set the glass back on the counter the yellow suds ran down inside and joined what remained of the head. It was strange, Quirke reflected, but in fact he did not much like drink and its attributes, the soapy reek of beer, the scald of whiskey. Even gin, which he considered hardly a drink at all, had a metallic clatter in the mouth that made him want to shiver. And yet the glow, that inward glow, that was a thing he did not wish to live without, whatever the state of his liver or his brain.

He thought of Isabel last night, the warm gin and tonic, the scummy chips and putrid rissole—he would remember that rissole for a long time—then the ritual of the tea, the faint taste of her lipstick on his cigarette, and the stronger taste when she kissed him. He thought of lying in the faint glow of her bedroom, and of her sleeping, her heavy head cradled in the crook of his arm. Was it a mistake to take up with her again? Probably. And yet in a sequestered corner of what he called his heart the fact of her glowed like an ember he had thought was ash but that the mere sight of her had quickened again into warm life.

What everyone told him was true: he was too much among the dead. But who was going to venture down into the underworld and fetch him up into the light? Isabel? Well, why not? Why not she, as good as any other? If it was not too late.

'I suppose,' the inspector said thoughtfully, leaning his elbows on the bar, 'we might go and have a word with him, the same Mr Clancy.'

'"We"?'

Hackett looked at him in surprise and feigned dismay. 'Ah, now, Doctor, you wouldn't think of abandoning me at this stage of the proceedings, would you? I'm not up to these fancy folk, you know that. You're the one that speaks their lingo.'

Quirke toyed with his glass, revolving the bulbous knob at the base between his fingers. 'You know, Inspector,' he said, 'you really have some peculiar ideas about me.'

Now that the funeral was over Maggie Delahaye wondered if she might return to Ashgrove and finish her holiday. It shocked her a little that she should entertain such a notion, with her brother hardly cold in his grave, and yet why should she not go back to Cork? In fact, since Victor's death it had crossed her mind more than once that really there was nothing to stop her from moving permanently to Ashgrove.

When she looked at the thing dispassionately she had to ask what was keeping her here. When Victor's first wife had died, Maggie had sold her own little house in Foxrock and moved into the red-brick barn on Northumberland

Road to look after her brother. She supposed now it had been a mistake. She had grown up in that house, and should have known she could not go back there without encountering ghosts. But her father after his stroke was becoming increasingly difficult, and the twins were still in college and were running wild, as young people often did after the loss of their mother. Victor simply would not have been able to cope on his own. But then, after only a couple of years, Victor out of the blue had announced his intention to remarry.

Nothing had been the same after Mona's arrival in the household. Victor was besotted with her, to an extent that to Maggie seemed, she had to admit, to border on the indecent. He had adored Lisa, and now he adored her successor even more. That could not be right. It was not that Maggie would have expected Victor to spend the rest of his days pining for his lost wife, but there was such a thing as moderation.

She did not hold Victor responsible for this state of affairs. Victor was only a man, after all, and Mona, though a vixen, was beautiful and probably—Maggie had to search delicately for the word—probably very passionate, and that was important for a man like Victor, well into his forties yet vigorous still. For Victor was just as childish as his wife, though in a different way, of course. Mona was greedy and grasping, and had a child's instinctive cleverness when it came to getting her own way; poor Victor, on the other hand, was like one of those schoolboy heroes in the books he used to read when he was young, full of high ideals and silly romantic notions of what other people were like. He was entirely taken in by Mona's little-girl act, and could not see how she was manipulating him, making him hop to her every command and laughing at him behind his back. Oh, yes, Maggie had the measure of Mona. Her brother, her lovely, brave, silly brother, was wasted on that woman.

And yet for all Victor's besottedness, Maggie was still convinced that deep down he had recognised something unpleasant in his wife, something cheap and ugly and in some way—yes, in some way *soiled*. She wondered if that was part of the attraction for him. Some men liked that kind of thing, liked to think of women being dirty and depraved. Maggie knew how possessive Victor had been of Mona, and how jealously he had watched over her. He had tried to hide his vulnerability behind the famously sophisticated façade that he maintained, but he could not deceive his sister. They had always been close, she and Victor. They had grown up together as allies against their father's bullying and their mother's neglectfulness. One day, in their hiding-place among the trees at Ashgrove, they had made a solemn vow that when they grew up they would marry each other, no matter what anyone said. And, in a way, Maggie had always felt that they *were* married, if only in spirit.

It had been hard for her when Victor actually did marry, and harder still when he married a second time, but she had said nothing on either occasion—what could she have said?—yet it had pained her to watch him throwing himself away on those two women who were worth so much less than he was. Lisa at least had been harmless, a timid, rather gawky girl always anxious to please, who when she fell ill had surprised everyone by putting up a brave, uncomplaining but in the end useless fight for survival. Mona, however, was not timid; Mona was not harmless.

Maggie had been as baffled as anyone by her brother's death. She could not accept that he had taken his own life. People had assured her it was the case, but still she could not accept it. She had tried at first to convince herself that Davy Clancy must have done it—why had he thrown away the gun?—but it was no good: she knew that Davy was weak and incapable surely of killing anyone, least of all a Delahaye. But why had Victor taken him out in the boat—why him? It had been Victor's way of sending a message, of leaving a signal as to why he had done what he had done. But what message was it, and to whom did he think he was directing it?

No: if Davy Clancy had not been the cause of Victor's death, then Maggie was convinced that Mona must have been involved, in some way that she could not explain or account for. She would have to get away from this house, the horrible, oppressive atmosphere, the awful sense of there being some secret in the air, hidden from her but known to others. Yes, she would go back to Ashgrove. She would have peace there.

She put her book away—pages of it had gone by without her registering a word—and went and sat in front of the mirror of her dressing-table and took up a tortoise-shell brush and applied it fiercely to her hair. Brushing her hair was usually a thing that soothed her, but today she went at it almost violently, with hard long strokes that drew the skin of her forehead tight and made her eyes widen, so that in the glass she looked a little mad. But then, she thought, perhaps she was a little mad. There was a streak of insanity in the family, on her mother's side, and neither had her father's people been the sanest, with their Bible-thumping and their furious hatred and fear of Catholics. They had never forgiven her father for moving south and going into business with a Taig, which was what they would have called Phil Clancy—a dirty Taig.

She put down the hairbrush and stared at her reflection, her eyes still wide. Maybe that was what had happened to Victor, maybe it had been an attack of temporary insanity. But no, Victor had not been mad. Passionate, yes, and fanciful, with all kinds of wild notions about himself and the people around him, but not mad. Something or someone had driven him to take himself and Davy Clancy in that boat out of Slievemore Bay that day with a gun in his pocket and despair in his heart.

When she came downstairs she found her father in the drawing room, slumped in his wheelchair at the window above the garden. She thought at first he was asleep but when she approached him she saw that was not so. She saw, too, that his eyes were damp. This startled her. She did not think she had ever seen her father in tears before— he had not wept even at the funeral of his only son. 'Are you all right, Daddy?' she asked, but it was not until she put a hand lightly on his shoulder that he responded, jerking himself away from her touch and glaring up at her, first in surprise and then in fury. He had been away somewhere in his thoughts.

He did not speak, and she could not think what else to

say to him. She felt compassion for him, but in a detached way; it was as she would feel for someone whose misfortune she had been told about, or had read about in the papers. She had never been close to her father. He had not welcomed closeness, in fact had discouraged it, by his remoteness, his wounding sarcasm, his sudden rages. Yet, for all that, she admired him. He was tough, self-sufficient, unforgiving, which were qualities she held in high regard. As for love, well, love did not come into it.

Tea arrived, wheeled in on a trolley by Sarah, the red-haired maid. The taking of afternoon tea was something Victor's first wife had instituted—poor Lisa, she had been so thrilled to find herself married into the grand and mighty Delahayes. Sarah manoeuvred the trolley into the bay of the big window. Maggie said that she would take over, and the maid smirked—a brazen girl, with scant respect for anything, but a good worker—and sauntered away, humming. Maggie poured a cup of tea for her father, adding milk and two spoonfuls of sugar as she knew he liked, and brought it to him. He waved it away with a violent sweep of his arm. 'Don't want tea,' he growled. 'I'm sick of drinking tea.'

Maggie sighed. 'Have you taken your pill?'

'No, I have not!'

'You know what the doctor said about—'

'Ach, to blazes with that. What do the doctors know? Look at the state they've left me in'—he had got himself convinced somehow that his stroke was due to medical incompetence—'stuck in this blasted contraption and wheeled around like an infant.'

Maggie might have laughed at that—the idea of her

father letting anyone wheel him anywhere! She waited patiently, standing back a little, then proffered the cup again. 'Take your tea,' she said.

He let her put the cup and saucer into his hands. She was afraid he would spill the tea, scald himself perhaps, but one of the things the doctors had told her was that he must be allowed to fend for himself as much as possible. He set the saucer in his lap, the cup clattering. He did not drink; he was glaring into the garden.

'Are you sure you didn't take your pill?' Maggie said.

He turned his head and looked at her with furious contempt. 'What was the good Lord thinking,' he said, 'to take my only son from me and leave me *you*?'

He watched her, almost smiling, eager to see the barb strike home. Maggie was thinking how remarkable it was that his accent had never softened, though he had lived down here in the South for half a century. It was another of the things he clung to, unrelenting, that Northern growl. 'Drink your tea,' she said again, mildly.

She brought a chair and sat down by the trolley and poured a cup of tea for herself. They both turned their eyes now to the garden. How strange to see everything in bloom and the sun shining so gloriously. But then, why was it strange? Death did not come only in times of dark and cold. It must have been beautiful, out in the bay, when Victor turned the gun against himself and fired. What would have been going through his mind, what terrors, what memories? She felt tears welling in her eyes but held them back by force of will. Her father was furious that he had let her see him weeping; she would not allow him to have redress by weeping herself, now.

'I was watching the birds,' the old man said. 'Thrushes, blackbirds. There's a robin, too, that comes and goes. Fierce creature, the robin—did you know that? Courage a hundred times his size. Aye, he holds on, that bird, doesn't weaken and let go.' He made a fist of his left hand and brought it down with a thump on the arm of the wheel-chair, slopping the tea.

It occurred to Maggie that what pained her father most about his son's death was the shame of it, the disgrace. Or was she being unfair? He was as capable of grief as she was. She speculated as to whether he might know what had driven Victor to do what he had done. Should she ask him? Surely a time such as this should permit them to speak as otherwise they never would. She glanced at her father, his carved profile, his poet's shock of silver hair. She knew nothing about him, next to nothing. He had never bothered with her; a daughter was nothing to him. And now he had no son. How would he not be furious? And heartbroken, perhaps; perhaps that, too.

Jonas came in. Automatically she looked to the door to see James entering behind him, as always. But Jonas was alone. This was so unusual that she gave him a questioning look, which he ignored. 'Any tea in that pot?' he asked.

Maggie laid her hand against the teapot's cheek. 'It's gone cold. Sarah can bring a fresh pot.'

Jonas shrugged. 'Doesn't matter. It's too hot to drink tea anyway.' He threw himself down in an armchair. He had changed out of the black suit he had put on for the funeral, and wore dark slacks and a white silk shirt and loafers with no socks. His slender ankles were tanned. He had not wept at the graveside either. The suspicion came to Maggie sometimes that she allowed herself to feel things far too deeply. Her brother's death had set going in her a rushing underground river of grief that would in time slow down but that would be there always, running under everything. There were other streams from the past that were still flowing. Billy Thompson, a boy she had been sweet on when she was young—he had died, and she mourned him yet, all these years later. She looked at Jonas draped there in the armchair, a dazzling creature, so seemingly at ease. Surely he, too, was grieving for his father, in his own subterranean fashion.

'How are you feeling, Grandad?' he asked.

The old man lifted a hand and let it fall again limply in a gesture of weary dismissal. 'I'm no better than the rest of us,' he said, still eyeing the garden, his jaw working.

Jonas turned to Maggie. 'And what about you, Auntie?' he enquired, jaunty and ironical. He addressed his aunt always in a tone of half-fond raillery. He seemed, she thought without rancour, to find her something of a joke. But then, she supposed she was a joke—the spinster sister living in the home she had always lived in, despised by her father, mocked by her nephews, abandoned now by her beloved brother; even Sarah the maid paid her no regard. Yes, she should retire to Ashgrove, live there alone, keep cats and become the local eccentric. 'By the way,' Jonas said, in an undertone, 'you and I need to have a talk.'

'Yes? What about?'

He frowned, and glanced in the direction of his grandfather. 'I'll tell you later.'

*

Mona, too, had changed out of black, into a silk dress of dark sapphire that set off her milky pallor and the rich bronze textures of her hair. When she entered the drawing room she paused in the doorway, seeing the three of them—Maggie, her father-in-law, one of the twins—in their separate places at the far end of the big bright room, posed there like actors awaiting the entrance of the leading lady.

She came forward, stopping at the sideboard to take a cigarette from the box on the mantelpiece and light it with the fat heavy lighter. She was conscious of the three of them watching her. She was accustomed to being the centre of attention but this was different. Becoming a widow had given her a new role. It was a curiously pleasant, light-headed feeling. A widow, at her age!—it seemed absurd, like something in a stage musical. The merry widow. She was still herself, of course, and yet she was someone else, at the same time, the Mona Vander-weert she had always been and now Mrs Victor Delahaye, whose husband was dead. It made her feel—well, it made her feel grown-up, in a way she had not felt before.

'Oh,' she said, 'am I late for tea?'

It was not tea she wanted, anyway, but a drink, though she supposed she had better not ask for one. It had been a trying day and did not seem set to get any easier. Everything felt flat. She would have liked the mourners to come back to the house after the funeral but her father-in-law had not wanted it. It would have been interesting to stand here being sad but brave among all those people.

Maggie had risen from her chair by the tea trolley. 'How are you, my dear?' she asked. *As if she cared*, Mona thought.

'I'm fine, thank you. I seem to be a bit—dizzy.' Her sister-in-law stood before her with her hands clasped under her bosom, what there was of it, gazing at her with a forlorn expression. All at once she had a vision of time stretching before her like a tunnel, or no, like an avenue in a cemetery, lined with dark trees, and a person standing mournfully under each tree, looking at her in just this way. A silent scream formed inside her. Boredom was one of her acutest fears. 'Really,' she said, turning away, 'I'm fine.'

None of them liked her. She had taken their precious Victor away from them, which was bad enough, but now they seemed to think she was somehow responsible for his death. They would not say so, of course, but she could feel them thinking it. She looked at the twin—was it James? for she was never quite sure which of them was which, even after all this time—and wondered what he knew. Both twins had been very cold towards her at the funeral, not that they were ever exactly warm where she was concerned. She would have to be careful. She supposed she had been foolish, had taken a foolish risk. Had Victor found out? Had that been why . . . ? No: she would not let herself think that, she would not: it was too absurd.

She turned to the young man in the armchair. 'Where's Jonas?' she asked.

He sighed, and his mouth tightened. 'I'm Jonas.' He held up his left hand and showed her the ring on his little finger. 'Jonas is the one who wears this, remember?'

She laughed, and put a hand to her mouth. 'Oh, sorry, yes, I didn't look.' His angry sarcasm amused her. Did they really expect her to check their little fingers every time she met them? It was not her fault that he and his brother were a pair of freaks. 'Sorry,' she said again, and looked around for an ashtray.

Samuel Delahaye sat slumped in the wheelchair with his chin sunk on his breast, glowering out into the garden. Mona went and stood beside him. He was the only one of them she had any time for. She had tried to get him to like her, and believed she had been successful, though of course he would never let on. He was such a grouch, shouting at everyone, insulting everyone. Often, when he was in one of his rages, she had an awful urge to laugh, but knew that if she did he would probably come rearing up out of that chair and slap her face. It would be interesting, to be hit like that. Old Sam was still handsome, and rather cruel-looking, like his grandsons. Only not weak like them; when he smiled, if what he did could be called a smile, he bared his lower teeth, just as Victor used to do.

Suddenly, at the thought of Victor, she felt sad. It was hard to grasp that he was actually gone, that he was in that wooden box, in the ground, already beginning to rot. She shivered. She had liked Victor. He had been handsome, too, more handsome than his father, in fact, but in a different way: *softer around the edges*, she thought. Yes, that was it, softer around the edges.

He had known nothing about her, she knew that. She had preferred it that way. Being married to Victor had been like living inside a fine, sound, well-appointed house, a house that was not hers but that gave her shelter and protected her and yet left her free to come and go as she pleased, a little gold key safe in her palm. She recalled his smell, of tobacco and pomade and that special soap he used to wash his hands with—the skin of his hands was sensitive and chapped easily. She tried now to see those hands in her mind, and was slightly shocked to realise that she could not. Had she ever really looked at them? Had she ever paid genuine attention to her husband? These were not questions that troubled her, but it was odd to find herself asking them. She was always careful how she positioned herself in front of things, looking, and being looked at. Sometimes she thought of herself as a separate object, a figure outside herself that she could regard from a distance, appraising, approving, admiring.

Victor had thought she loved him. It would have been unfair to let him think otherwise.

'Look,' her father-in-law said suddenly, dragging himself up in the wheelchair and pointing beyond the window to the garden with a trembling finger. 'Robin Redbreast! Aha, the wee warrior.'

It was nearly midnight when he left Bella's house, after his second visit. It was not two weeks since Victor had died, but it seemed far longer ago than that. Bella stood in the doorway watching him go. When he was turning the corner at the bottom of the road and glanced behind him she was still there: he could see her figure silhouetted in black against the light from the hall. He stopped, and stood looking back at her, hearing himself breathe. Why was she still there? The night was calm and mild, and the soft feel of the air made him think of summer nights in the past, and of himself walking away from some other girl's door, smelling the dew on the privet and the salt

reek of the sea, and hearing the birds far out in the bay
calling and crying. He had an urge suddenly to hurry back,
before Bella closed the door, and make her take him inside
again, and lie down with him and hold him in her arms.
He did not want to be out here, alone.

He went on, and turned the corner.

There was a big moon shining above the bay, it seemed
to him a huge gold eye watching him askew. He hoped
Sylvia would be asleep, but probably she would not be.
She knew he was in trouble, and that the trouble was
connected with Victor Delahaye's death. She had not
challenged him, of course, had not made even the mildest
enquiry. That was his wife's way, ever careful, ever discreet.

He knew he should have told her what was going on,
what he was up to; surely he had owed her that. Instead
he had kept it all to himself. It was not that he did not
trust her, only how could he have told her, what would he
have said—how would he have phrased it? *Well, you see,
dear, the thing is, over the past couple of years I've been
positioning myself to elbow Victor aside and take over the jolly
old firm—what do you think of that?* He knew what she
would think of it. He knew very well. Would she leave
him? She was English, and the English had a funny sense
of what was right and proper and what was not. He could
say to her it was just business—and what was it except
business?—but she would throw that back in his face. Yet
what did she expect? Did she think he should be content
to spend the rest of his working life with his neck under
Victor Delahaye's boot—no, under the heel of his John
Lobb penny-loafer with the hand-stitched seams and
scalloped tongue?

Victor Delahaye was what Sylvia would have called an ass: stupid, smug, conceited and lazy. All his life Victor had coasted in the shelter of the business that both their fathers, Samuel Delahaye and his partner Phil Clancy, had built up through hard work, shrewdness and unremitting ruthlessness. Had Victor been in sole control the thing would have done no more than drift and, who knows, might have foundered, if Jack had not been there to keep a firm grip on the tiller.

How many dangers had Jack steered them past? There had been that strike the dockers went on after the war, the strike old Samuel thought he could break and that Jack had been left to fix, by paying off the union bosses and cracking the heads of a few hard-chaws who would not be brought on board. And what about the time Clem Morrissy and his brothers had tried to set up that rival chain of garages and once again Jack had been called on to send in the muscle and keep the monopoly safe for Delahaye & Clancy? Always it was Jack who had done the dirty work, while Victor preened and boasted and played the gentleman. And then—

And then. Who would have thought Victor would have it in him to go out that way? Who would have thought it would affect him so disastrously, to discover himself sidelined? Who would have thought? There must have been something else; something else must have driven him to put a bullet through his heart, Jack was convinced of it. But what? If he could find out, maybe all was not lost, maybe something of all he had been working for could be saved.

Should he make one last try? Did he have it in him?

He had always been a fighter, unlike Victor, who had had everything handed to him on a silver platter. Yes, he would keep on: he would not be done down by that bastard Maverley and Victor's wastrel sons. That was what would keep him going, the thought of the twins and Maverley using Victor's death to defeat him. For they would get shot of him entirely if they could—oh, yes, they would. Already Maverley was putting the machinery in place that would grind him up and spit him out on the street. Did he imagine Jack had not seen him, after the funeral, sloping off for a quiet word with that detective, the one with the cow-shit still on his boots, and his sidekick in the black suit? Jack could imagine the book-keeper, with his grey jaw and his brown breath, counting out the insinuations like so many pounds, shillings and pence, blackening the name of Jack Clancy, accusing him by innuendo and trying to undo by stealth all that he had put in place with such care, such finesse, such inventiveness.

The front was deserted, and yet, as he walked along, it seemed to him somehow that he was not alone. More than once he stopped, and turned, and peered back along the path beside the sea. Was it a shadow that had slipped behind that bush? He stood, his nerves tingling, and strained to see into the gloom, listening past the washing of small waves against the seafront wall. There was nothing to be seen, nothing to be heard.

The grass was silver in the moonlight. He walked on, wanting to hasten his steps yet dreading the thought of reaching home. He pictured himself at the front door, easing the key into the lock and wincing at the crunch it made, and then standing in the shadows in the hallway, taking the measure of the house, trying to guess if Sylvia was asleep or if Davy was in, and feeling, too, the lingering damp warmth in his groin. The guilt that he felt was part of the thrill, always had been, although being thrilled by his guilt made him feel guiltier still. Such a tangle his life had always been. But who was it that had made it tangled? Whom was there to blame, but himself?

He came to the house and stopped, and stood with his hands on the coolly clammy top bar of the gate, looking up at his own bedroom window, where a faint light glowed. Sylvia would be awake, propped up in bed, with her spectacles on the end of her nose, reading, or at her sewing. Since Victor's death she had been sleeping badly— well, who had not? She would know, of course, or guess, what he had been up to tonight. She would not know the details—she was not aware of Bella's existence, he was confident of that—but she would not need to. He some- times thought she was glad to be rid of him for so much of the time. She had her own life. He was not a prime requirement in it.

He lit a cigarette, turning away in case the match-flame might be visible from that far window, and then walked aimlessly on, musing on his wife, of whom, if truth were told, he knew so little. He had loved her, once, this cool, pale, slender, distant woman. He had wanted her because she was so different from the women he had known before he knew her, and whom he continued to know, despite being married. And she had loved him—loved him still, probably. Despite everything.

He passed by the bandstand. It looked eerie, a filigreed iron gazebo standing in the moonlight, silent and brooding.

Stop. Listen. There was definitely someone behind him.

He was suddenly hot with fear, and the skin on the back of his neck crawled. He dared not turn, but then he did turn. Still there was no one to be seen, yet he knew there was someone, the same someone who had started up after him when he left Bella's house. 'Who's there?' he called out softly, feeling foolish, his voice unsteady. 'Who is it? Show yourself!'

Silence, with the sense in it of stifled, jeering laughter. He slipped into the bandstand and stood in the webbed shadows there under the wrought-iron canopy. The concrete floor gave off a mingled smell of piss and fag-ends. He thought with desperate yearning of how it would have been here earlier, when the mail boat was getting ready to set out, the passengers hurrying and people shouting farewells, the porters bumping luggage up the gangplank and the ship sounding its grave, portentous note. He could have lost himself in all that bustle, could have slipped away, and been safe.

A woman was approaching along the pavement. He shrank back into the shadows. Why had he come in here?—the bandstand offered no protection, it was open on all sides. He turned his head this way and that. The woman's footsteps were closer now. He seemed to hear his name spoken, very softly, but thought he must have imagined it. He was looking all around, trying to see in all directions. He almost laughed to think of himself, like a wooden doll, his head spinning and his eyes starting in fright. Always, behind everything, there was a part of him that stood back sceptically. Now he told himself he was being ridiculous, that there was no one after him, that all this fear and foreboding was the product of a fevered and guilty mind.

The woman had drawn level with the bandstand. He stepped forward, lifting a hand, ready to speak to her. He knew her! What was she doing here, at this hour? He began to say her name. The blow landed behind his right ear. He felt it distinctly, a dull shock without pain, and thought of a felled tree crashing to the ground. As he pitched forward he saw the moon slide sideways down the sky and disappear in darkness.

8

It turned out the Delahaye twins were at the party. Phoebe and Sinclair met one of them coming down the stairs just after they arrived. He was with his girlfriend—Phoebe recognised her but did not remember her name—and they stopped to talk, although they could hardly hear themselves above the din. The house was on a cobbled back-street in the North Strand with an iron railway bridge running over it. It was a funny little tumbledown place, with everything on a miniature scale, the tiny windows, the low front door, the narrow staircase leading up to two cramped bedrooms and a bathroom hardly bigger than a cupboard. Whenever a train went past the entire place wobbled and shook like a jelly out of its mould. Breen, the fellow whose house it was, had been at college with Sinclair, and fitted well with the place, being short and stout, with a shock of black curls and rimless glasses that kept sliding down the glistening, concave bridge of his snub nose.

Neither Phoebe nor Sinclair cared much for parties, and they had only come to this one because they had worried no one else would, since poor Breen was not exactly known as a social magnet. To their surprise they found the house throbbing with people and noise. Breen came bustling to meet them, sweaty and shiny and snuffling with happy laughter. He took the bottle of Bordeaux they had brought and glanced appreciatively at the label and said there was wine open in the kitchen. He gestured with pride at the heaving mass of people around them. 'The joint,' he said, 'is jumping.' He wore plimsolls and checked tweed trousers, hoist at half-mast by a pair of bright red braces, and a shirt of emerald green with a floppy collar. He used to profess a desire to be a painter, Sinclair recalled. He worked in the Coombe Hospital, delivering babies, 'by the yard, like sausages', as he said.

Now he plunged off, with their bottle of claret under his arm, and the last they saw of him was his tweed-clad Bunteresque backside disappearing into the crowd. They looked at each other, smiling in dismay. Phoebe took Sinclair's hand and they set off upstairs, where it might be less crowded, and met the Delahaye twin and his girlfriend coming down. 'Don't bother,' Delahaye said, or yelled, rather, '—it's bedlam up there!'

They went together, the four of them, down the short hall to the back of the house. Phoebe plucked at Sinclair's sleeve and put her mouth close to his ear. *'Which one of them is it?'* she asked, but Sinclair only lifted his hands helplessly and shook his head.

In the crowded kitchen they found paper cups and sloshed them full of Mooney's Spanish Burgundy and went on out to the garden, where the soft night air was a sudden balm. The garden was really no more than a walled yard, smelling of drains and dustbins, with a square of weed-choked clay and in one corner a privy with a broken door. There was a crowd of people out here, too, smoking and drinking. A couple were kissing in the shadow of the privy. Beyond the back wall the moon was perched on a distant chimney pot.

'This is Tanya Somers, by the way,' the young Delahaye said. He wore a black blazer and white sailing trousers with a Trinity tie for a belt. 'And I'm Jonas, in case you're wondering.' Phoebe and Sinclair smiled and shrugged as if to say that of course they had known which twin he was. 'People are never sure, I know,' Jonas said. 'James is here somewhere,' he added.

Tanya Somers had lazy good looks and a jaded manner. She wore her hair long, in a smooth, gleaming black swath that she kept pushing from her shoulders with negligent sweeps of the hand. She made no attempt to hide the fact that she did not know who Phoebe and Sinclair were, and that she was not much interested in finding out. When she spoke, Phoebe recognised the Rathgar accent. 'This wine is filthy,' she said. With a deft flick she emptied the contents of her cup into the weeds. 'I'm going to see if there's any beer.' She went off at an insolent slouch, tossing her hair back.

'I'm sorry about your father,' Phoebe said to Jonas.

He shrugged. 'Yes—I think people were a bit shocked to see me—us—here, considering it happened so recently. I suppose they expected us to go into mourning for a year and a day, like in the old songs.'

'Oh, I'm sure they'd understand,' Phoebe said, too quickly. Jonas Delahaye looked at her, the corners of his mouth twitching with amusement, and she felt herself flush and was glad of the darkness. 'I mean,' she went on, 'it's not like the old days, when everybody used to go into mourning for months, it seemed.' She felt Sinclair's elbow nudge her gently in the side. 'Anyway, that's what I think,' she finished lamely.

'Yes, well, I daresay you're right,' Jonas said, doing his patrician drawl. He looked into the paper cup and frowned. 'Tanny is right, this stuff is awful.' And he, too, threw the wine into the weeds and, giving them both a quick little smile, stepped past them and went into the kitchen.

'Oh, God,' Phoebe wailed softly.

'I don't really think he was offended,' Sinclair said drily.

'And you, just standing there—you could have said something!'

He laughed. 'Such as what? You were doing perfectly well yourself, digging the hole deeper and deeper.' He cupped a hand fondly against her cheek. 'Anyway,' he said, 'you're getting as bad as your father.'

'What do you mean!'

'You know very well what I mean—poking your nose into other people's business, asking questions and looking for clues.' Again he laughed, and this time pinched her cheek. 'Our own Nancy Drew, female investigator.'

She took a step backwards. 'You—!' He reached out and took her in his arms. She beat her fists softly against his chest, and now she, too, was laughing. 'Pig,' she said.

'That's a nice thing to call a Jew.'

She kissed him. '*My* Jew,' she said softly, her breath mingling with his.

They went inside and for several minutes wandered about in the party, going in single file, Sinclair ahead and leading Phoebe by the hand, the two of them pressing themselves sideways through the dense, hot-smelling crowd. There was a gramophone somewhere, and now a new record began—Elvis Presley, of course, whining about his blue suede shoes. Phoebe had no ear for pop music.

They encountered the second Delahaye twin standing in the doorway of one of the bedrooms, talking to a dark-haired girl with a fringe. He had backed her against the door-jamb, and she was looking up at him out of large, luminous eyes as he leaned over her, one hand on the jamb and the other against the wall, enclosing her in an almost-embrace, as if he would menace and at the same time caress her. He had a paper cup of wine in one hand and a smouldering cigarette in the other. A bright red handkerchief drooped from the breast pocket of his pale linen jacket. Sinclair tapped him on the shoulder. 'Hello, James.'

Delahaye turned his head. There was a bleared look in his eye. 'Oh, hello, Sinclair,' he said, slurring a little. 'You here too? God, what a scrum, eh? This is'—he turned back to the girl—'what did you say your name was?'

'I didn't,' the girl said, and smirked.

'Anyway, you're a smasher.' He turned again and this time addressed Phoebe. 'Isn't she a smasher?'

Phoebe gave him a cool, bland smile and moved on, but not before she had linked a finger around Sinclair's thumb and tugged at it.

'Take care, James,' Sinclair said. He smiled at the girl. 'You, too.'

They found a corner of the bedroom that was inexplicably free of people and immediately took possession of it. Breen's bed was heaped with discarded jackets and cardigans, and in the midst of the heap a couple lay on their sides facing each other, glued mouth to mouth. The boy's hand kept moving up the girl's stockinged leg, trying to get under the hem of her skirt, and she kept batting it away, with an almost lazy gesture. Phoebe and Sinclair tried to ignore them.

'You must admit,' Phoebe said, 'it's very strange, the way that man died.'

'Which man?' Sinclair asked innocently. She smacked his hand.

'Don't tease, you,' she said. 'The twins' father, I mean, as you very well know.'

'Funny,' Sinclair said, 'calling them twins. You never think of grown-ups being twins—but they certainly are. You never see one but you see the other.'

Phoebe gave a little shudder. 'I'd hate to be a twin—wouldn't you?'

He offered her a cigarette, but she shook her head, and he lit one for himself, thinking. 'I don't know,' he said. 'I haven't even got a sibling.'

'Well, neither have I.'

They were silent briefly. The subject of Phoebe's past and parentage was a delicate one, not to be lightly alluded to. Quirke had not been a good father.

'I must say,' Sinclair said, 'they don't seem very—well, they don't seem very upset. Would you do it?—go out to a party?'

'I don't know.'

The girl on the bed moaned softly. The boy had succeeded in getting his hand under her skirt and was rummaging urgently in her lap. Phoebe turned away. Sinclair was half sitting against the sill of the little square window, and she had an urge to sit on his knee, but did not.

There was a square of moonlight in the window with two bars of shadow making an out-of-kilter cross. She realised that she had never before considered the possibility of her father dying, of his being dead. For the first nineteen years of her life she had thought Quirke was her uncle, and even still she was wrestling with the fact of what he really was to her. *Father* was not a word that sat easily in her mind, but father he was, and very much living. How would she feel if he were dead? She did not know, and this surprised her, and faintly appalled her.

'Of course, I know what you think,' Sinclair said, mock-innocently again. 'I heard you telling Jonas Delahaye— you're all for casting aside those old fuddy-duddy notions about mourning and all the rest of it.'

'Oh, stop,' she said distractedly. She was still puzzling over the prospect of Quirke's projected demise. Would she be sad? Of course she would. Would she suffer, would she grieve? That was an altogether different question.

The girl on the bed wriggled out of the boy's embrace and struggled up and sat there among the crumpled clothes, blinking, a hand plunged in her hair. The boy sat up, too, more slowly, and pawed at her shoulder entreatingly. The girl wriggled again, and disconsolately he let fall his hand. The two of them seemed unaware that anyone else was in the room, although there were people milling at the foot of the bed and in the doorway.

In the moonlight at the window Sinclair, still seated awkwardly, put an arm around Phoebe's hips and drew her close to him. 'I'm sorry,' he said.

'Why?' She touched him under the chin and made him look up at her. 'What are you sorry for?'

He glanced aside. 'Oh, you know. Fathers. Death. All that.'

'Yes,' she said distantly, as if not to him but to someone else. 'All that.'

He woke, if it could be called waking, into liquid darkness. Everything was moving under him with a slewing, sideways roll that was familiar. He thought of his student days, when he was starting to drink, and after half a dozen beers he would wake in the middle of the night with a parched mouth and a thudding headache, while the bed on which he lay revolved slowly around him like a broken carousel. Also, he was wet. He was lying on his side with his legs drawn up to his chest and half his head submerged in water. It was seawater, he knew from the texture of it. A boat, then, but a boat that had something wrong with it. There was none of the sense of a boat's trim lightness; this vessel felt stodgy, like the barely floating hollowed-out stump of a tree.

He tried to sit up, and indeed saw himself doing it, as in a piece of trick photography, a wraith rising up out of himself while his body lay there lumpy and inert. The pain in the back of his head seemed a kind of noise, a dully pulsing roar that made the bones of his skull vibrate. He turned his head and peered up at the stars. They, too, seemed to be vibrating, zigzagging about, like fireflies. The last thing he had seen was the moon sliding down the sky—where was it now?

At last, with a groan, he got himself up to a sitting position. He had been wedged in the space between the two thwarts. His clothes were sopping. He put a hand cautiously to the back of his head and winced when he felt the pulpy knot under his ear. What had he been hit with? Something wooden. He looked about. Ahead there was only the darkly gleaming sea to the horizon, behind him were the lights of Dun Laoghaire, a long way off. And what was that?—a boat, gliding away from him landwards, silent, white-sailed, a white light glimmering at the tip of its mast. He tried to shout but his voice would not work. He was shivering now, sitting there in the slopping, warmish, deepening water. He looked to the mast. There was no sail; it had been taken away.

Deepening. The water was deepening.

He pressed forward on to his hands and knees and felt about, under the puddle of water. Sound workmanship, clinker-built. It was—could it be?—yes, it was the *Rascal*, his own twelve-footer. His questing hands, scrabbling and splashing, found what they had been looking for, what he had known they would find. Someone had taken a crowbar to the bottom of the boat and opened a crack between the boards six inches long and a good half-inch wide; he could feel the current of colder water coming up through it, a silken flow. He had been scuttled. A feeling of strange calm came over him. *She's sinking*, he thought, *and I'm going to drown*.

It seemed almost a joke, a prank someone had played

on him. Then panic surged up like bile and he plunged both his hands over the rent in the boards, as if that way he could stop the water coming in. But water was a thing that would not be stopped. He groaned and cursed. This was wrong, this was all wrong—he could not drown, it was impossible. He looked over his shoulder towards the other boat, but all he could see of it now was the mast-light, swaying and winking. He tried again to cry out—*Help! Wait!*—but the paltry words stuck in his swollen throat. He began to weep helplessly. The bruise on the back of his head, as if angered by his tears, set up a violent hammering that drove him down on all fours again, with his head hanging.

The water was coming in faster now. He tried to stand but the blood rushed from his head and he fell over, making a great splash. The boat tipped heavily sideways and then righted itself, the water sloshing around his knees. He was very cold now, shivering in rhythmic spasms, and his teeth chattered. His mind raced, skittering this way and that, like a rat in a trap.

He stood up again, and this time managed to stay upright. He gazed at the far dark shore with its swaying lights. He thought of the people there, sleeping, dreaming, and of the ones who were awake, doing ordinary things, making love, drinking, fighting—alive, all of them. Would Sylvia be asleep? Maybe she was lying awake in the dark, wondering where he was. Or maybe she had got up: maybe she was standing at the window in the living room, looking out anxiously into the night, watching for him.

The water was up to the gunwales now, and lapping round his knees. Terror had tightened his throat and he could not swallow. The mast-light of the other boat was no longer to be seen. He held his cold face in his hands.

No, he would not go this way, he would not let the boat take him with her. He sucked in a deep breath, the air rasping in his throat, then closed his eyes and clambered over the side.

How black the water was, wrapping him round like swathes of icy satin. He was a good swimmer, always had been. He should have taken off his clothes.

Mother! Oh, Jesus. Oh, God.

The pain pounded in his head. His arms were tired already, his muscles were beginning to lock.

The lights of shore seemed further off than ever.

He stopped flailing.

No good, no good.

Convolvulus.

II

9

ANOTHER FUNERAL, with the same mourners as before, save the one who was in the coffin. Yet to Quirke the atmosphere this time was different, even though he could not at first say what the difference was. Perhaps it was just the weather. On the day of Victor Delahaye's funeral the sun had shone as if for a festival, but today there was rain, a fine warm mist that drifted down absently yet still managed to soak its way rapidly into everyone's clothes, so that the inside of the church smelt like a sheep pen.

He stood at the back as the priest, up at the altar, droned his way through the funeral Mass. He looked over the heads of the congregation, trying to identify individuals from behind. That was surely Mona Delahaye in the big floppy black hat, while the tall upright woman with the greying blonde hair must be Jack Clancy's widow; and that would be her son beside her. There was no mistaking the Delahaye twins, of course, with their long, straw-pale heads. Hackett was there too, in an aisle seat halfway up. Hackett without his hat, shiny-haired, with a bald patch, always seemed to Quirke somehow incomplete, a novice monk, perhaps, tonsured and prematurely aged.

There was another blonde woman, younger than Mrs Clancy, and nearer the back. She wore not a hat but a navy-blue beret, jauntily tipped to the side, and a purple silk shawl over a dress of scarlet corduroy. In this flaunted outfit she had the look of a passion-flower stuck in among a funeral wreath.

Two days after Jack Clancy's disappearance his sunken boat, lodged on a sandbank five miles off the Muglins, had got tangled in a trawler's net and was dragged up. The trawler's skipper saw at once where the boards in the bottom had been pried apart and called the guards. Another two days had elapsed before Clancy's body was washed into a stony cove at the back of Howth Head. Quirke had left the post-mortem to Sinclair. Death by drowning, but there was the question of a bruise behind the ear. The old conundrum: did he jump, or was he pushed?—did he sail out into the bay and make the hole in the bottom of the boat himself, or did someone bang him on the head and load him unconscious into the *Rascal* and force those boards apart?

It had been all over the papers. *Second Tragedy Strikes City Firm. Dead Man's Business Partner Drowns.* 'By the Lord Harry,' Inspector Hackett had said, lifting his hat and scratching his head with his little finger, 'they're certainly doing an awful lot of dying, these folk.'

When the Mass ended the undertaker's men carried the coffin to the waiting hearse, and the churchyard became a mass of blossoming black umbrellas. The woman in the blue beret was alone, and seemed to Quirke lost. He made his way to her, a little surprised at himself, and offered her a cigarette. She, too, was surprised, and gave him a questioning look.

'The name is Quirke,' he said.

'Are you—?' She hesitated. 'Are you a friend of the family?' He shook his head, offering her his lighter. She gave a tight, small laugh. 'No, neither am I.' She leaned down to the lighter's flame, then lifted her head back and blew smoke into the air. 'Bella Wintour. With an oh-you.' He looked baffled, and she laughed again, and spelled the name in full.

'Ah,' he said, 'I see.' They were both aware of getting wet. Out of the corner of his eye Quirke saw Hackett making his way towards them. He touched a finger to Bella Wintour's elbow. 'I'm not going to the cemetery, are you? No? Cup of tea, then?'

As they moved towards the gate they passed by Mona Delahaye, standing beside her father-in-law in his wheel-chair, holding an umbrella over them both. She smiled at Quirke in her deliberately sultry way, and he tipped his hat to her, and cleared his throat.

'My my,' Bella Wintour murmured, as they went on, 'widows everywhere you turn.'

They went to the Royal Marine Hotel and sat in armchairs in the lounge. Bella's beret and the shoulders of Quirke's suit were greyly furred from the fine rain. When the waitress came Bella said that what she needed was not tea but a vodka and tonic. 'It is noon,' she said. 'Sun and yard-arm and all that.' Quirke asked for whiskey, and the waitress sniffed and went away. 'What is a yard-arm, anyway?' Bella asked. 'I've always wondered.'

'No idea,' Quirke said, producing his cigarettes again. 'Not a sailing man, myself.'

'No,' she said, looking him up and down with a faint, sardonic glint, 'I wouldn't have thought so.'

She glanced about. He could see her sensing him watching her. The rain-light gave to the air in the room a quicksilver, melancholy sheen. Her wandering gaze came to rest on him again, a slightly strained amusement in her grey eyes. 'I was Jack Clancy's girlfriend,' she said. 'One of them, at any rate.' She twirled her cigarette in the ashtray and made a glowing pencil-point of the tip. 'Are you shocked?'

'Not shocked, no,' Quirke said. 'Curious.'

'What's there to be curious about? If you knew anything about Jack you'd know he was fond of the ladies.'

'I don't know much about him at all.'

'That's obvious.' She leaned back against the dingy plush of the chair. 'Are you'—she smiled in the surprise of hearing herself ask it—'are you a policeman?'

He shook his head. 'Pathologist.'

'I see. You must be dedicated to your job, if you attend the funerals of your—what do you call the people you pathologise? Not patients, surely.'

'I don't think there is a word. Corpse. Cadaver.'

'No longer people, then, just things.'

He did not answer that.

The waitress came with their drinks. As the girl was setting them out, Bella continued to examine Quirke with a quizzical eye. Quirke paid and the waitress went off with another disapproving sniff. 'Cheers,' Bella said, lifting her glass. 'Here's to life, eh?'

They drank in silence for a time, both looking off in different directions now, aware of a constraint. They were strangers, after all.

'So you knew Jack Clancy,' Quirke said.

She was looking towards the windows still, towards the pools of silvery light congregated there. 'Yes, I knew him. On and off—you know. He used to call in, now and then.' She glanced at him, and shrugged, and gave her mouth a sadly grim little twist. Then she looked away again. When she lifted her glass it cast a metallic uplight on her throat. Quirke tried to guess her age. Forty? More? A woman on her own, beginning to wonder if independence was all it was cracked up to be. 'In fact,' she said, 'he called in that night, the night that he—the night that he died.'

'Did he?' Quirke said, keeping all emphasis out of his voice.

Bella nodded, sucking in her underlip. 'I keep going over it,' she said, 'over and over what he said, how he seemed, the way he looked.'

'And?'

She shrugged again. 'And nothing.' She stubbed her cigarette into the ashtray. The butt kept burning, sending up a skein of acrid smoke. 'There was something on his mind, all right,' she said. 'It was his second visit to me in the space of days, though I hadn't seen him in—oh, I don't know. Years.'

'And what did he say?'

She gave him a sharp look. 'What did he say about what?'

He opened his hands in front of her, showing his palms. 'I don't know. You said there was something on his mind.'

'And so there was. But he didn't *say* anything.' She seemed angry suddenly. 'He wasn't the kind of person to *say* things. Or maybe'—she sighed, and shook her head—'maybe he was but he just didn't say them to me. We weren't what you'd call close, at least not in that way.'

Quirke was aware of a faint but burgeoning inner warmth, as if a pilot light in his breast had flickered into life. He recognised the sensation. He savoured slightly illicit occasions such as this, a rainy lunchtime in a shabby hotel bar, with the fumes of strong drink in his nostrils and sitting opposite him a blonde of a certain age, circumspect and feisty, whose game eye seemed to offer possibilities that, if followed up in the right way, might lend a larger glow to the long afternoon stretching before them. He was supposed to be at the hospital, but Sinclair would cover for him. He thought of Isabel Galloway. She was rehearsing something by Chekhov that was coming to the Gate.

'Shall we have another?' he said to Bella Wintour.

He liked her little light-filled house. She made coffee for them, and they sat side by side on the sofa in the garden room, facing the big window. She told him this was where she had last sat with Jack Clancy. At such a moment another woman would have shed a tear, or produced a sorrowful sniff, but not this one. The rain had stopped and a watery sun was struggling to shine, and the garden

sparkled, and a virtuoso thrush was doing its liquid whistling. Quirke would have preferred a drink but sipped his
coffee with as good grace as he could muster.

Bella had kicked off her shoes and sat sideways on the
sofa with her bare, pink-soled feet drawn up. She was
smoking one of his cigarettes. She had set a big glass
ashtray on the sofa between them. Quirke was eyeing the
chipped crimson polish on her toenails. He found women's
feet at once endearing and slightly repellent. He made
himself look into the garden. 'What's that flower?' he
asked. 'The one with the white blossoms shaped like the
end of a trumpet.'

'It's a weed,' Bella said. 'I can't remember the name.'

'There's a lot of it.'

'Yes. It'll choke everything else, apparently, if I don't
do something about it.' She shifted the position of her
legs, grunting, and refolded them under her. 'Tell me what
your interest is,' she said.

'What?'

'In Jack Clancy. In his death.'

He said nothing for a moment, tapping his cigarette on
the edge of the ashtray, his eyes hooded. 'Why do you
think,' he said, 'he would have committed suicide?'

She widened her eyes. 'Is that what they're saying, that
he killed himself? The papers only said he drowned.'

'He was an expert sailor—he had trophies to prove it.'

'Even experts make mistakes.'

He nodded, still with his gaze downcast. 'There was
some bruising, to the head.'

'Bruising? What sort of bruising?'

'To the back, just here.' He lifted a hand to his own

head to show her. 'A bad one. The blow would have knocked him unconscious.'

'He had a fall, then?'

'Maybe. There was no sail on the boat.'

'What happened to it?'

He shrugged. 'Currents tore it off, maybe.'

'Is that possible?'

'I don't know. *I*'m certainly no expert when it comes to boats.'

She sat very still, hardly breathing, looking into his eyes. 'You think he was killed, don't you?' she said.

'I don't know. Someone might have hit him on the head and put him in the boat and taken the sail away so that if he woke up he wouldn't be able to hoist it and get back to land.'

'Someone?'

He stubbed out his cigarette and rose and walked to the window and stood with his back to the room, looking out. 'You remind me of Jack,' Bella said behind him, 'standing there. Only you're bigger.'

Quirke made no comment. 'You're sure he didn't tell you, that night, what was on his mind?' he asked.

'I told you,' she said. 'Jack and I weren't like that, we weren't—intimate.'

He glanced at her over his shoulder. 'You weren't?'

'I *told* you—not that way. And for God's sake don't keep standing there like that, will you?'

He came back to the sofa, but did not sit. 'I think I should go,' he said. He found he was as much surprised by this as she was.

She looked up at him, tightening her lips and moving

her teeth as if she were nibbling on a small hard seed. 'Why did you come here?' she asked.

'Because you invited me.'

She was still watching him, her eyes narrowed. 'You came to see what you could find out about Jack, didn't you?'

'Yes.'

At the front door, as he was putting on his hat, she asked if he would come to see her again. He chose to misunderstand, and said that if there was anything she wanted to tell him, or to ask him, she could call him at the hospital. She smiled coldly. 'That wasn't what I meant,' she said. 'But it doesn't matter.'

Before he reached the garden gate she had shut the door.

Inspector Hackett felt put out. He had caught Quirke pretending not to see him in the churchyard, before he went off with the woman in the beret. He tried not to mind, but he did. Of course, he knew about Quirke and women, but all the same.

Who was the blonde, anyway? he wondered. Somehow he did not think she was a relative of the dead man. He had spent his working life studying people, how they looked, the stances they took, the way they moved, and he had seen at once that this woman did not belong among the Clancys or the Delahayes. He guessed she must be one of Jack Clancy's old flames—Jack was rumoured to have had quite a few. And Quirke would have spotted her straight away for who she was, being something of an expert himself in that particular field. The blonde, he thought, would be well able for Quirke. He chuckled. Poor old Quirke, always getting himself in the soup.

Once out of the church gate he walked down to the seafront and turned right along Queen's Road. A pleasant way, with the trees in heavy leaf and the fine houses standing back in seclusion behind them. A feeble rain was falling; he disregarded it. He liked the smell of rain on grass and leaves; it reminded him of his boyhood and his grandfather's farm. Happy times, long gone.

This was a peculiar business. First Delahaye had done away with himself and now Jack Clancy was drowned. What the connection was between the two deaths he did not know; not yet. But there had to be a connection. Quirke was convinced Clancy had been murdered because of the knock to the head. This seemed fanciful to Hackett, but he trusted Quirke's instincts in these matters. Quirke knew the dead the way he himself knew the living. He chuckled again.

It was only a bit after noon but he realised he was hungry. He retraced his steps, leaving the seafront behind and climbing the hill towards the town. Halfway up he stopped at a pub—Clancy's; now there was a coincidence—and sat on a stool at the bar and ordered a ham sandwich and a glass of red lemonade. The barman, a pustular fellow with a missing front tooth, lent him a copy of the *Press* to read. *Minister Urges Higher Turf Production.* Emigration was up, burglaries were down—the one, no doubt, the consequence of the other. *Animal Gang Member Sentenced.* He sipped his lemonade, the syrupy sweet taste another echo of boyhood days. As his eye skimmed the columns of print his mind kept drifting back to the question of Jack Clancy's death, touching it lightly here and there, as if it were the man's corpse itself. Clancy's son had been on the boat when Delahaye had shot himself—his presence there a thing for which no explanation had yet presented itself—and then Clancy himself goes down in a boat that either he or some other or others had scuttled. An eye for an eye, a tooth for a tooth? That had to be it. Vengeance. But who was the avenger, and what was the cause?

There was a flurry of movement and a young man with red hair perched himself on the stool next to his. Hackett sighed. The bloody pub was empty yet this fellow had to choose to sit right here beside him. He concentrated on the paper, frowning irritably. *Productivity, the Minister said, was the key to solving the country's economic and social problems.*

'Hello, Inspector,' the young man beside him said. He turned. Widow's peak, narrow face, freckles. Who—? Reporter, yes. Jimmy somebody. The *Mail*? The young man seemed mildly offended not to have been recognised straight away. 'Minor,' he said. 'Jimmy Minor.'

'Ah, yes.' Hackett put on a large, slow smile. 'One of our representatives from the fourth estate, if I'm not greatly mistaken.'

Jimmy Minor took out a packet of Gold Flake, lit one, put the packet away. 'Thanks, no, I won't,' the inspector said, with soft sarcasm. Minor took no notice. Hackett took a bite of his sandwich.

'You were at the funeral,' Jimmy Minor said.

'Were you there?' the inspector said, chewing. 'I didn't see you.'

'We blend into the crowd, us fourth-estaters.'

Hackett was fascinated by the way the young man smoked, almost violently, twisting up his mouth and sucking at the cigarette as if he were performing an unpleasant task that had been imposed on him and that he was condemned to keep carrying out, over and over. He had ordered a glass of stout and a sandwich, and now the barman brought them.

'Were you there for the paper?' the inspector asked.

'No.'

'Ah.' Minor had lifted a corner of the sandwich and was examining doubtfully the slice of bright-orange cheese underneath and the thin smear of butter. 'Just curiosity, then?' Hackett said. It came to him that Minor was a friend of Quirke's daughter Phoebe. A sort of friend, anyhow—friendship, he surmised, was not likely to be a thing that Minor would give much energy to. The barman, idling behind a skittle-row of beer-taps, was fingering an angry red crater on his chin. Hackett watched him, regretting the sandwich he had just eaten, which those fingers had probably assembled.

'Well,' Minor said, with the air of a man getting down to business, wiping a thin line of creamy beer-froth from his upper lip. '—what do you think?'

Hackett could not take his appalled eye off the barman and those probing fingernails. 'What do I think of what?' he asked distractedly.

Minor snickered. 'This business with Clancy and Delahaye, the two of them gone within less than a fortnight of each other.'

'A remarkable coincidence, all right,' the inspector said mildly, and took a sip of his lemonade.

Minor turned to him with an exaggerated stare of incredulity. 'A coincidence?' he said. 'Do you think I came down in the last shower, or what?'

Hackett brought out a packet of Player's and with pointed courtesy offered Minor a cigarette, which Minor was about to take when he realised he already had a Gold Flake going.

'So tell me,' the inspector said, 'what do you think these two misfortunate deaths were due to, if not coincidence?'

'There's no such thing as coincidence.' Minor was waggling his empty glass, trying to catch the attention of the dreamy barman. 'I think,' he said, 'there's something distinctly—another glass here!—something distinctly queer about the whole thing. I hear, for instance, that Clancy had half his head knocked off before the boat went down. He hardly did that to himself.'

Hackett sighed. This, he reflected, was how things got about, to muddy the water and darken the air. 'Half his head, you say? I hadn't heard that.'

It was clear that Minor did not believe him.

'And furthermore,' Minor said, as the barman slid a second glass of Guinness across the counter to him, 'I hear there's something going on behind the stout high walls of Delahaye and Clancy Limited.' He waggled his fingers. 'Hands in tills, that kind of thing.'

Inspector Hackett, taking a slow draw of his cigarette, leaned back on the stool and squinted at the ceiling. 'Is that so?' he said, eyeing the light fixtures. 'I must say, Mr Minor, you seem to hear an awful lot of things, in the course of your day.' Two forty-watt bulbs in flowerpot-shaped lampshades made of that tallow-coloured stuff that looked like stretched human skin. Mrs Hackett, he thought, would not be impressed. 'And do you hear,' he asked, 'whose hand it was that got slammed in the till?'

Minor drank his Guinness, giving himself another moustache of lather. 'I'm guessing the late Mr Clancy was involved.'

'Ah, yes,' Hackett said, 'that would be a reason for the poor man to put an end to himself, if he had been found out.'

Minor stared at him sideways. 'You think it was suicide?' he said incredulously.

Hackett waved a hand in mild dismissal. 'I don't think anything,' he said. 'You're the one that's doing all the thinking.'

Minor was silent for a moment, watching the policeman out of a narrowed eye. 'Look, Inspector,' he said, lowering his voice, 'you and I could help each other in this.'

'Could we?' Hackett asked, in a tone of large surprise. 'How would that be, now?'

Minor would have none of the policeman's feigned innocence, and shook his head impatiently. 'I hear things, you know things,' he said. 'What's wrong with a fair trade?'

The inspector smiled almost indulgently. 'Ah, Jimmy my lad, I don't think it works that way.' He took his hat from the bar and stepped down off the stool. 'I don't think it works that way at all.'

He nodded, and put on his hat, and sauntered away, whistling softly.

It rained at first, a nasty drizzle that clung like grease to the windscreen, but once Maggie had got past Carlow the clouds broke and the sun struggled through. Drifts of cottony white mist clung to the tops of the mountains off to the left—hills, really, she could not remember what they were called—and everything shimmered and glowed, the trees and the wet green fields and the tarmac of the road before her. It would be so lovely at Ashgrove: the countryside there always looked so dramatic in weather like this. The only blemish on the day was the guilty niggle that she could not free herself of. Was she running away? But even if she was, what of it? They had hardly noticed her going, the twins, and Mona, of course, but even her father, too. They were probably glad to be rid of her, the lot of them. After all, was she not, in her heart, glad to be rid of them?

She tried to think of things to distract herself from these troubling matters. Her name, for instance. Marguerite Delahaye. It was a nice name, she thought. She should never have allowed herself to be called Maggie: it sounded so common. Miss Marguerite Delahaye, late of Dublin and now of Ashgrove House in the County of Cork.

Everything felt strange. It was strange the way time went on, calmly as ever; it seemed shameful, somehow.

Surely there should be another pace for things to move at, after all that had happened. Death had stepped so suddenly into her life, like a thief, no, like a robber, brutal and violent. She had wept for Victor so much and for so long that she felt dried up now. Arid, that was the word; she felt arid. The bitterness had not abated. She suspected it never would abate. She imagined it, a sort of knot inside her. She had thought it would shift after Jack Clancy died, but it had not, it was still there, a hard dry chancre of bitterness lodged under her heart. And yet she felt lightened, too, lightened in spirit. It was as if a burden had been set on her shoulders but she had managed to shrug it off. She was free. The road unwound before her as if it would never end. All that hate and horror was behind her. Yes, she was free.

She closed her eyes for a second and when she opened them there was a child on a bicycle in the road in front of her. She pressed hard on the brake pedal and wrenched the wheel first to the right and then to the left, and the car bounced on to the grass verge and the engine gave a great roar, as if enraged, and abruptly cut out. There was a smell of exhaust smoke and hot rubber. She looked in the driving mirror. The child had stopped too, a girl of eight or nine, with dirty curls and a dirtier face. It was an adult's bike she had, much too big for her, so that she had to reach up to grasp the handlebars. Where had she come from, as if out of nowhere? Maggie in her mind saw with awful clarity what so easily might have been, the mangled bike on its side, its front wheel spinning, and beside it the motionless form lying on the road, like a little pile of bloodstained rags. *It's following me*, she thought. *Death is following me.*

She stopped in the next town—she did not notice its name—and found a hotel, a dingy place smelling of boiled cabbage, and sat in a corner of the bar and drank a glass of brandy. It made her cough at first, for she was not used to spirits. A man came in and sat at the next table. He was a big, florid fellow, with thick lips and starting eyes. He wore a tweed jacket and a yellow waistcoat, and gaiters—she had not seen anyone wearing gaiters since she was a child. He went to the bar and ordered whiskey—*a ball of malt*, she heard him say—and came swaggering back to the table, grinning at her as he went past.

She tried to ignore him but there was something grossly fascinating about him. He sat at the table with his legs opened wide, showing off the big round bulge in the crotch of his trousers. Each time he took a sip of his drink he would let the whiskey flow back into the glass, mixed with spit that sank to the bottom of the glass, stringy and white. He spoke to her, remarking what a grand day it was, thank God, now that the rain had cleared. She did not answer, only gave a quick cool smile, nodding. He asked if she was staying in the hotel. No, she said; she was on her way to West Cork. 'Cork!' he said, '—sure, I'm from Bandon, myself.' She nodded again. She had gone hot, and could feel a flush rising up from her throat. The man asked if she would care for another drink—'A bird never flew on one wing!'—but she thanked him and said, no, that she would have to be on her way. He grinned again, and wished her a safe journey, and asked her, with a laugh, to say hello to Bandon for him, if she happened to be going in that direction.

She gathered her things, her handbag, the car keys, her chiffon scarf, and stood up. She was afraid that he would reach out and touch her as she went past, would catch hold of her cardigan or try to grab her hand. But then she noticed that he was looking at her strangely; his expression had changed and he seemed surprised, even shocked. She must have said something to him, though she had no idea what. She often did that nowadays, blurted things out without thinking. Sometimes she even spoke without knowing she had done so, and she would not realise it until she saw people backing away from her, looking offended or frightened. Her father had threatened more than once to have her put away; especially now, she would have to be careful and guard her tongue.

In the car she had to sit quite still for a minute to calm herself, but then it occurred to her that the man in the gaiters might come out and try to accost her again, and she started up the engine and drove away quickly.

She could not wait to get to Ashgrove.

10

MONA DELAHAYE telephoned him at the hospital. The girl on the switchboard got the name wrong, and said there was a Mrs Delaney wishing to speak to him. He knew no Mrs Delaney, but asked for her to be put through anyway. When he heard Mona's voice he felt a sudden tightness under his shirt collar that surprised him. As she spoke he pictured her thin, wide, crimson mouth, curved in a smile of malicious enjoyment—he had told her of the mix-up in the names, and she had laughed delightedly— and he could almost feel her hot breath coming to him all the way down the line. He asked what he could do for her and she suggested he might come to the house, as there were things she wanted to speak to him about. 'No one will tell me anything,' she said, with a pout in her voice. He did not know what she meant by this. What were the things she was not being told, he wondered, and who were the people who were not telling them to her?

He put his head in at the door of the dissecting room. Sinclair was there, getting ready to operate on the corpse of a tinker girl who had drowned herself in the sea off Connemara. 'Have to go out,' Quirke said. 'You'll hold the fort?' Sinclair looked at him. Sinclair was used to holding the fort. 'Mrs Victor Delahaye wants to see me,' Quirke added, thinking an explanation was required. Sinclair had the gift of making him feel guilty.

Sinclair considered the scalpel in his hand. 'Maybe she's going to confess to killing Jack Clancy,' he said.

'Oh, I'm sure,' Quirke said. 'I'll be back in an hour.'

On Northumberland Road the recently rained-on pavements were steaming in the sun, and the humid perfume of sodden flowers and wet loam hung heavy on the air. The maid with the rusty curls opened the door to him. With her grin and her green eyes she reminded him of a young woman he had encountered years before, in a convent. Maisie, she was called. He wondered what had become of her. Nothing good, he suspected. He had not even known her surname.

He was shown into the drawing room, where he stood in front of the sofa with his hands in his pockets, looking idly at the Mainie Jellett abstract and rocking back and forth on his heels. The window and the sunlit garden beyond were reflected in the glass, so that he had to move his head this way and that to see the picture properly. He did not think much of it but supposed he must be missing something. Around him the house was drowsily silent. It still did not feel like a house in mourning.

Mona Delahaye entered. She shut the door and stood leaning against it with her hands behind her back, her head lowered, smiling up at him. Today she wore black slacks and a green silk blouse and gold-painted sandals. Her toenail polish matched her scarlet lipstick. 'Thanks for coming,' she said. 'Like a drink?' She went to the big rosewood sideboard, where bottles were set out in ranks on a silver charger. 'Gin?' she said. 'Or are you a whiskey man?'

'Jameson's, if you have it.'

'Oh, we have everything.' She glanced over her shoulder, doing her cat-smile. 'I'll join you.'

She came to him bearing two glasses and handed one to him.

'Thanks,' he said.

'Chin chin.' She drank, and grimaced. 'God,' she said hoarsely, 'I don't know how you drink this stuff—liquid fire.'

She stood very close to him, half a head shorter, her civet scent stinging his nostrils. The top three buttons of her blouse were open, and he looked down between her small pale breasts and saw the sprinkling of freckles there. 'There was something you wanted to speak to me about?' he said.

'Did I?'

'That's what you said on the phone.'

'Oh, yes.' She was gazing vaguely at his tie. 'It's just that no one tells me anything.' She lifted her eyes to his. 'Your friend the detective—what's his name?'

'Hackett. Inspector Hackett.'

'That's it. He has a way of talking without saying anything. Have you noticed?'

'Yes,' Quirke said, 'I've noticed that. What would you like him to say?'

She was looking into her glass now. 'I think I've had enough of this, thank you,' she said. She returned to the sideboard and put down the undrunk whiskey and took another glass and poured into it an inch of gin and a generous splash of tonic. She lifted the lid of a silver bucket and swore under her breath. 'No ice again,' she said.

There were certain women, Quirke was thinking, who seemed doubly present in a room. It was as if there was the woman herself and along with her a more vivid version of her, an invisible other self that emanated from her and surrounded her like an aura. It came to him that he very much wanted to see Mona Delahaye without her clothes on. His grip tightened on the whiskey glass. Her husband was hardly cold in his grave.

'The thing is,' she said, turning with her glass and moving towards the white sofa, 'people think I'm stupid.' She glanced back at him. 'You, for instance—you think I'm completely brainless, don't you?' He could see no way of replying to this. She sat down on the sofa with a not unhappy little sigh. 'That's why you'd like to go to bed with me.' She smiled and drank at the same time, looking up at him merrily. 'Come,' she said softly, patting the place beside her, 'come and sit down.' He hesitated. It was the playful lightness of her tone that made the moment seem all the more dangerous. 'Oh, come on,' she said, 'I won't bite you.'

He went to the sideboard and poured another whiskey, trying not to let the neck of the bottle rattle against the glass. He could feel her watching him, smiling. He went and perched on the arm of the sofa, at the opposite end from where she sat, as he had done the first time he was here, with Hackett. 'What is it you want to know?' he asked. 'The reason why your husband killed himself?'

'Oh, no,' she said. 'I know that, more or less.' She

crossed her legs and draped one arm along the back of the sofa. She lifted her glass to her lips, but did not drink, and wrinkled her nose instead. 'Gin without ice is sort of disgusting, isn't it?' Quirke thought of another woman, sitting on another sofa, with a glass of warm gin in her hand. Mona Delahaye was watching him, reading his mind. 'Are you married, Dr Quirke?' she asked.

'No.'

'You have a sort of married look about you.'

'I was married a long time ago. My wife died.'

Mona nodded. 'That's sad,' she said, with calm indifference. She went on scanning his face, her thin mouth lifted at the corners. 'So you're a gay bachelor, then.'

'More or less.' He swirled the whiskey in his glass. 'Why *did* your husband kill himself?'

She took her arm from the back of the sofa and leaned forward. 'Oh, I didn't mean that I *know*,' she said dismissively. 'I sort of do.' She paused, looking at the narrow gold band on the third finger of her left hand. 'He was terribly—well, terribly jealous, in a ridiculous sort of way. He used to worry that I had a lover'—she smiled—'or lovers, even.'

'And did you?'

She ignored the question. 'He was forever going on about it,' she said, 'until I got bored, and then of course I'd start to tease him. Awful of me, I know, but I couldn't resist it.' She looked at him again, frowning. 'Did you know my husband?'

'I met him at a reception once. I can't remember where.'

'Was I there?'

'I believe you were.'

'That's odd. Surely I would have remembered meeting you.' She smiled slyly, then frowned again, and let her eyes slide away from his until she was gazing at nothing. 'He had no sense of humour, that was the trouble—none at all. And that really is very boring, you know, if you're married to the person.' She finished her drink and rolled the empty glass between her palms. The shadow of a cloud darkened the window for a second and then the brightness flooded back. 'Honestly,' Mona said, glancing towards the window, 'you'd think it was April, wouldn't you?' She looked at him again. 'He left a note, did I mention that?'

'No,' Quirke said, 'you didn't mention that.'

'Well, he did. But look'—she shook her head at him with pretended displeasure—'I wish you wouldn't sit there like that, all tensed up like a corkscrew. Sit here, beside me—come on.'

'Mrs Delahaye,' Quirke said, 'I'm really not sure why you asked me here today.'

'No,' she said brightly, 'neither am I. But it would be nice if you came and sat down.' She smiled. 'We could discuss the matter,' she said, in a husky tone of mock-solemnity. 'You like discussing things, don't you?'

He got to his feet and stood irresolute. His glass was empty again. He felt dizzy. What was he to do? The woman on the sofa sat at her ease, looking up at him, with what might have been a warmly sympathetic smile, as if she understood his dilemma. She held up her glass. 'Get us both another drink,' she said. 'I'd like one, and I think you need one.'

He took his time at the sideboard, pouring the drinks. When he carried them to the sofa Mona tasted hers and shook her head. 'No,' she said, 'I can't drink another one without ice. Would you be a dear——? The kitchen is at the end of the hall.' She indicated with her thumb. 'Sarah will be there, she'll show you.'

He took the ice bucket and walked with it down the hall, into the dim recesses of the house. Sarah the maid was not to be found; he had once been in love with a woman named Sarah, who was dead, now. The kitchen was large and impersonal, and smelt faintly of gas. The squat refrigerator stood in a corner murmuring to itself, like a white-clad figure kneeling in rapt prayer. He extracted the crackling ice tray from its compartment and took it to the sink and struggled with it, the pads of his fingers sticking to the plump cubes sunk in their metal chambers. At last he thought of turning the tray over and running the tap on it, and then of course the cubes all fell out at once with a clatter and he had to chase them round the bottom of the sink with fingers that by now were turning numb.

At last he got the cubes into the bucket and set off back through the house. In the hallway he heard voices, and as he was passing by a door it opened suddenly and one of the Delahaye twins, coming out, stopped on the threshold and looked at him in surprise. He was dressed in white, as usual—white sports shirt, duck trousers, plimsolls—and carried a wooden tray with glasses on it. Quirke glanced past the young man's shoulder into the room. There was a billiard table, and a darkly pretty girl was sitting on it, with her left foot on the floor and her right leg raised, her hands clasped around her knee. The other twin stood in front of her, with a hand resting on her hip.

Impassive, they returned his stare. No one spoke. In a second or two the little tableau—Quirke in the hall, the twin in the doorway and the couple at the table—was over, and Quirke passed on. He had a strange feeling of lightness, as if he were passing through a dream.

Mona Delahaye was reclining now against the back of the sofa. She uncrossed her legs slowly and leaned forward, holding up her glass, into which he dropped a handful of ice from the bucket. 'You're such a pet,' she said, watching the cubes jostle amid the tonic bubbles.

Quirke retrieved his whiskey glass and sat down again on the arm of the sofa. 'You say your husband left a note,' he said.

'Yes.' She frowned, as if petulantly. 'I threw it away. Burned it, actually. Or did I flush it down the you-know-what?' She twinkled at him. 'You see?—I'm such a scatterbrain.'

'May I ask what he said—what he wrote?'

'Oh, silly stuff. How much he loved me and how jealous he was—all that, the usual.' She sipped her drink thoughtfully. 'There's really nothing you can do for people who are jealous, is there? And they make such a—such a *spectacle* of themselves. It's always too pitiful.' She looked at him. 'Don't you think?'

He drank his whiskey, then brought out his cigarettes and offered her one, and took one himself. Leaning down with his lighter he looked again into the front of her blouse. Her skin was so pale there, and would be so soft to touch. 'Was he jealous of Jack Clancy?' he asked.

She gave a little silvery laugh. 'Oh, he was jealous of

everyone,' she said. She pushed out her lower lip and directed a thin stream of smoke upwards past his face.

'Is that why he tried to kill his son?'

She frowned in puzzlement. 'What?'

'Because he was jealous, is that why he abandoned young Clancy in the boat miles offshore and left him to fry in the sun? To get back at his father?'

She gave him an odd look, tight-lipped and wide-eyed, as if he had said something richly funny at which she must not allow herself to laugh. 'I hadn't thought of that,' she said, blinking slowly, trying to show him how impressed she was by his perceptiveness. 'I'm sure you're right. In fact, I'm sure he intended to kill Davy, but lost his nerve at the last minute and shot himself instead. It would be just the kind of thing Victor would do. He really wasn't very—he wasn't very *competent*, you know. He had this reputation as a ruthless businessman'—she broke off for a second to laugh again, almost in delight—'but it was all nonsense. He hadn't an idea. It was his father who kept the business going, even after he was supposed to have retired. Then when poor old Sam had his stroke that creep Maverley stepped in and took charge. And there was Jack, of course—Jack knew the business inside out.' She darted her cigarette in the direction of the ashtray that she had set on the floor beside her foot. 'Victor's trouble was his mother. You wouldn't have known her—a real monster, hiding behind a mask of niceness. She ruined him, gave him ridiculous ideas of how clever and important he was, at the same time working away to undermine his confidence. *Oh, Victor, don't try to be like your father*, she'd say, *you couldn't possibly be like him.* And she'd smile, very sweetly, and pat his hand. It's her he should have killed, though conveniently she died.'

Forgetting himself, he slid down from his place on the sofa arm until he was sitting beside her. She smiled, and it seemed for a moment she might move sideways and lean her head on his shoulder, or nestle against his chest. 'Will you tell me what was in the note—the suicide note?' he asked.

She stared at him, again with that look of almost laughing. 'I didn't say it was a *suicide* note,' she said. 'Just a note. He often wrote things down that he couldn't bring himself to say.'

'And what was it he wrote that last time—what was it he couldn't say?'

'I told you—about being jealous.'

'Of Jack Clancy?'

'Um.' She dipped a finger into her glass and stirred the gin and what was left of the ice cubes, then put the tip of the finger into her mouth and sucked it, looking at him sidelong. He held her gaze. He was acutely aware of the presence of others in the house, of Sarah the maid, of the twins, and that dark-haired girl. What had the three of them been up to in the billiard room? Nothing good, he was sure of that.

'Did you know what he was going to do?' he asked. She shook her head, still with her finger in her mouth. 'But you weren't surprised,' he said softly.

She took his glass from his hand and rose and walked to the sideboard and poured them each yet another drink.

'What do you know about me?' she asked, busy with bottles, glasses, ice.

'Know about you?'

'Yes. Where I'm from, for instance. Can you tell from my accent?' He had not noticed an accent. 'Maybe I've lost it,' she said.

She brought their drinks and gave him his and sat down again beside him.

'We'll both be drunk,' Quirke said.

She folded one leg under her with balletic grace. 'Yes,' she said gaily, 'that's my aim.' She clinked her glass against his. 'Bottoms up.'

The whiskey this time burned his throat. He needed to eat something. He was beginning to hear himself breathe, and that was always a bad sign. Drink seemed not to affect Mona Delahaye, except to lend her expression a brightly impish gleam.

'So,' he said, 'where are you from?'

'You really can't tell? I don't know whether to be glad or not—I mean about having lost my accent. I'm from South Africa. My name, my'—she giggled—'my maiden name, used to be Vanderweert.' Quirke nodded. He could not imagine this woman ever having been a maiden. 'I was born in Cape Town,' she said. 'Ever been there? Very beautiful.'

'You're a long way from home, then.'

Her look became pensive. 'Yes, I suppose so. Though it's hardly home, any more.' She glanced at him, smiling. 'I suppose you're thinking of diamond mines, and kaffirs being flogged, and so on, while I loll on the veranda in the cool of evening drinking something tall with ice in it and admiring the sun setting behind Table Mountain. Not like that, I'm afraid, not like that at all. My father was —is—a civil servant, third class, as they say. I grew up in a bungalow in Parow.'

'Where's that?'

'Suburb of Cape Town. Not the loveliest spot on earth.'

'How did you meet your husband?'

'Victor?' she said, as if she had forgotten that she had once had a husband. 'He was visiting Cape Town, pretending to be on business—he loved to travel about the world, being the high-powered executive—and I was working as a typist in the office of one of the firms he called in to. He took me to dinner, we danced, the moon rose, and by morning the deal was clinched.' She was watching him, ironical and amused. 'The way things really happen is always grubby, isn't it? I could have lied to you, you realise that. I could have said I was a De Beers heiress, and that Victor had to plead for my hand with my father the plutocrat, and you wouldn't have known any better. But I thought you'd prefer the truth. I thought you *deserved* the truth, dull as it is.' She chuckled. 'Victor would be furious—he liked to pretend I was the daughter of some grand colonial family. Poor Victor.'

She looked convincingly sad for a moment. Quirke had an urge to take her hand; he must not drink any more, he must not. 'I'm sorry,' he said. 'I never properly offered you my condolences.'

She brightened. 'Oh, how sweet!' she said. 'But really, it's all right. In fact, at times like this you need someone absolutely heartless around to buck you up.' She turned her head and peered at him, looking deep into his eyes. 'You do want to go to bed with me, don't you?' she said. 'I wasn't wrong about that, was I?'

He did not know how to reply. The feline candour of her gaze both unnerved and excited him. He was sweating a little. He was glad of the commonplace things around them, the room, the sunlight in the garden, the presence of other people in the house. Surely she was teasing him, being scandalous to see how he would take it.

'Tell me what you think about Jack Clancy,' he said, to be saying something.

'What I think about him?' she said. The light in her eye was more erratic now, and when she frowned it was as if she had lost the thread of something and was having trouble finding it again. The gin having its effect at last; he was faintly relieved.

'About what happened to him, in the boat,' he said.

'Don't you know? I thought you knew everything, you and your detective friend.'

He leaned forward and put his glass carefully on the floor and clasped his hands before him. He could clearly hear the air rushing in his nostrils, in his chest, and knew he was drunk. Not seriously drunk, not drunk drunk, but drunk all the same.

'Jack Clancy drowned,' he said, 'but before he did, someone or something hit him on the head.'

'Oh, yes?' she said absently. He was not sure she had been listening. She leaned down to pick up his glass from where it stood on the carpet between his feet. He moved to stop her. 'Come on,' she said, 'just one more, and then we can go and see if there's anything to eat for lunch.'

He would not let her have his glass, but took hers and walked with both to the sideboard. He had intended to leave them firmly there, yet found himself refilling them instead. Just one more, as she had said; a last one. The skin of his forehead had tightened alarmingly, and there seemed a very faint mist in front of his eyes that would not clear no matter how often he blinked. He carried the glasses back to the sofa. Something was scratching at the back of his mind, insistently, but he ignored it. Just this one, and then he would leave.

He realised he was leaning over her, she seated and he standing, grinning, and swaying a little. A great wash of happiness, childish and vacant, swept through him like a thrilling gust of wind. *Quirke*, he told himself, *you are a damned fool*.

He woke with a start and did not know where he was. The light in the room was shadowed, but there was a rich warm tint to it of old gold. High ceiling, a plaster cornice on four sides, the walls painted apple green. Two windows, lofty, the curtains of heavy yellow silk, drawn, with sunlight in them. Wardrobe, dressing-table, a hinged screen, silk again, swooping birds painted on it. He lay amid tangled sheets, under a satin eiderdown, much too hot. There was sweat on his upper lip and in the hollow above his clavicle. His tongue burned, whiskey-raw. He remembered, of course. *Oh, Lord*.

She lay at his side, her back turned to him, her hair splashed like a rich dark stain on the pillow. She was snoring softly. He eased himself out of the bed, sliding his legs sideways under the eiderdown and setting his feet cautiously on the floor, and crossed the room at a crouch, looking for his clothes.

'Going already?' she said behind him. He straightened, turned, his heart sinking. She was lying on her back now, with an arm under her head, looking at him along the lumpy length of the eiderdown. 'Give us a fag before you go,' she said.

When he bent to pick up his clothes from where he had discarded them on the floor something began beating angrily in his head. He pulled on his trousers. His jacket was draped over the back of a little gilt chair in front of the dressing-table. He found his cigarettes and his lighter and returned with them to the bed. Mona still lay with her head resting on her arm. One pale small breast was exposed.

'Sorry,' he said.

'For what?'

'I should be at the hospital.'

'Oh, of course you should. Busy busy busy.' She pulled herself up in the bed, leaning on her elbows. He put a cigarette between her lips and held the lighter for her. 'Anyway,' she said, 'I'm used to men creeping out of my bed.' She laughed, a subdued little hoot. 'That sounds awful, doesn't it? What a slut I must seem.' She peered more closely at him in the curtained gloom. 'You are a big fellow, aren't you?' she said. 'All muscle and fur. Come back to bed—come on.'

He brought an ashtray from the dressing-table and put it on the bed where she could reach it. Her breasts, palely pendent, made him think of a small, soft, big-eyed animal—a lemur, was it? He sat down and the mattress springs gave a faint, distant jangle of protest. She had scrambled higher still in the bed and was lying back against a mound of pillows, watching him—no, *surveying* him, he thought—as if she were measuring him against a model in her head and finding him sadly though perhaps not hopelessly wanting. The ashtray bore the legend *Hôtel Métropole Monte-Carlo.* She saw him looking. 'Stolen,' Mona said. 'By me. I like to steal things. Nothing valuable, just things that take my fancy. People's husbands, for instance.'

'I told you,' Quirke said, 'I'm not married.'

'Yes. Pity.' She squirmed a little, making a face. 'Ach— I'm leaking.' She saw him flinch, and smiled. 'Why are you so afraid of women?' she asked, with no hint of accusation or disapproval, but seeming curious only. 'I suppose your mother is to blame.'

'I have no mother,' Quirke said. '—*had* no.'

'She died?'

He shrugged. 'I never knew her. Or my father.'

'Dear dear,' she said, with an odd, harsh edge to her voice, 'a poor little orphan boy, then. Let me picture it. There was the workhouse, and the beatings, and the bowls of gruel, and you a little lad scrambling up chimneys for tuppence and a rub of soap, yes?'

He did not smile. 'Something like that, yes.'

'So how did you get from there to here?'

'That's a long story—'

'I like long bedtime stories.'

'—and a boring one.'

She drew on her cigarette. 'I suppose we shouldn't risk

another drink? No, no, you're right, goodness knows what we'd be driven to do.' She leaned forward, draping her bare arms over her knees. 'So,' she said. 'No mummy, and afraid of women ever since.'

'Why do you think I'm afraid of women?'

She shook her head mock-ruefully. 'A girl can always tell things like that. It's not so bad, you know, being nervous. Quite appealing, in its way.' She ran a fingertip over the back of his hand where it rested on the sheet. 'Quite attractive, sometimes.'

The sweat had dried on his skin and he felt chilled suddenly. He went and found his shirt and pulled it on, then returned to the bed. 'Tell me what's going on,' he said.

She stared. 'How do you mean? What's going on where?'

'Here. All this. Your husband killing himself, then Jack Clancy dying too. The business. Davy Clancy. Your sister-in-law—'

'My *sister-in-law*?' She was staring at him incredulously. 'You mean Maggie?'

'Your husband's sister, yes.'

'What about her?'

'What about any of you? There's something behind all this. It's tangled up together somehow.'

'Well, of course it is. How would it not be? Two families, in business together and living in each other's ears. How would it not be *tangled*?'

Of the many things this young woman might be, he reflected, brainless was not one of them.

Suddenly she leaned forward and kissed him on the

lips, hard, almost violently, almost in anger, it seemed. Her mouth tasted of cigarette smoke and, faintly, of gin. So many things that were happening had happened before, in identical circumstances, with another woman, other women. He felt the tremulous coolness of her breasts against his skin. She drew back a little way and stared at him. Her eyes seemed huge at such close range. 'What a fool you are,' she said, as if fondly. 'What a hopeless, foolish man.'

He went on tiptoe along the hallway towards the front door with his hat in his hand. There were indistinct voices behind him in the house. He hoped he would not have to encounter again the twins or the girl. They were so cool, that trio, so seemingly detached, looking at him in that amused, measured way, tossing their secret knowledge from one to another, like a tensely springy, soft-furred tennis ball. He would find out what it was, that secret, the secret they were all playing with.

As he drew open the front door—still no sign of Sarah the maid, thank God—he saw himself as a kind of clown, in outsize trousers and long, bulbous shoes, staggering this way and that between two laughing teams of white-clad players, jumping clumsily, vainly, for the ball that they kept lobbing over his head with negligent, mocking ease. Yes, he would find out.

11

PHOEBE COULD NOT GET the Delahaye twins out of her thoughts. She had not really wanted to go to the party that night in Breen's tiny gingerbread house under the railway bridge. She did not like parties: they always left her feeling unsettled and giddy for days afterwards, but she had felt she had to go, since that was what girlfriends did with their boyfriends.

Girlfriend. Boyfriend. The words brought her up short, and almost made her blush, not for shyness or bashful pleasure, but out of an embarrassment she could not quite account for.

What was it about the Delahaye brothers that made them so striking? Of course, twins were always a little bit uncanny, but with the Delahayes it was not only that. A fascinating aura surrounded them, fascinating, alarming, worrying. There was their colouring, so blond, with that dead-white skin, waxy and almost translucent, and their strange, silvery-blue eyes, transparent almost, like the eyes of a seagull. But mostly what drew her to them was their manner, remote, and with such stillness, as if they were always posing for their portraits, as if—

Drew her to them. Once again she was struck. Was that what she had meant to think? Was she drawn to them?

Gulls, yes, that was what they were like, those two, standing always at a remove, pale-eyed, watchful, disdaining.

She was thinking about them the day she met Inspector Hackett. It was lunchtime and she had come out of the shop she worked in, on Grafton Street, the Maison des Chapeaux, and there was the detective, strolling along in his shiny blue suit with his hands in his pockets and his little pot-belly sticking out, his braces on show and his battered old hat pushed to the back of his head. It seemed that every time she encountered Hackett he was out and about like this, at his ease, without a care. Today he was obviously enjoying the sunshine, and he greeted her warmly, with his elaborate, old-fashioned courtesy.

'Is it yourself, Miss Griffin!' he exclaimed, throwing back his head and puffing out his cheeks for pleasure. She believed he really was fond of her, but she could never understand why. She seemed to remember he had no children; maybe she made him think of the daughter he might have wished for.

'Hello, Inspector,' she said. 'Isn't it a lovely day?'

'It is that, indeed,' Hackett said, squinting at the sky and seeming at the same time to wink at her. She liked the way he exaggerated his quaintness for her amusement, playing the countryman come to town and exaggerating his thickest Midlands drawl. She knew very well how clever he was, how cunning. It occurred to her that she would not wish to be a miscreant upon whom Inspector Hackett had fixed his mild-seeming eye.

They went into Bewley's. It was crowded, as it always was at lunchtime, and there were the mingled smells of coffee and fried sausages and sugary pastry. They sat at a tiny marble table at the back of the big scarlet and black dining room.

Hackett, with his hat in his lap, asked the waitress for a ham roll and 'a sup of tea'—he was really putting on the clodhopper act today—and then turned back to beam at Phoebe, and enquired after her father. She was aware that of late the detective and Quirke had been seeing each other regularly again because of the Delahaye and Clancy business, so Hackett must know how her father was; nevertheless she said that Quirke was very well, very well indeed. This was a coded way of saying that Quirke was not drinking, or at least not drinking as he sometimes did, ruinously. Hackett nodded. He had a way of pursing his lips and letting his eyelids droop that always made her think of a fat old Roman bishop, a Vatican insider, worldly-wise, calculating, sly.

'Wasn't it awful,' she said, 'about that poor man, Clancy, who drowned? Such a terrible accident, and so soon after his partner had died.'

She watched him. Her breathless schoolgirl tone—he was not the only one who could put on an act—had not fooled him, of course. He nodded, his chin falling on his chest. 'Oh, aye, terrible,' he said, and gave her a quick, sharp glance from under those hooded lids.

'Do they know what happened to him?' she asked. She was not to be put off.

'They?' he asked, all puzzlement and mild innocence.

'The family,' she said. 'The authorities.' She smiled. 'You.'

The waitress brought their orders. Phoebe had asked for a cup of coffee and a slice of toast. Hackett eyed her plate dubiously. 'You won't grow fat on that, my girl,' he said.

She nodded. 'That's the point.'

Hackett slopped milk into his tea and added three heaped spoonfuls of sugar. The rim of his hat had etched a line across his forehead and the skin above it was as pink and tender-looking as a baby's. His oily-black hair was plastered flat against his skull—she wondered if he ever washed it. What did she know about him? Not much. He was married, she knew that, and he lived somewhere in the suburbs. Beyond these scant facts, nothing.

He reminded her of a dog she had once owned, when she was a little girl. Ruff was his name. He was a mongrel, with black-and-white markings and half an ear missing. He loved to play, and would fetch sticks she had thrown for him, and would drop them at her feet for her to throw again, sitting back on his haunches and grinning up at her, his impossibly long pink tongue hanging out. One day, when she was staying in Rosslare on a holiday, she had seen Ruff out on the Burrow, the strip of grass and sand between the hotel and the beach. He had caught something in the grass, a young hare, she thought it was, a leveret, and she had stood watching in horror as he tore the poor creature to pieces. Ruff had not seen her and, unsupervised, had reverted to being a wild creature, all fang and claw. At last she had called out his name, and he had glanced at her guiltily and then run off, with what was left of the baby hare in his mouth. Later, when he came back, he was once again the Ruff she knew, grinning and happy, with that ragged half ear flapping. No doubt he expected her to have forgotten the scene on the Burrow, the torn fur and the gleaming dark blood and the white, rending teeth. But she had not forgotten; she never would forget.

She did not know whether it was she or Hackett who had brought up the subject of the Delahaye twins. To be talking about them was like an extension of her thoughts, and she realised how much indeed they must be on her mind. She told of seeing them at the party at Breen's house, and how surprised she had been that they were there, at a party, so recently after their father's death.

'When was that, exactly?' the inspector asked, stirring a spoon round and round in his tea.

'Saturday,' she said. 'Saturday night.'

'Ah.'

She waited, but he seemed to have no more to say on the subject. Then she remembered. Saturday night was the night Jack Clancy had died, out in a boat too, on the lonely sea, like his partner.

She saw Jimmy Minor come in. He had stopped in the entrance to the dining room and was lighting a cigarette. Quickly, on instinct, she turned her face aside so that he might not see her. This surprised her, but then, she often found herself surprised by things she did. Yet why had she wanted to avoid Jimmy? He was supposed to be her friend.

Feeling guilty, she half rose from her chair and waved, so that he could not miss seeing her. He waved in return, and began to make his way through the crowded room, weaving between the tables and trailing smoke from his cigarette. She could not imagine Jimmy without a cigarette.

He reminded her of a boat of some kind, a tramp steamer, perhaps, with his red hair like a flag and that plume of smoke always billowing behind him.

When he caught sight of Inspector Hackett he raised his eyebrows and hesitated, but Phoebe waved again and he came up. 'Hello, Pheebs,' he said. 'In the embrace of the long arm of the law, I see.'

Inspector Hackett nodded amiably. 'Mr Minor,' he said. 'We meet again. Will you join us?'

Jimmy gave Phoebe another twitch of his eyebrows, and borrowed a chair from the next table, and sat down. He wore a ragged tweed jacket, a white shirt, or a shirt that had been white some days ago, and a narrow green tie with a crooked knot. His bright-red hair was trimmed close to his skull and came to a point in the centre of his pale, freckled forehead. His hands had a chain-smoker's tremor. Inspector Hackett was watching him, was *inspecting* him, with a sardonic expression. There was something between the detective and the reporter, that was clear: they had the air of two wrestlers circling each other, on the look-out for an opening.

The waitress came and Jimmy ordered a cup of black coffee. 'No food?' the waitress said. She was a delicate girl with the face of a Madonna. Jimmy shook his head and she went off. Jimmy, it seemed, rarely noticed girls.

'Tell me, Mr Minor,' Hackett said, 'have you been hearing anything interesting since last we met?'

Jimmy Minor shot him a look. 'A thing or two,' he said. 'A thing or two.'

'Any one of which you might care to share?'

'Well now, Inspector, I doubt I'd have anything to tell you that you don't know already.'

'You could try me with something.'

Jimmy winked at Phoebe. He was rolling the tip of his cigarette along the edge of the ashtray, shedding ash neatly into the cup. It occurred to Phoebe that if you smoked as much as Jimmy did you would always have something to do. Perhaps that was why he did it.

Years before, when she was little, her father, her supposed father, Malachy Griffin, had smoked a pipe for a while. She had envied all the things he had to play with: the tobacco pouch of wonderfully soft leather with a buttoned flap, and the little knife with the tamper on the end of it, and paper packets of woolly white pipe cleaners, and those special imported matches—Swan Vestas, they were called—that could only be got from Fox's on College Green. She had liked the smell of the tobacco he smoked, one that he had made up specially, also at Fox's, a blend of Cavendish and Perique—how was it she could remember so many of these names from the past?—and more than once when he had set down his pipe and gone off to do something she had pretended to take a puff from it, not minding the sour wet feel of the stem in her mouth. How warmly the bowl sat in her palm, how smooth it felt. The silver ring where the stem was fitted into the bowl had a tiny hallmark on the underside; it was like the silver band Malachy wore on his little finger, that had once belonged to his father—

She frowned, staring at her empty cup. Something had snagged in her mind, like a ragged fingernail catching in silk. Something to do, again, with the Delahaye twins—what was it? She remembered one of them, James, she thought it was, leaning over the girl in the doorway upstairs at Breen's house, his head turned to look at her, at Phoebe, his arm lifted and his hand pressed against the door-jamb.

What? What was it? No: gone.

Jimmy was saying something about the firm of Delahaye & Clancy. A clerk there had told him—what had he told him? She had missed the beginning of it. '—a whole trail of transfers,' he was saying, 'thousands of shares shifted between one place and another, and nobody knowing what was going on.'

Inspector Hackett, listening, nodded slowly, in an absent-minded way, once more stirring the spoon in his tea, which by now must have gone quite cold. 'Tell me,' he said, 'are you doing a story about this?'

Jimmy gave a scoffing laugh. 'Are you joking?' he said. 'Do you think my rag would print anything that might suggest something peculiar was going on at the highly respected firm of Delahaye and Clancy?'

'I don't know,' the inspector said, playing the innocent again. 'Would it not?'

Jimmy turned to Phoebe. 'You know who we're talking about?'

'Oh, she does,' the inspector said. 'She knows the family, in fact. Don't you, Miss Griffin?'

An eager light had come into Jimmy's eye. 'Do you?' he asked.

'I've met the twins, Jonas and James, and Jonas's girlfriend, Tanya Somers. And Rose Griffin knows their aunt.'

Jimmy whistled, shaking his head. 'The small, tight

world of the gentry,' he said. He turned back to Hackett. 'Big fleas have little fleas, eh, Inspector? And so *ad infinitum.*'

Phoebe felt her forehead go red. Jimmy had a nasty side to him that he really should not let be seen. 'That's not a very nice image,' she said sharply, 'me as a flea, hopping on people's backs.'

Jimmy only grinned at her, the sharp tip of his dark-red tongue appearing briefly and then quickly withdrawing. Phoebe thought of a lizard on a rock.

'As a matter of fact,' Hackett said blandly, as if he had registered nothing of this sharp exchange, 'Miss Griffin was at a party with the Delahaye lads the night their father's partner died.'

Jimmy looked at her with a speculative light. Yes, she thought, Jimmy really could be ugly when he was after a story. She realised she was blushing again, not because of Jimmy's nastiness this time, but at the mention of the Delahayes. She felt a twinge of annoyance. What was the matter with her? 'It was at Andy Breen's place,' she said to Jimmy. 'I'm surprised you weren't there.'

'Down the country,' Jimmy said offhandedly. 'Following a lead.'

Phoebe smiled to herself. Jimmy had seen too many movies with hard-bitten newsmen in them—he even had a trace of a Hollywood accent, sometimes. She pictured him in a trenchcoat and a fedora with a *Press* sign stuck in the band. The image amused her, and she felt the blood subsiding from her face.

Inspector Hackett was watching her, amused in turn by her amusement. 'And was it a good party?' he asked.

Phoebe looked at him. The more innocent the detective's questions sounded the more pointed they seemed to be. She shrugged. 'Not particularly. But then, I don't much like parties.'

'Is that so?' the inspector said. Suddenly he stood up, and fished in his trouser pocket and brought out a florin and put it on the table. 'I'll say good day to you,' he said. 'Miss Griffin. Mr Minor.' And carrying his hat he turned and sauntered away.

Jimmy sat back on his chair and watched him go. 'He's a cute hoor, that one,' he said, almost admiringly.

Sunlight through the stained-glass window above them gave to the big room a churchly aspect, and the people at the tables round about might have been a congregation. Smoke as of incense drifted on the heavy air. Jimmy drank off the dregs of his coffee and now he, too, stood up. 'Go for a stroll?' he said.

Phoebe smiled up at him thinly. 'Haven't you things to do?' she asked sweetly. 'Leads to follow, that kind of thing?'

Jimmy's pale brow turned paler; other people flushed when they were angry, but Jimmy turned chalk-white. He was a tiny person, almost a miniature, with dainty little hands and feet, and he was easily offended.

Phoebe rose briskly and took his arm. 'Yes,' she said, 'come on, let's go for a stroll.' From her purse she took a shilling and added it to Hackett's florin. That's threepence for a tip, she thought, and for some reason wanted to laugh.

They went up to St Stephen's Green and walked in the cool inky shadows under the trees. They could hear the voices of children at play out on the grass. Somewhere above them an aeroplane was circling, making an insect drone.

It was almost time for Phoebe to be back at work. She looked up into the sea-green light under the dense canopy of leaves. At moments such as this, rare and precious, the possibility of happiness came to her with all the breath-taking force of something suddenly remembered from the past. Would she always be ahead of her own life, looking backwards?

'What are they like,' Jimmy said, 'the Delahayes?'

'Why do you ask?'

He had paused to light yet another cigarette. For a moment he had the look of a greedy baby, leaning over the match with the cigarette clamped in his pouted lips like a soother. He never seemed to have a girlfriend. She wondered, not for the first time, if he might be—that way inclined. It would explain the bitter brittleness of his manner, behind which she could always sense a tenta-tiveness, a yearning, almost. She felt a sudden rush of compassion for him, this fearsome, discontented, babyish little man. She linked her arm in his.

'There's a story in this business,' he said, staring hard ahead, 'if only I could tease it out.' He glanced at her. 'What does your father think?'

'You mean, does he think there's a story in it for you?'

Jimmy frowned at the tip of his cigarette. 'You know, Pheebs,' he said, 'humour really isn't your strong suit.'

'Well,' Phoebe said cheerfully, 'at least I try, not like some I could name.'

They went on, Jimmy scowling and Phoebe smiling at

her shoes. Were there any men, anywhere, she wondered, who were really grown-up?

'You know Jack Clancy was murdered,' Jimmy said. It seemed not quite a question.

A black-stockinged nanny went past, wheeling a black pram with enormous wheels and high, humped springs.

'Do I?' Did she? It shocked her a little to realise that she did not care about Jack Clancy and how he had died. Did any of them care? What was it to them, to her father, to Jimmy Minor, to Inspector Hackett, even—what was it to them, in the long run, whether the poor man had drowned himself or had been pushed under by someone else? They pretended, all of them, to be after the facts, truth, justice, but what they desired in the end was really just to satisfy their curiosity. At least Jimmy was honest about it. 'Do you know it for a fact that it was murder?' she asked.

'I have a feeling in my gut,' Jimmy said. 'It all seems wrong, somehow. They're covering up.'

'Who's covering up? My father? That detective?'

'I don't know.' He gave a sharp little laugh. 'When I was a kid I used to read detective stories, couldn't get enough of them. Arthur Conan Doyle, Dorothy L. Sayers, John Dickson Carr and Carter Dickson—those two were the same guy, in fact—Josephine Tey, Ngaio Marsh, whose name I never knew how to pronounce and didn't know whether it was a man or a woman. All those—I loved them. They made everything so squared off and neat, like a brown-paper parcel tied up with twine and sealing wax and an address label written out in copperplate.

There was a body, there were clues, there were suspects, then the detective came along and put it all together into a story, a true story, the story of the truth—the story of what happened.'

He laughed again, more softly this time. 'I used to get such a warm feeling when I reached the end and everything was explained, the killer identified and taken away by the police, and everybody else going back to their lives as if none of it mattered, as if nothing serious had taken place. I wanted to be Sherlock Holmes and Poirot and Lord Peter Wimsey, all rolled into one. I knew I could be. I knew I'd get all the clues and work out who had done it and at the end would get to point my finger at the culprit and say *You, Miss Murgatroyd—it was you who waited behind the curtains in the library with the stiletto in your hand* . . . And Miss Murgatroyd would be led away, cursing me, and everyone would gather round and congratulate me, and Major Bull-Trumpington's niece, the pretty one, would hang on my arm and tell me how wonderful I was.' He stopped, and laughed again, shortly. 'And then I grew up.'

It was odd, Phoebe thought, how they could walk along arm in arm like this, when a while ago, in the café, she had been so angry with him. But no, she corrected herself—they were not arm in arm. She had her arm linked in his, but he had his hand in his pocket, and was as stiff as he always was, stiff and vexed and simmering with resentment. Resentment at what, at whom? At her? She kicked a leaf. In this latitude there were fallen leaves all year round. The leaf—sycamore, was it?—looked like a hand, crook'd and clutching at the ground. She thought of those two men, out on the sea, in their separate boats, facing their separate deaths. Such a waste; all such a waste.

'But isn't that what you're doing still,' she said, 'trying to find out the story? You said so a minute ago. You're still trying to put it all together so everything will be explained.'

'Everything doesn't get explained,' he said. He sounded weary now, weary and almost old. 'You find a few pieces of the jigsaw puzzle, some of them fit together, some of them you just leave lying on the board, by themselves. That was the point of those detective stories I used to read—there was nothing that didn't mean something, nothing that wasn't a clue. It's not like that in real life.'

'What about red herrings? Didn't the people who wrote the stories put in things purposely to throw the reader off the scent?'

It came to her, so suddenly that it almost made her laugh. Two rings, on two little fingers. Or one, on two. 'Listen,' she said quickly, letting go of his arm, 'I have to go back to work. I'm late already.' She brushed her fingertips against his cheek. 'Cheer up,' she said. 'I'm sure you'll get your story.'

As she set off along the path under the trees, Jimmy turned to watch her go, a flickering figure moving through dappled shadow. He heard the children's voices again. That plane was still there too, buzzing at some edge of the sky. He lit another cigarette, and walked on.

*

Inspector Hackett ambled towards Pearse Street and his office. At the junction where D'Olier Street met up with College Green there was a concrete triangle with grass in it, too small and mean to be called a traffic island. The spot always annoyed him, he was not sure why. It was not the patch of grass itself, dry and brittle now from the summer heat, that he found provoking, but just the simple fact of its being there for no reason. Why grass? It could all have been of concrete, that would have done as well, and would have been better suited to the location. As it was the little triangle was no use to anyone, except for dogs to do their business on.

Yes, he supposed that was it: he felt sorry for the grass, and angry with those who had been so thoughtless in putting it there. Some damn-fool official in the Board of Works, he supposed, poring over papers on a wet Monday morning, licking his indelible pencil and putting a tick beside a line: *to wit, one triangle, with grass, junction of . . .* And look at the result: dry straw, baked clay, dog-shit, fag ends, a chewing-gum wrapper. Nobody cared enough about anything, and so everything was let go to hell. He was coming more and more to hate this city, its crowds, its dirt, its smells—the river was particularly foul today— its incurable dinginess. There were days when he longed for the fields and streams of childhood, as a man lost in the desert would thirst for water.

He tramped up the uncarpeted wooden stairs to his office, and at the return on the second landing he was assailed by another reminder of childhood. The hot sunlight coming in at the big window there made a fragrance in the dry dusty air that brought him back instantly, as if the years were nothing, to the little two-roomed school-house on the Grange Road outside Tulsk where Miss McLaverty had taught him his lessons when he was a little fellow. He had loved Miss McLaverty dearly. She used to look very stern, with her long tweed skirt and her rimless glasses and her hair tied back in a tight bun with a net over it. But she had had a soft spot for him, and often she would let him sit on her knee at break-time when all the senior infants had goody to eat—that was another smell he remembered, of the bread with the sugar on it soaked in hot milk—and helped him, too, when he could not add up his sums or got stuck on a hard word during reading lessons. She, too, had a smell, very different from his mother's smell, delicate and cool, like the scent of wet lilac. She would lean over him and point at the figures or the letters in his copybook with a wonderfully clean and polished fingernail. Such tears he had wept when the time came for him to be taken out of Miss McLaverty's care and sent to the Christian Brothers' school in Roscommon town.

He sighed, putting his knee to the office door, which was warped in its frame and always stuck. Old fool, he thought, maundering over the lost past. And look at that desk! There were files on it that had been sitting there for months, untouched, gathering dust. He took off his hat and, with a flick of his wrist, sent it sailing in the direction of the hat-stand, but it missed, of course, and he had to bend down, groaning, and retrieve it from where it had got wedged under the radiator and dust it off with his elbow and hang it on the hook, where it waggled from side to side as if mocking him. He sighed again, and slumped down in the swivel chair behind his desk and scrabbled crossly in his pockets for his cigarettes.

He knew what the matter was, of course. This moment came in every case when his thoughts, beginning at last to concentrate and yet not wanting to, would skitter off and fix on anything other than the business in hand. It was, he believed, what the mind doctors called transference. There was something all wrong about the deaths of Victor Delahaye and Jack Clancy. He could, if he wished, accept the thing for what it seemed: one had taken his own life for reasons only to be guessed at; the other, distracted by being caught out in a scheme to cheat his partner, had made a mistake at sea and fallen and hit his head and tumbled overboard and drowned. But he knew it was not that simple; it could not be. The course of events was unpredictable, sometimes chaotic, often farcical, but there was always a thread of logic to be grasped. This entire business felt wrong; a fume of heat came off it, like the steam off a dunghill on a winter morning.

He turned about in his chair. Through the grimed window behind his desk the sunlight on the chimney pots outside seemed unreal, a matt, honey-coloured glaze.

If the story had involved just Victor Delahaye and Jack Clancy it might well have been as simple as it seemed, the grotesque coincidence of Delahaye's suicide followed by Clancy's fatal accident. Yes, it was not the dead that troubled him, but the living. He thought of them, set them out in his mind one by one, like the pieces on a chessboard.

There were the Clancys, mother and son. What was he

to make of Sylvia Clancy, tall, straight, stately as a heron, with her hoity-toity accent and her shield of impenetrable politeness? Was she too good to be true? And the young fellow, Davy Clancy, the spoiled boy-child, his father's son, furtive, sly, too good-looking by far—what did he know that he was not telling?

Then there was Delahaye's widow, a shrewd and avid calculator whose trick it was to lie in wait behind the mask of an empty-headed minx—he had seen the way she looked at Quirke that day in the churchyard, with her husband not yet cold in the ground. That poor fool Delahaye would have been no match for her. Old Samuel, Delahaye's father, now, he would have had the measure of her, and indeed would probably have preferred her for a daughter to the daughter he did have. What was her name? Margaret? No—Marguerite. An odd party, that one. Keeper of secrets, storer of grudges, an ageing, embittered woman disguised as the long-suffering spinster daughter whose only care is for her family and ailing father, in her father's house. Oh, yes, he knew the type, hard done-by and sad but liable suddenly to turn and bite, and bite deep.

And there were the other Delahayes, the twins. A rich man's sons, too satisfied, too sure of themselves, dismissive, careless and uncaring. He thought again of the traffic island with its scorched grass.

He turned and pressed an electric bell on the corner of his desk, and presently heard heavy, dull footsteps on the stairs. There was a pause, then a brief knock on the door, and his assistant, young Jenkins, clattered in. Jenkins— pin-head on a long stalk of neck, cow's lick of hair across a narrow forehead, blue serge, boots, an ever-eager eye—was of a type that Headquarters seemed to think Hackett deserved; certainly at least they kept sending them to him, raw recruits fresh out of the Garda training college at Tullamore with less of an idea than the Man in the Moon of what a real policeman is and does.

'Yes, Boss?' Jenkins said.

'Couple of lads I want you to round up,' Hackett said. He wrote out the Northumberland Road address—it was always best to write things down for Jenkins—and handed over the slip of paper. Jenkins frowned at the address as if it were a line of hieroglyphics.

'Am I to arrest them?' he asked, his face brightening with eagerness.

Hackett put a hand to his forehead. 'No, no,' he said quietly, 'no. Just bring them in. Tell them we believe they might be able to help us with our enquiries.'

'Right.' The young man started to go.

'Oh, and, Jenkins—'

He put his head around the door again. 'Yes, Boss?'

'Go easy, right? This is the quality we're dealing with here.'

The young man nodded. 'Right-oh, Boss.' His head, at the end of that neck, resembled nothing so much as an oversized Indian club.

Maggie Delahaye was blissfully happy—blissful, yes, it was the only word. Mrs Hartigan had got everything ready for her before she arrived, had opened all the windows to air the house, had put fresh flowers on the hall table and made up her bed. She had even, Maggie saw with amusement, brought up a chamber pot from the back-stairs lavatory, for there was the china handle of it peeping out discreetly from under the frill of the old lace bedspread that had belonged to Maggie's grandmother.

She stood at the window in the sun, looking down at the lawn. No rabbits this afternoon; they would be out in the morning, at first light, hopping around on the grass in that funny, hesitating way they did, like faulty clockwork toys. How peaceful it was, how quiet! She gazed out over the sweltering fields to the far grey-blue mountains outlined against a hazy sky. This, this was where she belonged. Here she would rest, and let the great world pass over her, like a wave.

She deserved a little peace, a little contentment, at last. True, she felt guilty for having left her father. But he would manage. Her father always managed.

On the kitchen table she found that Mrs Hartigan had left a plate of salad and sliced ham for her, covered with a tea towel. There were wedges of soda bread, too, on another plate—Mrs Hartigan's soda bread was famous throughout the parish—and fresh milk in a glass jug with a little lace doily on it to keep the flies out. She realised that she was hungry, and sat down to eat. How pleasant it was to hear nothing but the clinking of knife and fork— she always liked to be silent at mealtimes, and wished others would follow her example. She poured some milk into a glass, but it was warm and tasted as if it might be on the turn, although perhaps it was just that she was not used to milk so fresh, straight from the dairy, heavy with cream. She pushed it aside, feeling slightly queasy, and went to the dresser and took another glass and brought it to the sink and held it under the tap, but paused, and did not fill it.

A faint savour remained of the brandy she had drunk in that hotel—was it the village of Horse and Jockey she had stopped in?—and now it occurred to her that a glass of wine might settle her stomach. Also, she should mark her arrival, her *homecoming*, as she thought of it, with a toast to herself—why not? There used to be bottles of wine at the back of the old stable—her father jokingly called it his cellar—and they were probably still there, if Jack Clancy had not guzzled them all. Why her father had ever let the Clancys come here to share the house each summer she did not know. Who were the Clancys, what were they to the Delahayes? In her heart she had always thought Jack Clancy common, for all his pretence of being a gentleman, with his swagger and his jokes and his genteel English wife.

She went out by the back door, leaving it on the latch, and made her way to the stables. There was a smell of horses still, after all these years! She thought of Tinsel, her pony that had died under her one day coming back from a ride—the poor thing's heart had given out, just like that. What age was she then? Eleven, twelve? Happy times. She had never got another horse, for she could not bear to think of replacing Tinsel.

The wine was there, in a long rack against the back wall, the bottles dusty, their labels tattered and faded. She took one out at random, and brushed off the grime. Château Montrose, 1934. Goodness! To think of all that had happened since then, in the world, and in the family—

her mother's death, then Victor's wife Lisa dying and Victor remarrying in such a rush, and then her father's stroke. The twins had not even been born in 1934. And now Victor, too, was gone. She lifted the bottle and held its cool flanks between her palms. She would not weep, no, she would not start weeping again. She had come here to be happy, to forget and be happy. But how could she forget? The daytime was all right, but the nights, ah, the nights. A shiver ran along her spine, or not a shiver but a sort of flinching sensation. Someone walking over her grave, as the old people used to say. Someone walking over her grave.

She was on the way back to the house, with the wine bottle cradled like a baby in the crook of one arm, when the idea came to her of clearing all of the Clancy things out of the house. They would not be coming here any more, surely, now that Jack was dead. Sylvia would not want to come, she was certain of that. By the time she got to the kitchen the plan had seized hold of her imagination, and in her excitement she almost overturned the bottle when she was trying to get the corkscrew into the cork. Yes, she would empty out all the bedrooms on the west side, the Clancys' side, so-called, and put the things, the clothes and bed linen and all the rest of it, into boxes and crates and ship them off to Dublin. Sylvia would find room for it all in that big house in Nelson Terrace, and what she did not need or want she could give to the St Vincent de Paul.

Carefully she poured out a glass of wine, holding the bottle in one hand and supporting the neck on the fingers of the other. At the first taste the wine seemed musty and dry as ink, but she took another sip, and another, and suddenly it blossomed in her mouth like a flower, so soft and velvety. It came to her that it was the past she was drinking, the past itself, that mysterious other place where sometimes it seemed to her she lived more immediately, more vividly, than she did in the present. She sat down and ate some of the salad and a thin sliver of ham. The wine had taken the edge off her hunger. She looked again at the mildewed label. 1934! A whole world away.

Who was it she had hit, that time, with the bottle? Some girl that Victor had brought home. She almost laughed to think of it. What age was she then? Old enough to know better. They had been at dinner here, the whole family and the Clancys, and the girl had said something to Victor, teasing him. She was a big, stupid girl with an enormous bosom, like two footballs under her blouse; Maggie could not take her eyes off it. When the girl laughed Maggie could see the food in her mouth, half chewed. Then, a moment later, the girl had been crying and holding her head and there was blood where her ear was cut. Someone had jumped up and taken the bottle out of Maggie's hand, she remembered—Jack Clancy, it was. Wine had spilled all down the front of her dress. It seemed she had hit the girl, had grabbed the bottle by the neck and swung it round and bashed her with it on the side of the head. She had no recollection of having done it, but she was not sorry that she had. It would teach Miss Big-bust not to laugh at her brother. Strange, how she could do things and forget having done them.

There was the question, of course, of what to do with the bedrooms once she had cleared the Clancys' things out of them. She knew a furniture dealer in Cork who would come and advise her. Anything she bought to replace the Clancys' things would have to be not only good but authentic; it would have to fit in. She had no intention of doing anything that would damage or compromise the delicate fabric of Ashgrove. She poured herself a little more of the wine. It would be a great house again, with all trace of the Clancys gone from it. And she would be the lady of the house.

She smiled, her lips curving on the rim of the glass. She would have visiting cards printed, with *Miss Marguerite Delahaye, of Ashgrove House, in the County of Cork* written in italic lettering. Why was there no word to go after a woman's name, like Esquire for a man? She could call herself *The Honourable Miss Marguerite Delahaye*— who was there that would challenge her right to a title? Anyway, she *was* honourable. Where honour was concerned, men did not have a monopoly. She had done the honourable thing.

The two young men arrived at Pearse Street with an air of polite but jaded interest, as if they were on a visit to a third-rate tourist site. Dressed alike in elegantly crumpled cream-coloured linen suits and open-necked white shirts, they glanced with indifference at the bare floorboards and the institution-green walls, the crowded notice board, the duty desk with its wooden flap and the duty sergeant presiding over his big black ledger, like St Peter, as Hackett often thought. The two avoided meeting each other's eye, seeming afraid they would burst into laughter.

At a sign from young Jenkins, the duty sergeant lifted the flap to let them through, and Jenkins led the way down a set of narrow wooden stairs to the basement. The atmosphere was close and dank and there was a smell of old cigarette smoke, sweat and stale urine, and the sunlit day outside suddenly seemed a distant memory. Inspector Hackett had directed that the twins be put in separate interrogation rooms, where they were to be locked in and left alone with only their thoughts for company. He had not told Jenkins what it was they were to be questioned about, exactly, but Jenkins trusted his boss, and went out to the yard at the back, where the Black Marias were parked, to smoke a cigarette, and dream of the promotion he had been dropping hints about to the boss for weeks.

In fact, Hackett himself was not sure what line of questioning to adopt with this pair, in their silk shirts and their expensive suits. He had gone out to the top of the stairs in time to glimpse Jenkins conducting them down to the basement. They were certainly not your usual suspects, who in Hackett's mind came in two varieties: the cringers and the swaggerers. The Delahayes would certainly not cringe but they did not swagger, either. They looked as if they had strolled in from a picnic, and were confident that they would be returning to it presently. Hackett wondered what it would be like to be so self-assured. And how was he to shake that self-assurance?

He went back to his office and sat with his feet on the desk and brooded, looking vacantly out of the grimy window and picking his teeth with a matchstick. He had never played chess, did not even know the rules, but he imagined that for grandmasters of the game the moves

they made on the board would be only a clumsy mani-
festation of altogether more subtle configurations in their
minds. It was something like that with him, too. The
people involved in this case, the Delahayes on one side
and the Clancys the other, shifted and glided in his
thoughts like so many black and white pieces executing
immensely intricate manoeuvres in a luminous mist.

Somewhere there was a pattern, if only he could find
it. Jack Clancy's death had been the direct result somehow
of Victor Delahaye's suicide, he was convinced of that.
He was convinced, too, that Clancy had been murdered.
Was it the twins who had murdered him? If so, why?—
had Clancy driven their father to kill himself? Had they
wreaked vengeance on him? There was also the question
of the alibi. Quirke's daughter had told him she had seen
the twins at a party on the night that Clancy died. How
then could they have taken Clancy out in his own boat in
Dublin Bay and drowned him? But somehow they had.
He knew it was they who had done it: a lifetime of
experience told him so.

He rose wearily, hitching up his trousers. The room
was unbearably stuffy, for the single window behind the
desk had been stuck fast for years. He sighed heavily;
nothing for it but to go down and deal with those two
buckos.

Jenkins, of course, did not know which one he had put
in which room. 'They're the spitting image of each other,
Boss,' he said defensively, with the hint of a whine that
never failed to set Hackett's teeth on edge.

'Yes,' Hackett said drily, pushing past the junior policeman, 'that's because they're twins.' Jenkins blushed. He was very susceptible to blushing, was young Jenkins.

They went down the wooden stairs, Hackett in the lead with his assistant clattering at his heels. The first door they came to had a brass number 7 nailed to it; no one knew how or why the room had come to be numbered so, since it was the first one in the corridor. Hackett thrust open the door and swept inside—it was always best to start off with noise and bustle. Young Delahaye, whichever one it might be, was sitting at his ease before the little square wooden table with the rickety legs. He was leaning back on the straight-backed chair with an ankle crossed on a knee. He looked over his shoulder and smiled at the two men as they entered, and for a second it seemed he might leap to his feet and welcome them warmly, as if he were in his own house and the unfurnished and windowless cell were a grandly appointed reception room.

'Good day to you,' Hackett said brusquely, coming forward and offering his hand. 'Which one are you?'

The young man cast a sceptical look at the hand being offered, then took it, and uncrossed his legs and rose slowly to his feet, seeming to unwind his long, slender frame as if it had been twined around the chair, all the while shaking Hackett's hand with a show of solemn courtesy. He was some inches taller than the detective. 'I'm Jonas Delahaye,' he said. 'Where's my brother?'

Hackett did not reply. He had given Jenkins a bulging cardboard file to carry, and Jenkins came forward now and dropped it on the table with a thump, and retreated and stood with his back against the door, his arms folded.

There was nothing in the cardboard file but a bundle of out-of-date documents that had nothing to do with the deaths of Victor Delahaye or Jack Clancy, but a file always looked impressive, and some people were unnerved by its bulky presence on the table. Not Jonas Delahaye, however, who hardly gave the thing a glance. Hackett walked around the table and sat down on the second of the two chairs, which, along with the table, were the sole items of furniture in the room. The walls were a sombre shade of bile-green and bore a shiny grey film of damp, as if they were sweating. Directly above the table a sixty-watt bare bulb dangled from a double-stranded flex. Below the bulb a trio of flies were circling slowly in a sort of dreamy waltz.

'Now then,' Hackett said briskly. He opened the file and riffled through the grubby documents and shut it again. 'Can you tell me where you were on Saturday night last?'

The young man opposite him, leaning forward with his elbows on the table and his fingers clasped, beamed, as if he had made a bet with himself as to what the first question would be, and was pleased to find he had won. 'Let me see,' he said, frowning and putting on an effortful show of remembering. 'That would be the night that Mr Clancy died, yes?' Hackett nodded. 'Then I was at a party. Stoney Road, North Strand. Home of a chap I know, a doctor. Breen is his name, Andy Breen. Why?'

Hackett leaned back and said nothing. In the silence Jenkins's stomach rumbled, like a roll of distant thunder, and he coughed and shuffled his feet. Jonas Delahaye was still smiling, holding the detective's scrutinising gaze.

From outside came the sound of an approaching siren, a plaintive keening muffled by the thickness of the walls.

'A bit strange, wouldn't you think,' Hackett said, 'going out to a party so soon after the death of your father?'

The young man paused a moment, and frowned again, to show that he was giving the question judicious consideration. 'Ye-es,' he said, 'I suppose it might seem like that. I didn't think of it at the time, but I see what you mean.'

Hackett waited, but the young man merely sat, bright and attentive, with his hands still clasped before him, waiting for the next question. Long ago, at school, Hackett had known a fellow that this one reminded him of. What was his name? Geoffrey something. Tall, pale, with a shock of yellow hair and uncannily pale grey eyes. Geoffrey, never Geoff. His people had a big house out on the Longford Road. Well-off Catholics with a Protestant name—what was it? Geoffrey was a delicate youth, and used to get two days off school at the start of every month to be brought up to Dublin for some special medical treatment that he never spoke about. There was something about him, an air of separateness, of detachment, and a sense, too, that he knew some amusing thing that no one else did.—Pettit! That was his name. Geoffrey Pettit. What had become of him? At the end of the summer holidays one year he had not turned up, and no one had heard any more of him. But Hackett remembered him well, and surely others did, for he was the kind of person people would remember. He leaned back on his chair. If he was not mistaken, Geoffrey Pettit, too, had worn a signet ring, on his little finger, just like this blandly smiling, sinister young man sitting opposite him now.

This was for Hackett the pivotal moment in every investigation, the moment when he sat down face to face with a person he believed had killed another human being. There was always the problem of plausibility. Killers never looked like killers, for what would a killer look like? Of the handful of proven murderers he had come across, the only thing seemingly out of the ordinary he had detected in them was a certain quality of self-absorption, of being somehow removed, turned inwards and lost in awe before the breathtaking enormity of the deed they had committed. It was there in all of them, even the most careful and crafty, this sense of hushed wonderment. Did he detect it in Jonas Delahaye? He was not sure there was anything detectable in him, behind that hard, smooth, bright exterior. The detective felt a faint shimmer along his backbone. It occurred to him he might be in the presence of a refined and intricate madness.

'So you went to a party,' he said, 'you and your brother. Was your girlfriend there—what's her name?'

'Tanya. Tanya Somers.' The young man nodded. 'Yes, she was there.'

'Good party, was it?'

Jonas smiled; his teeth were wonderfully white. 'Middling. The usual, you know. Brown-paper bags of stout, charred bangers and sliced pan to eat, the girls tipsy and half the fellows looking for a fight. We didn't stay long.'

'Oh? What time did you leave, would you say?'

'Midnight? One o'clock? Something like that.' His smile turned mischievous. 'If it was the pictures, this would be the moment for me to ask, *Just what are you driving at, Inspector?* Wouldn't it?'

Jenkins, at the door, made a sound in his throat suspiciously like laughter quickly stifled; Hackett decided to ignore it. He brought out a packet of Player's and pushed it across the table, sliding it open with his thumb as he did so. Jonas shook his head. 'You don't smoke?' Hackett said.

'I do,' the young man answered pleasantly. He was still smiling.

Hackett stood up and began to pace back and forth at his side of the table, smoking his cigarette, a fist pressed to the small of his back. He was wondering idly for how many hours of the day in this place did he have his behind planted on a chair. What would life be like elsewhere? He thought again of Geoffrey Pettit, and of the Pettits' home, a square white mansion set on the side of a green hill above the Shannon looking south towards Lough Ree. The Pettits and the Delahayes of this world had it soft.

'So let's refresh our memories here,' he said. 'Your father dies, and a bit over a week afterwards you and your brother and your girlfriend are at a party in your friend's house in North Strand, the very night, as it happens, that your father's business partner is drowned out in Dublin Bay. Would that be right? Is that the right sequence?'

The young man again made a show of considering the question, then nodded. 'Yes,' he said calmly, 'that's right.'

'Did your mother know you were intending to go to a party that night?'

For the first time something like a shadow passed over the young man's features. 'My mother?'

'Your stepmother.'

'Oh. Mona.' He gave a faint snicker. 'Who can say

what Mona knows or doesn't know? Things go in'—he pointed to one ear—'and then'—pointing to the other—'out again, usually without pausing on the way.'

'You're not fond of your stepmother?'

The young man pursed his lips and shrugged. 'Are people ever fond of their stepmothers? Isn't that what they're for, to be feared and disliked?'

Hackett paused in his pacing. 'Feared?' he said softly.

'Oh, you know what I mean,' Jonas snapped, with an impatient gesture. 'Snow White, the poisoned apple, all that. Mona is not the wicked witch, she's just Mona. We pay her no attention.'

Hackett sat down again. 'But she'll inherit the business, and so on?'

The young man placed his hands flat on the table before him and leaned back with a large, slow smile. 'These are very personal questions, Inspector,' he said calmly. 'Impertinent, I'd almost say.'

Hackett was wondering where this young man had gone to school; somewhere in England, surely, chosen probably by his Unionist grandfather. He, too, smiled broadly. 'Sure, aren't we in a police barracks,' he said jovially, 'where all kinds of liberties are allowed?'

The young man, though maintaining his smile, was watching him with a certain narrowness now. 'I've seen my father's will,' he said. 'It's quite clear. Mona will be well provided for. The business stays with my brother and me.'

'Ah,' Hackett said, nodding. 'I see. That sounds right and fair.'

'Yes. My father had his weak points, but he was always fair.' He widened his smile again. 'It's a family tradition.'

'And the Clancys?' Hackett asked quietly.

The corner of Jonas's mouth twitched in faint amusement. 'There'll be some money for Mrs Clancy. He—Jack—was a partner more in name than anything else. Did you know he'd been buying up shares in the business on the quiet? We've made sure to get them back, of course. Chap of ours, Duncan Maverley, handled that—what'll we call it?—that readjustment.'

Hackett stubbed out his cigarette in the tin ashtray on the table, and offered the packet to the young man again—'You're sure you won't join me?'—then lit a fresh one for himself. He sat back, rubbing a hand vigorously along the side of his jaw, making a sandpapery sound. 'There'd be plenty of people would have seen you at the party,' he said, 'that would remember you being there, yes?'

'Of course. In fact, your friend Quirke, the pathologist, his daughter was there, with her boyfriend, who's Dr Quirke's assistant, as it happens.'

'Ah. Miss Griffin and young Dr Sinclair. I see. And you spoke to them?'

'I met them as they were arriving.'

'And did you see them later on?'

'I'm sure I did. I must have—it's a tiny house, built for gnomes.'

'And your brother, he spoke to them?'

The young man bit his lip to stop himself from smirking. 'You'll have to ask him that yourself,' he said, 'won't you, Inspector?'

Over at the door, young Jenkins's stomach was rumbling again.

Each morning when she woke, Sylvia Clancy had to adjust herself anew to a transformed world. Shock, bewilderment, grief, these were the things she would naturally have expected after the death of her husband, and when they came she found she could cope with them more easily than she had ever thought she would. But this sense of everything having suddenly become unfamiliar left her feeling helpless and lost. Things looked skewed, tilted off-balance; even the daylight had a sort of acid tinge that had not been there before.

She did not know how or why Jack had died. He was a master yachtsman, easily the best sailor in his class, here and in Cork, though Victor, of course, had imagined he was the more experienced and skilled of the two. What was Jack doing out on the bay that night, so late, and alone? Why had he not told her he was going out? Jack had his secrets, but he was considerate, and always let her know when he was going to be away, or out sailing, even though she knew that 'sailing' was often a cover for other activities. She had been careful not to give him any sense that she was keeping tabs on him; he had his freedom, and knew it; that had been how it was between them from the start. Had she been wrong? Should she have insisted on rules, limits, demarcations? She did not know; she was not sure of anything, any more.

That night, the night of his death, she had sat in bed reading until quite late; it had been close to midnight when she had put her book aside and turned out the bedside lamp and opened the curtains. She always slept with the curtains open, for she loved to see the lights of the harbour shining in the darkness like jewels, white, emerald, ruby-red, laid out on a velvet cloth, and to hear the mast ropes clinking in the wind. Had she been awake while Jack was drowning? She had felt no intimation of it, no start of dread, no inexplicable shiver, no sigh or whisper on the air. She could not bear to think of him dying out there alone and helpless, with no hand to hold, no one to cling to, no one to bid him farewell on his final voyage, into the dark and silent depths. He had loved her in his way, as best he could, she knew that. What did she care, now, about his girlfriends, his flings, his 'bits on the side', as the wags in the club would say, smirking behind their hands?

It tormented her to think that she would never know the true circumstances of his death. Had it been an accident? It seemed impossible—though he was impulsive in many ways, when it came to boats he had never been one to take risks, to cut a corner. Perhaps he had been tipsy, and had stumbled somehow and fallen overboard and hit his head as he was falling. He was a strong swimmer, and would surely have survived if he had been conscious when he fell into the sea. It had been a summer night; the cold would not have hampered him and made his limbs cramp up. But what other possibility was there? She did not like to think about other possibilities, yet she was aware of them, thronging just beyond the borders of her mind, clamouring to be let in.

Despite everything she knew to be the case she could

not believe that Jack was gone. She knew he was dead, of course, yet she could not accept it. She kept thinking that he was being held up somewhere and prevented from coming back, and that if she did certain things, performed certain as yet unknown rites, and waited long enough, he would return. At moments in the day she would stop whatever she was doing and stand very still, listening, as if to hear his step in the hall, as if the door would open and he would come walking in, whistling, with the paper under his arm. At night especially she listened for him, for the small, distant sound of his key in the front-door lock, for the creak of the loose board on the first step of the stairs, for the bathroom tap to run, for the lavatory to flush, for the light switch to click off. It was all nonsense, she knew, this breathless waiting for the impossible to happen, yet she could not stop herself. It comforted her, imagining that he would come back.

She was glad of Davy's presence in the house, infrequent though it was. He stayed out as much as he could, but when he was there he was some kind of company. They did not talk about his father, or the circumstances of his death. Death, she had discovered, causes an awkwardness, a kind of embarrassment, among the bereaved. The thing was too big to be dwelt on. It was as if some huge thing had been thrust into their midst, as if a great stone ball had come crashing through the roof and sat now immovable between them, so that they had to negotiate their way round it and at the same time pretend it was not there.

Davy shied from her, and would hardly meet her eye. He had been like that before his father died, throughout the week after Victor Delahaye's death. She was reminded of when he was a boy and she had walked into his room one day without knocking—she could not believe she had been so careless—and found him lying on the bed with his trousers open and doing that thing to himself that men did. For weeks afterwards he would not look at her and blushed furiously if she came near him. Now it was like that again, only worse. Did he hold her responsible in some way for Jack's death? She had read somewhere that when children lose a parent they sometimes blame the one who has survived, and Davy in so many respects was still a kind of child. But what about Victor's death?—how could he think she had any responsibility for that? It was Davy himself whom Victor had taken with him on that last terrible trip out to sea.

Did Davy know more than he was saying, about both deaths? Not that he said much. These days he was like an animal in hiding, folded into himself, showing nothing but sharp spines.

She tried her best to bring him out of himself, to make him talk to her, to tell her whatever things it was he knew and was keeping secret. She had him drive her to visit Jack's grave every day. They ate lunch together, in the kitchen, in silence. She cooked dinner for him, too, but as often as not he stayed out until long after dinnertime, and she would make up a plate and leave it for him on top of the stove. It was an eerie sensation to come down in the morning and find the food eaten, the plate washed and put away. Her son was more of a ghost for her than Jack was. Unlike Davy, however, Jack was not a presence but a vast absence. She might wait in constant expectation for him to come back, but he would not come back, not ever again.

On Davy's twenty-fifth birthday she took him for a treat to lunch at the Hibernian Hotel. She could see he did not want to go, but she insisted he should put on a suit and tie, while she wore a dark-blue suit that she did not think looked too much like widow's weeds—the occasion was supposed to be a celebration, after all—and together they took a taxi in from Dun Laoghaire. They were late, but they still managed to get a good table, by the window, looking out on Dawson Street. She had fish while Davy ate a steak. She persuaded him to drink a glass of wine, although usually he drank only beer, and not much of that.

She watched him across the table as he ate, and a lump came to her throat to see how much like his father he was becoming, with the same deftness, the same attentiveness to the smallest things. He was a good boy, she thought— and was glad he was not able to hear her refer to him as a boy—even if he could be difficult at times. She knew so little about him, what he did, where he went, who his friends were. Did he mean to be secretive, to keep things from her, or was that just the way all grown-up sons were with their mothers? Lonely though her own life would be from now on, she must not attempt to pry into his affairs or make him think she expected him to share things with her. After all, he was not a boy, he was a man, and his own man, at that. Just like his father.

Glancing about, she caught sight of someone at a table on the other side of the dining room whose face she knew although for a moment she could not put a name to it. He was large, and wore a double-breasted black suit. There was a woman with him, who was also somewhat familiar, though Sylvia was sure she had never met her. When the couple had finished their lunch they passed close by on their way out, and the man stopped, and a second before he spoke she remembered who he was.

'Mrs Clancy,' he said, 'how are you? My name is Quirke. I'm a—I'm an associate of Detective Inspector Hackett's. I was at your husband's funeral. I'm very sorry for your loss.'

She thanked him, and introduced Davy, who gave him an openly hostile stare and turned away and glared out of the window into the sunlit street. Quirke's lady-friend had gone on a few paces, and stopped now and looked back with a polite vague smile. She was that actress, Sylvia suddenly recognised her—what was her name? Galligan? Galloway? She was good-looking, in an actressy sort of way.

Quirke was still standing there, beside the table, as if he expected her to say something more, to do something more. She was keenly aware of his dark bulk, which seemed to lean over her a little, and suddenly something gave way inside her, and she thought she might be about to weep. What was the matter with her? She did not know this man, had only glimpsed him once before, in the churchyard, and now here she was, ready to clasp his hand and bury her face in his sleeve and shed hot tears. She tried to speak. 'I—I wonder if—' She snatched up her handbag from the floor where she had left it leaning against the leg of her chair and opened it and rummaged in it for a handkerchief. She must not cry, not here, in front of these people, this man, this stranger!

He had started to move on. She twisted about on the chair, looking up at him urgently. What did she want of him? He paused, seeing the silent appeal in her look. He frowned and smiled, seeming to understand. But to understand what?—she did not herself understand what was happening, why she wanted him not to go but to stay here beside her. 'I'll come back,' he said. 'Just a minute.' He stepped away, and touched a finger to the actress's elbow and they went on, moving between the tables, and a moment later Sylvia saw them outside on the pavement, Quirke speaking and the actress looking at him with a quizzical smile and then shrugging and turning to walk away. Quirke, feeling himself watched, glanced back and caught Sylvia's eye through the window, and they continued gazing at each other for a long moment.

They sat in armchairs in the lobby with a little table between them on which a waitress had set out a pot of coffee and cups and saucers and plates of biscuits and thin square sandwiches. When Quirke had come back into the dining room, Davy had put down his napkin and gone off angrily, so it seemed to his mother. What was there for him to be angry about? Surely she could speak to whomever she liked.

She no longer felt like crying, and anyway the tears that had threatened would have been tears not of sorrow but relief. Yes, relief. There was something about this man sitting before her that she felt she could trust. It was not that he seemed particularly warm or sympathetic. Quite the opposite, in fact. She felt he was the kind of man she could speak to precisely because of a certain coolness, a certain stoniness, she detected in him. She could tell him her secrets and he would keep them, not out of discretion or consideration for her, but out of—what? Disinterest? Indifference? Well, that would be fine. Indifference would be fine.

'Tell me, Mr—what did you say your name was?'

'Quirke.'

'Tell me, Mr Quirke, why did you come to the funeral? You didn't know my husband, did you?'

'No, I didn't.'

She waited, but obviously nothing more was coming. She poured herself a cup of coffee. 'Do I remember seeing you at Victor Delahaye's funeral, too?'

'Yes, I was there.' He had ordered a glass of whiskey with his coffee. She could smell the sharp, hot fragrance of the liquor. 'A tragic business,' he said. 'First Mr Delahaye, and then your husband. You must be very shocked.' His hands were quite delicate, she noticed, pale and soft-looking. His feet were small too, for such a large man.

'Yes, we're all shocked, of course,' she said, with a flicker of impatience; she had no time for small-talk now.

He drank his whiskey. She could see him watching her without seeming to. She did not know what she wanted to say to him, what secrets they were she thought she might trust him with. Yet something was pressing inside her, like some small trapped thing pressing to be released.

'Your husband was an experienced sailor, I think,' he said.

'Yes, he was. Very experienced, very expert. He had won trophies—' She broke off; how fatuous that sounded. 'He had,' she said levelly, 'a great love and knowledge of the sea. I think—' She stopped again. What on earth was it that was coming? 'I think my husband was killed.' She swallowed, making a gulping noise. 'I don't think he died by accident. I think he was murdered.'

She was not sure what she would have expected him to do, but whatever it might have been he did not do it. He merely sat there, with his elbows on his knees and the whiskey glass in one hand, gazing at her without the slightest expression that she could see. She thought what a peculiar man he was. 'Why do you think he was murdered?' he asked.

She almost laughed. 'Do you mean why was he murdered, or why do I think he was?'

He shrugged. 'Both, I suppose.'

'I have no idea!' It was almost a cry, the way she said it. She could hardly believe that she was uttering these things aloud, to this bizarre man, in a hotel lobby, on what was otherwise a perfectly ordinary afternoon in summer. *Did* she believe Jack had been murdered? As far as she was aware the possibility had not entered her head before she had blurted it out just now. Was this what had been inside her all along, struggling to get out, without her knowing what it was? She felt as if she were standing on the very brink of a dizzyingly deep abyss. What things were down there, at the bottom, writhing and struggling? 'I'm sure I'm being fanciful,' she said. 'You must forgive me.' Her coffee cup rattled in the saucer when she set it down.

'It's probably hysteria—certainly that must be what you're thinking. I'm sorry.'

Quirke nodded; she had the impression his mind was elsewhere.

'Mrs Clancy,' he said, 'I wonder if you're aware that I'm a doctor, and that a post-mortem was carried out on your husband?'

She gazed at him, appalled, yet fascinated, too. She must not look at his hands again, she must not; to think what they had done to Jack. 'I knew a post-mortem had been carried out, of course,' she said, controlling herself.

He nodded again. 'And there'll be an inquest. I'll be giving evidence to it.'

'Oh, yes?' She felt a thrill of dread. 'And what will it be, your evidence?'

'That your husband died by drowning.'

She waited; talking to this man was like making a long-distance telephone call on a faulty line. 'Nothing else?' she said.

He took the last sip of his whiskey and set the empty glass down on the table. For such a large man his gestures were curiously precise, even finical. 'There was a bruise on the back of his head, on the right side, just under his ear.' He touched a finger to his own head to show her the place.

'Yes,' she said, 'someone told me that.' She was breathless, as if with excitement. What did this man know? What things had he found out?

'The blow he suffered,' he said, 'was the kind of blow it would have been difficult for him to inflict on himself,

I mean by falling and hitting his head on some part of the boat, say.'

'Maybe the sail, I mean the mast, the what-do-you-call-it, the boom, maybe it swung somehow and hit him on the head.'

He made a show of considering this, and gave her a squinting look. 'Do you sail, Mrs Clancy?'

'No, no. Jack took me out sometimes, but I had no feel for it. To be honest, I've always been a little afraid of the sea.' Her mouth twitched in a faint smile. 'I must have had a premonition.'

Quirke smiled too, lifting his shoulders. 'I don't know much about boats either,' he said. 'But I know that the night your husband died there was hardly a breath of wind. I think there would have to have been a gale for the boom to swing hard enough to make such a traumatic bruise.'

There was a silence. She gazed at him as if hypnotised, her eyes very wide. 'Are you saying, Dr Quirke, that you agree with me?—that you think my husband was killed?'

'I don't know. I'm not a detective.'

This amused her. 'A person could be forgiven for thinking otherwise.'

He inclined his head in a small bow of ironical acknowledgement. 'I have a great curiosity,' he said. 'If I were a cat I'd have been dead long ago.'

The sunlight was gone from the street outside, and when she looked past Quirke to the glass front door she saw that a summer shower had started up. She imagined being out there, in the damp coolness, with the soft rain falling on her face, her hands. She closed her eyes for a moment. She tried to picture Jack as he was the last time she had seen him and could not; poor dear foolish Jack, who was dead.

'Tell me why you think your husband was murdered,' Quirke said.

She opened her eyes. 'You asked me that already.'

'I'm asking again.'

The rain was heavier now, and she fancied she could hear faintly the hiss and drum of it as it beat down on the city. When she was a little girl she used to love to watch the rain. She saw herself at the window of her granny Morgan's house in Colwyn Bay, leaning on the sill with her chin on her hands, smelling the dusty cretonne of the curtains. What a dreamer she was in those days. Every July the family came up from London to stay for a week with her grandmother. Wales was nice. Such friendly people, with that lovely lilting accent. Granny Morgan's house was at the top of a steep street, and when the rain was heavy the drops would hit the road and hop up again, and she would imagine a vast corps of tiny silver ballerinas pirouetting down the hill.

'I think he was having an affair,' she said.

Once again she had startled herself. The man opposite her cleared his throat and shifted heavily in the armchair. She looked down and saw his preposterously dainty feet, crossed at the ankles, and again she felt she might laugh in delight. It was a very long time since she had spoken like this to anyone, let alone a man she hardly knew. Or had she spoken like this before, ever?

'I'm sorry,' Quirke said. 'This is no business of mine.'

'Would it be, if you were a real policeman?' The tone

of her own voice, teasing and playful, shocked her. Was she *flirting* with this man? One is never too old or too distressed, she reflected, to make a bloody fool of oneself. 'Forgive me,' she said, with a faint laugh. 'I don't know why I'm being so—so giddy.' Quirke, his eyes downcast, was lighting a cigarette, and she could not make out his expression. A sudden crimson flash of pain struck along her spine and made her catch her breath. She forced herself to sit up straight and stay very still. Her pain was like a child she was carrying inside her: she had to nurse it, to lull it, so that it would not wake fully and set to clawing at her with its tiny sharp nails.

Quirke picked up the empty whiskey glass and turned it in his fingers. She gazed at him. 'I'm sorry,' she said, 'I shouldn't have blurted that out about Jack and—and my suspicions. If he was having an affair it wasn't the first time.' She looked at him almost pleadingly. 'I suppose that detective has found out about my husband's reputation. Unlike many men, Jack genuinely liked women. He found them'—she gave a rueful laugh—'interesting. To talk to, I mean. That makes a man very attractive, if women feel he's interested, and will listen to them. And he could be funny, too. That's another attraction. So, all in all, there was nothing for me to do but grin and bear it. He always came back to me in the end—'

She broke off and laughed again, more sadly this time. 'That's what every woman in my position says, isn't it? Pathetic.' She took a sip from her cup; the coffee had gone cold, and had a bitter taste. 'It's a thing you discover, how hackneyed it all is. You hear yourself saying things that you'd laugh at if you read them in a magazine story. It makes it all the harder.'

Quirke lifted his hand and signalled to the waitress, and when she came he ordered another whiskey, then turned and asked if she would like something else. 'More coffee, perhaps?'

'No, thank you.' The girl began to move away. 'Or wait, yes, I will have something.' She thought. 'I'll have a sherry, please. Dry.' When the girl had gone she smiled at Quirke a little shamefacedly. 'I shouldn't, really—I had a glass of wine at lunch. Alcohol goes straight to my head, I'm afraid. I'll get tipsy and you'll think me a complete idiot.'

Quirke leaned back in the chair, watching her, the smoke from his cigarette curling up past his jaw, so that he had to half close one eye, which gave him the look of a screen villain, and she had to bite her lip to keep from smiling.

'If your husband was—involved with someone,' Quirke asked, 'do you think it's connected with the way he died?'

'I don't *know*,' she cried. 'Maybe some irate husband went after him—maybe there was a fight.'

'Is there anyone you can think of that might have been that angry with him?'

She shook her head. 'Jack never talked about the people he saw, for obvious reasons. And I never asked, for the same reasons.' She made a fist and struck it into the palm of her other hand. 'My God, why does it all have to be so banal, so—so grubby?'

Their drinks came. She tasted the sherry; it was sweet,

of course. She did not have the heart to send it back. In the street the rain had stopped, and suddenly the sun came out, as if a curtain had been drawn swiftly aside, and the tarmac shone and car roofs threw off big floppy flashes of light, like huge bubbles forming and bursting. Quirke's face had retreated into shadow, but she could see his eyes, fixed on her speculatively.

'Did your husband talk about work, at all?' he asked.

'Work?' she said. 'You mean the office and all that? Hardly.' She laughed. 'I don't think the affairs of Delahaye and Clancy were ever uppermost in his mind.'

'So he didn't ever say anything to you about there being—disputes, that kind of thing?'

'What do you mean, disputes? With the office staff? Strikes?'

'No, no.' He hesitated. 'It seems there was something going on inside the company. Shares were being manipulated, moved around.'

'Shares,' she said blankly. 'Company shares, you mean?' She stopped, then began slowly again. 'Are you saying— are you saying my husband was—I don't know—embezzling money from the business?'

'No, not embezzling.'

'What, then?' Under the sleeves of her suit she had a crawling sensation along the inner sides of her arms.

'Do you know a person called Maverley?' he asked.

'Duncan Maverley?' Her mouth took on a sour twist. 'Of course. What about him?'

'At the funeral—the funeral of Mr Delahaye—this man Maverley spoke to Inspector Hackett and me. He wasn't very clear, I mean he wasn't very forthcoming, but what he seemed to be intimating was that your husband was planning, was in fact carrying out, a wholesale takeover of the business, to put himself in Victor Delahaye's position as head of the firm.'

She reached out gropingly and grasped the sherry glass and took a gulp of the oily sweet drink. She had hoped the alcohol would steady her nerves but it was only making her feel more shaky still. This was madness, all madness. That dreadful little man Maverley, what kind of mischief was he attempting? 'I don't know what to say, it seems an insane accusation. Jack didn't have that kind of ambition. He was content to be the Junior Boss—you know that's how everyone referred to him, and how he often referred to himself—and sail his boat and see his friends at the yacht club and—' She stopped. *And play at love with his girls*, was what she might have said, too.

And yet. Who knows what goes on inside the minds of other people? She had been married to Jack Clancy for more than a quarter of a century, but could she put her hand on her heart and swear that she had known him? What had he been like when he was with one of his 'bits on the side', for instance? If she had seen him cavorting with some trollop—and, thank God, she never had— would she have recognised him? He had despised and resented Victor Delahaye, she knew that, but surely he had long ago reconciled himself to a secondary position in the house of Delahaye & Clancy. But then, what if he had not? What if these accusations the poisonous Duncan Maverley had made were true? She felt pity, suddenly. Poor Jack, scheming and plotting like a little boy, planning, for years probably, to do down the Delahayes and make himself the Senior Boss, without ever a word of it to anyone, not even to her. Had his life been nothing but shame and humiliation, as he chafed under the disdainful patronage of a man for whom he felt nothing but contempt? Was that why he had chased after girls, in order to have a little success in some aspect of his life? Had they given him the admiration and sympathy that everyone else had withheld from him? Everyone else, including her. Yes, surely that was it. How had she not seen it? If she had seen it before now, she might have been able to help him, might have done something to assuage his shame and frustration, his rage against himself and the world.

But no, she told herself, no—she *had* known, of course she had. She had known and had chosen not to know. It was exactly what she had always secretly despised in the Irish, that capacity for self-delusion, that two-faced way of dealing with the world. She was just as dishonest, as hypocritical, as anyone else, and may as well admit it.

She stood up suddenly, clutching her handbag and looking about her wildly. Her lower lip was trembling. She needed the lavatory urgently. Quirke, too, rose to his feet, and she reared back almost in fright—she had almost forgotten that he was there. He was saying something but she was not listening. She shook her head and stepped back. 'I must go,' she said, in a choked voice. 'I'm sorry, I have to—' And she turned and fled.

12

THE FIRST THING that struck Phoebe was the fact that they had known where to find her. But how had they known? She had been in the habit of stopping at the coffee shop two or three evenings a week on her way home from work. It was a place where she could be on her own—she had not even told David Sinclair about it. The owner of the shop, Mr Baldini, an Italian man of middle age with wonderfully soft eyes and a melancholy smile, knew her well by now, and would greet her when she came in, and would show her to her favourite table by the window, as if she were a regular at some grand restaurant and he the maître d'. She would sit at the plastic-topped table in a wedge of evening sunlight and read the paper, and drink a cup of milky coffee and eat one of the dismayingly sweet little cakes that the owner's wife baked in the kitchen at the back, from where there wafted warm smells of vanilla and chocolate and roasted coffee beans. She prized these intervals of solitude, and was shocked this evening when the Delahaye twins came in and, without being invited, sat down at her table.

She could not get used to the uncanny likeness between them. Looking at them, sitting there smilingly side by side, she had the unnerving sensation, as she always had in their presence, that a fiendish and immensely complicated trick was being played on her, by means of mirrors and revolving chairs and walls that only looked like walls. They were dressed alike, in brown corduroy slacks and short-sleeved grey woollen shirts, and each had a cricket sweater slung over his back with the sleeves loosely knotted in front. She would not have been surprised if they had begun to speak to her in unison, like a pair of characters out of the Alice books.

'Hello,' she said, keeping her voice steady and her tone light. 'I thought I was the only one who knew about this place.'

'Ah,' the one on the left said, 'but you see, we're good at nosing out secrets.' He pressed his smiling face forwards across the table, making snuffling noises, like a pig after a truffle. Then he lifted a hand and showed her the signet ring on his little finger. 'I'm Jonas, by the way, to save you having to ask.'

The other one, James, laughed. She looked at him. She had noted before how strange his eyes were, hazed-over somehow and yet alight with eagerness, as if he lived in constant expectation of some grand and hilariously violent event that he was convinced would begin to unfold at any moment. She wondered uneasily if his mind was quite right. 'Where's your boyfriend this evening?' he asked, with a sort of playful truculence.

'Yes, where is he?' Jonas said. 'We thought one of you was never seen without the other, like James and me.'

James at this gave a snort of laughter, as if it were richly funny.

'He's at work, I think,' Phoebe said. These days he always seemed to be at work, whatever the time of day. That was why she was here now, trying to fill in some of the long night that was ahead of her.

'*Mit* ze cadavers, *ja*?' Jonas said, putting on a comic accent and making a broad slicing gesture, as with a scalpel. 'Professor Frankenstein in his laboratory.'

She did not know what to reply. She pushed her coffee cup aside and gathered up her handbag and her *Irish Times* and made to rise, but Jonas reached across and pressed an index finger to the back of her hand, quite hard, and she sat down again, slowly. 'Don't go,' he said pleasantly. 'We've only just arrived.'

Mr Baldini came to take the twins' order. He was from a hill town in Tuscany, he had told her. She often wondered how he had ended up here, but did not like to ask. The twins said they would have coffee and a cake, like her. Mr Baldini nodded, unsmiling. His soft brown eyes slid sideways and met hers, as if to send a warning signal. Had the twins been here before? Did he know something about them that she did not? 'For you, *signorina*?' he said. 'Something else, perhaps?' She shook her head and he turned to go, as if reluctantly, and gave her again that odd, cautioning look.

'Enjoy the party?' Jonas said.

'The one at Breen's house?'

'Where we saw you, yes.'

'It was all right. A bit too noisy for me.'

Jonas played a brief tattoo on the edge of the table with his fingers. 'Good old Breen, eh?' he said. 'Good old Breen.' He was looking at her with what seemed a dreamily calculating air. She wondered what he was thinking, but decided it was probably better not to know.

'Breen is a brick,' James said, more loudly than was necessary. 'A real brick.'

'James is fond of rhyming slang,' Jonas said, and grinned, and winked.

Mr Baldini brought the coffee and the cakes. 'Two and eightpence,' he said.

Jonas glanced up at him, and the Italian stared back stonily. For a moment there was the sense of something teetering in the air, dipping first this way and then that. Then Jonas shrugged. 'Pay the man, Jamesey,' he said quietly, smiling at Phoebe, and began to hum under his breath the tune of 'O Sole Mio'. James handed over a ten-shilling note, and Mr Baldini went off again.

Jonas, pushing aside the coffee and the plate with the cake on it, extended his arms straight out in front of him across the table, almost touching Phoebe's face, and turned his hands backwards and linked his fingers and pressed them against each other, making his knuckles crack. Then he gave himself a shivery shake and blew loudly through slack lips like a horse. 'Seeing your chap later, are you?' he asked. Phoebe nodded. 'Jolly good,' Jonas said, giving her again that narrow, speculative stare. 'In the meantime,' he said, 'why not come along with us?'

She stared back. 'Come along where?'

'We're off to the ancestral pile. Have a glass of something, bite to eat, listen to the wind-up gramophone. Typical relaxed evening *chez* Delahaye. What do you say? The stepmater is home, I'm sure she'd love to meet you.

She's a bit of a party girl herself, though you mightn't think it to see her in her widow's weeds.'

She looked at the two of them, Jonas lazily smiling and James with that avid light in his eye. It would be foolish to go with them, she knew, and yet, to her surprise, a small sharp voice in her head immediately spoke up, urging her to accept.

'All right,' she heard herself say, with an insouciance she did not really feel, 'but just for an hour.'

'That's settled, then!' Jonas exclaimed, and smacked both his palms flat on the table and stood up. He was wearing a Trinity tie for a belt. '*Avanti!*'

He went first, with Phoebe after him and James following. Phoebe could feel the twin's eye on her, and a tiny tremor made her shoulder-blades twitch. At the door she glanced back and saw Mr Baldini standing by the big silver espresso machine, looking after her with a grave and melancholy gaze.

The evening was smoky and hot. They walked along by the railings of St Stephen's Green, the two young men sauntering with their hands in their pockets and Phoebe in the middle, to where Jonas's car, a low-slung, two-door red Jaguar, was parked under the trees. 'See that shop?' Jonas said, pointing across the road to Smyth's. 'I once bought a jar of honey there with bumble bees drowned in it. And a box of chocolate-covered ants.'

'Why did you do that?' Phoebe asked.

Jonas was unlocking the car door on the driver's side. 'Wedding presents,' he said, 'for our new mummy, when Daddy bethought himself to marry again.'

Phoebe was not sure if she was meant to laugh. 'And did she like them, your stepmother?'

'Scoffed the lot. You should have heard her crack those ants between her little pearly teeth.'

James climbed into the narrow back seat while Jonas took the wheel, with Phoebe beside him. They roared off in a cloud of tyre smoke. Phoebe was aware of her heart madly beating. What was she thinking of—how had she dared?

In Northumberland Road the tree-lined pavements were dappled with late gold, and midges in clouds bobbed and rose like bubbles in a champagne glass. Jonas slewed the car in at the gate almost without slowing, making the gravel fly, and drew to a bucking stop beside the front steps.

As they walked up to the door, James lagged behind again, to have another look at her, Phoebe felt sure. The phrase came to her, *drawing up the rear*, and she smiled somewhat bleakly to herself. Would she tell David about this exploit she had allowed herself to be taken on? She thought not. She could imagine the look he would give her, out of those liquid brown eyes of his, with his head sceptically tilted and his chin tucked in.

The hall was cool. A seething patch of sunlight from the open doorway settled briefly on the parquet. 'Welcome to the House of Usher,' Jonas said gaily, and James did another of his snorting laughs. Phoebe, despite herself, rather liked the idea of being the menaced innocent in a Gothic tale. A red-haired maid, young, with thick ankles, appeared at the other end of the hall and, seeing Phoebe with the twins, gave a sardonic half-grin and withdrew to wherever she had come from. 'The staff, as you see,' Jonas said, 'lack a certain polish.' He made a deep bow, with an arm extended. 'This way to the funhouse, ladies and gents!'

The drawing room glowed with greenish light from the garden. Phoebe noted the vast white sofa, the Mainie Jellett on the wall behind it, the sideboard with bottles, cut-glass decanters, a soda siphon. There was a big bunch of red and yellow roses in a china bowl on the table.

'A drink,' Jonas said, making for the sideboard. 'My dear, what will you take?'

Phoebe hesitated. Should she drink? Probably not. 'Gin,' she said firmly. 'I'd like a gin and tonic.'

'That's my girl! James, be a dear and fetch some ice from the kitchen. And see if there's a lime, will you?' He grinned at Phoebe. 'Lemons are so *common*, don't you think?'

Phoebe walked to the window and stood looking into the garden. She was conscious of herself as a figure there, as if she were posing for her portrait. *Young Woman by a Window*. She had grown up in a house like this, not so large or luxuriously appointed, but with the same hushed air, the same high ceilings, the same fragrance of roses and floor polish. Here, though, there was something else. What was it? The faintest hint of something sickly, as in a room where lately an invalid had lived, and that even the musky scent of the roses could not mask.

James came back with the ice, lobbing a lime high into the air and catching it expertly in his palm with a small sharp smack.

'By the way,' Jonas said, plopping ice cubes into Phoebe's glass and handing it to her, 'we were questioned by the rozzers—did you know?'

She thought at first he was making a joke, but decided he was not. 'No,' she said carefully. 'What did they want to ask you about?'

'Yes,' he said, ignoring her question, 'the good old third degree. Shall we sit?'

They took to the sofa, with Phoebe perched in the middle, Jonas lounging to her right and James sitting a little too close to her on the left. Now that she was seeing them properly and had a chance to study them, she realised that far from being identical they were in fact entirely distinct. The circumstance of looking so alike might be no more than an ingenious piece of mimicry, the putting on of a kind of camouflage behind which they could hide in order to spy on the world. Jonas was the brighter of the two. He was clever and quick, and funny in a brittle sort of way, while James, with that laugh and that air of avid anticipation, was distinctly alarming. Yet if she were to be afraid of them, she knew, it was Jonas who would frighten her the most.

'It was just like in the movies,' Jonas was saying now. 'They took us downstairs, to the basement, and put us in separate cells, so we wouldn't be able to co-ordinate our stories, and asked us all kinds of things.' He nodded at her glass. 'Need some more ice?'

She shook her head. 'What kinds of things did they ask?'

'Oh, silly stuff. It was that pal of your dad's, In-spector—what's it?'

'Hackett?' she said, surprised.

At the name, for some reason, James, on her other side, laughed. She thought of the monkey house at the zoo.

'Yes, that's it,' Jonas said. 'Hackett. Good name for a detective. Bit of a rough diamond. Country-cute, I'll grant you, but not what you'd call bright. *Can you tell me now, young lad,*' he said, doing an uncannily close imitation of Hackett's tone and accent, '*where you were on the night of the full moon, and can you produce a witness to prove it?*' He smiled at her, and his voice sank to a purr. 'That would be you, my dear. Our witness.'

'Me?'

'Yes. At Breen's place, the night of the party. I told you already.'

'Why did he want to know where you were?—why that night?'

The brothers glanced at each other. Jonas laughed. 'Because, my dear, that was the night Jack Clancy fell out of his boat and drowned.'

She looked away. Yes; yes, of course.

Abruptly Jonas sprang up from the sofa. 'Music,' he said. 'Let's have some music.'

At the other end of the room there was a radiogram, a great mahogany brute standing on four little braced peg-like legs. Jonas opened wide the cabinet doors and leaned down to read the spines of the record sleeves. 'Eeny meeny minee mo,' he murmured, and extracted an album, '—catch old Frankie by the toe!' He turned, showing the record cover with its stylised portrait of the singer—the hat, the cigarette—standing in a melancholy mood on a street corner at night. 'Frankie-boy,' he said, 'every bobby-soxer's damp dream. Here we go.' He took out the disc and put it on the turntable. There was a faint hiss and then came the first plinking notes of the tune picked out against a soupy orchestral background. *In the wee small hours of the morning.* Jonas struck a pose, head back, nostrils flared, his arms encircling an invisible partner, then danced a sweeping step or two, singing along with the record. Phoebe could feel James beside her laughing without sound. Still singing, Jonas now supplied his own lyrics.

> *Where were you, lad, on that fatal evening?*
> *Can you prooooove your whe-ere-abouts?*
> *If I ask Miss Griffin if she saw you*
> *Will she back up your cast-iron al-i-biiieee?*

He danced now in the direction of the sofa, and as he swept past he grabbed Phoebe's wrist and drew her stumbling to her feet and took her in his arms and waltzed her off around the room at such a pace she felt her feet were hardly touching the floor. His brother, meanwhile, threw himself back on the sofa, clapping his hands and raucously whinnying.

Phoebe, her heart hammering in its cage, saw the room spinning around her. She was dizzy already. She could smell the man who was holding her, his odour a mingling of sweat, cologne and something else, sharp and sour, a faint acid reek. On the second turn around the room she glimpsed over Jonas's shoulder the door opening, and someone, a woman, coming in. For a second the woman's face, slender and pale, was a point of stillness in the general whirl, then Jonas swept on, whirling Phoebe with him. They passed by James, asprawl with his arms stretched out at either side along the back of the sofa, watching her with huge enjoyment. Then in rapid succession came the window, the sideboard, the sofa and James seated, the Jellett abstract, and then the woman again, in the doorway.

Jonas, too, had seen her, and veered towards her now, and letting go of Phoebe's left hand he caught the woman by the wrist and pulled her into the dance with them. On they dashed, three of them now, whirling and whirling. The woman seemed quite calm, and merely amused, as if she were used to this kind of thing. Smiling, she kept her eye fixed on Phoebe. Abruptly Jonas let go of both of them and flung himself down with a great laughing gasp to sprawl beside his brother. Phoebe stumbled, and would have fallen if the woman had not put an arm round her waist and held her firmly. They waltzed on together, the woman keeping no better time to the music than Jonas had. She was wearing a green silk blouse and a black skirt with petticoats underneath it.

'I'm Mona,' she said. 'Mona Delahaye. And you're Phoebe, yes? I know your father, a little.'

The song ended and they stopped, and Phoebe stood panting, and smiled back at the smiling woman, and thought how little like a widow she seemed. Both twins now regarded them with keen interest. Mona ignored them, and walked to the rosewood sideboard and poured herself a gin, and added a splash of tonic. 'You two,' she said accusingly, addressing the twins over her shoulder, 'you've used all the ice again!'

Jonas looked sideways at his brother, and James put his hands on his knees and heaved himself to his feet with a histrionic sigh. 'Oh, all right,' he said, 'I'll go.'

When he had left Mona went and sat where he had been sitting, pressing down her skirt and ballooning petticoats with a careless gesture, and smiled at Phoebe again and patted the place beside her. 'Come,' she said, 'come and sit.' She turned her head and spoke to Jonas. 'Move over, you.'

Phoebe did as she was invited and came and sat down beside Mona. She felt exhilarated, but dizzy, too, more than dizzy—how much gin had she drunk?—and her tongue felt thick and she had difficulty focusing her eyes. Mona had grabbed Jonas's glass and with her fingers fished out what remained of the ice cubes in it and dropped them into her own drink.

'Hey!' Jonas said, laughing as he attempted to take back his glass. 'You are a cow.'

'And you're a pig,' Mona answered complacently.

They were like a pair of spoilt siblings fighting over a toy, Phoebe thought. This observation seemed to her at once profound and funny. She blinked—could she be tipsy already?

Mona turned to her. Mona had the most extraordinary violet eyes that tapered at their outer edges and turned up into points. Her scarlet lipstick made her face seem all the more pale. She was very lovely, though her lips were a little thin. Phoebe wondered what it would feel like to be a man kissing that mouth. At that moment, as if Mona had read Phoebe's thoughts, she parted her lips and Phoebe glimpsed between them the fire-pink sharp little tip of her tongue. That was what she would do if she were being kissed: she would open her mouth like that, just barely parting the lips, and the tip of her tongue would dart out.

'You look quite wild,' Mona said. 'What have these two brutes been doing to you?'

'Oh, just—dancing,' Phoebe said. Her head felt terribly heavy all of a sudden, and she leaned back against the sofa, letting her shoulders droop.

'She's a very good dancer.' Jonas spoke in a soberly judicious tone.

'Yes, she is,' Mona said.

She was still smiling and gazing searchingly at Phoebe.

'She has wings on her heels.' Jonas, too, was looking at Phoebe, leaning forward to see past Mona.

'Have you?' Mona said, still gazing at Phoebe. 'Have you wings at your heels?'

With both those pairs of eyes fixed on her, Phoebe felt as if she were an exotic creature perched in a cage and being stared at. What a narrow face Jonas had, a narrow face and a wide mouth, which gave him a faintly cruel look.

James came back with the ice and Jonas insisted that they all have another gin and tonic. Phoebe protested feebly that she did not want anything more to drink, but was ignored. She was still sitting with her head leaning against the back of the sofa and her hands resting limply in her lap. Mona, beside her, touched her hair, peering more deeply still into her eyes. 'Jonas,' she said, 'you haven't given her anything, have you?'

Jonas, at the sideboard again pouring drinks, threw her

a look of exaggerated outrage. 'As if I would!' He brought them their glasses. Phoebe had difficulty holding hers, though it felt wonderfully cool. She lifted it before her face in both hands and watched with fascination a drop of condensed moisture making its way in a gleaming zigzag down the misted side. It seemed to her magical, a thing never witnessed before now. She wanted to tell the others about it but did not think she would be able to find the words.

'Come along,' Jonas said briskly, extending a hand to each of them and taking Phoebe's glass. 'Let's us face the music, my dears, and dance!'

The two women stood up. Phoebe's knees wobbled, and she reached out before her for support, and Mona took her hand and put an arm round her waist again, and slowly they began to dance. James and Jonas, too, were dancing together now. Round and round the floor they went, the two couples, in opposite directions. Each time they passed each other Jonas would make an elaborate eighteenth-century bow, and James would laugh his laugh.

Phoebe, her head spinning, felt herself gliding off into a sort of trance. Her feet seemed very far away, and glancing down she saw with surprise that they were moving as if by themselves, to their own rhythm, pacing out the measure of the dance. Once her arm brushed against the side of Mona's breast, but Mona seemed not to notice. The scarab-green silk of Mona's blouse felt as if there were electricity running through it.

On the record, Sinatra's voice had a sad little sob in it.

Someone kicked the door from outside and it flew open and an old man in a wheelchair, with a mane of grey hair, propelled himself over the threshold. He glared at the dancing couples and his face darkened with fury, and there was a sort of rumbling sound in his chest as the words gathered there, and he made a fist of his right hand and smashed it down on the arm of the wheelchair. *'This is a house of mourning!'* he bellowed, in the thundering tones of a hellfire preacher.

The dancers halted. Phoebe swayed on her feet. Mona's arm was still encircling her waist. She seemed to be laughing, very softly.

'Hello, Grandad,' Jonas said brightly. 'Care for a snorter?'

The man in the wheelchair looked at him, his head trembling and his eyes blazing. 'You young whelp!' he said, half choking on the words.

Everything in front of Phoebe had begun to swim. Her head felt so heavy, so heavy. She took a step forward and leaned her forehead on Mona's shoulder. 'I think,' she said, and her voice was so thick now she could hardly make it out herself, 'I think I'm going to . . .'

Isabel was late, as so often. Quirke did not mind. He was in McGonagle's, in the back snug, known for some reason as the Casbah, where only the most regular of regulars were allowed to enter. He had the *Evening Mail* before him on the table, quarter-folded, which was the way he liked to read a newspaper, and a large whiskey at his elbow. The Casbah, cramped and cosy, struck a faintly nautical note. It might have been the cabin of a trawler. There was a lot of dark brown wood that somehow was always faintly and stickily damp to the touch, and the head-high wooden partition that separated it from the rest of the pub had a row of small, low-set frosted-glass windows that were reminiscent of portholes. The air was shadowed and smoky, but a chink of evening sunlight from somewhere had set a glowing jewel in the bottom of the whiskey glass.

He was reading a story about a case of criminal conversation, in which a man had sued his business partner for having an affair with his wife. 'Criminal conversation'. Who thought up these terms? Maybe it was a direct translation from the Latin. The case was a nasty one, with evidence not only from the three people involved but also from hotel clerks and chambermaids and even from one of the conductors on the Howth tram. What must the woman feel? Perhaps he might ask Isabel.

He knew very well he should not be drinking whiskey so early in the evening. In fact, he should not be drinking spirits at all. He had promised Phoebe he would keep to wine only, and that even wine he would take in moderation, yet here he was, breaking that promise. It was a familiar sensation, this slight buzz of shame at the back of his mind.

There were certain conditions, most of them bad, that had become ingrained in him over the years, so that now he could not imagine his life without them. First and foremost of these conditions was dislike of himself, a mild but irresolvable distaste for what he did and what he was. In his better moments, his rare self-absolving moments, he regarded this permanent state of self-deprecation as, paradoxically, a sign of some virtue. For if he disapproved of himself, must there not be a finer side to him, however firmly it was turned away, that was doing the disapproving? Surely the truly wicked ones thought nothing of their wickedness, were not even aware of it, or if they were they gloried in it, like Iago, or Milton's Satan. Of course, by maintaining a low regard for himself he was giving himself the excuse to carry on as he wished to, with no thought for anyone else. Being bad, as he was, and as he acknowledged he was, lifted a weight of responsibility from his soul. *I do as I do and can do no other*. That was a motto a man could live with.

Isabel arrived at last, a vision of summer itself in a loose white linen dress and red slingback shoes with high heels. She plonked her leather handbag down on the folded *Mail* and began to scrabble about in it.

'Here,' Quirke said, offering her his packet of Senior Service, 'have one of mine.'

'Thanks,' she said, taking a cigarette and leaning down to the flame of his lighter. 'And for Christ's sake get me a drink, will you? Vodka and ice. I feel as if my head is about to burst.'

She sat down opposite him on the stool, exhaling an angry cone of cigarette smoke. She was having trouble with the director of the play she was rehearsing. Quirke braced himself for a tirade, and went to the hatch and signalled to the barman. When he sat down again Isabel suddenly laughed. 'I'm sorry,' she said. 'I won't start, I promise.' She took another long drag on her cigarette. 'But that *bastard*, honestly—that little *bastard*!'

'What's he done now?'

She opened her mouth to speak but shut it again, and

again laughed. 'No,' she said. 'I said I wouldn't, and I won't. It's a lovely evening outside, I'm going to have one drink with you, then we're going to take a taxi home and you're going to—well, you know what you're going to do, being the gentleman that you are and ever ready to lay a cool hand on a hot girl's brow. I mean a girl's hot brow. Or do I?'

She leaned across the table and kissed him. The barman, his big moon face looming at the hatch, cleared his throat pointedly.

They drank their drinks, the little fingers of their free left hands entwined on the table between them. Quirke admired the way the glowing spot of gold reappeared in the bottom of his glass each time he set it down. Where was the light coming from? He could not see. He did not care. Maybe Isabel was the one who would save him. From what? From himself, first.

To keep herself from complaining about the director, Isabel complained about the play instead. 'Talk about kitchen sink, my God!' she said, throwing her eyes to the ceiling and putting on what he thought of as her comical El Greco face. 'Sink, tin bathtub, chamber pot and all. Can life really be like that?'

'Mostly it is,' Quirke said.

'And the jokes! All of them seem to be about cows— the thing is set in the bog somewhere. Is that how country people are?'

He laughed. 'How do you mean?'

'Oh, you know—stupid and comical.'

'We're all like that.'

'I'm not!' she said indignantly. 'You're not. Well'—her

lips trembled on a laugh—'I'm not, anyway. You know I play the mother? The one playing the daughter, so-called, is forty if she's a day. And my husband is about eighteen, and has spots.'

Quirke squeezed her finger more tightly. He liked to listen to these rants of hers: they amused and soothed him. He watched her long, pale, animated face. She was a handsome woman still. She worried that she might be too old to have children; she had told him so one night over an after-show dinner in the Trocadero, tears shining in her eyes and her mouth slack. She had been a bit drunk. He wondered if she remembered. They both worried about babies, but his worry was of a different order from hers.

He tried to imagine himself bouncing a damp and odoriferous infant on his knee. 'Have another drink,' he said.

Isabel stood up. 'No—I said just the one. Come on. I have to be at the Gate at half nine—I'm in the second act.'

They had left the snug and were making their way towards the door among the dim forms of early drinkers when the barman spoke Quirke's name. 'Call for you, Doctor,' he said, holding up the receiver of the phone that stood beside the cash register. Quirke frowned. Who would be calling him here? Who would have known where to find him?

He took the receiver and crouched over it at the bar. Isabel waited, tapping her foot. She was uneasy, feeling eyes on her from the shadows, trying to see through her clothes. She had wanted Quirke to meet her in the Gresham but of course he had insisted on McGonagle's.

She could not think what he saw in the place. She imagined him sitting here like these other ones, lurking in the dimness with his drink and his cigarette, eyeing someone else's woman. She banished the image. She tapped her foot. At last Quirke handed the receiver back to the barman and turned and took her by the elbow and steered her to the door.

'Sinclair,' he said. 'Something about Phoebe.'

He put her into a taxi in the rank at the corner of the Green. Her face at the side window was white with anger. She had wanted to know what the 'something about Phoebe' was, but he had said he did not know, that it was confused, that the line had been bad and he had not been able to hear Sinclair properly and what he had heard he had found hard to understand.

All this, most of it, was a lie. He had not mentioned Mona Delahaye. She had tried to call him at the hospital and the woman on the switchboard had put her through to the pathology lab and Sinclair had answered, and then Sinclair had phoned him. Phoebe was at the Delahayes' house and was unwell, it seemed, and needed to be collected—Sinclair was working late, he was in the middle of a post-mortem, he could not get away. Quirke would have to go. Sinclair gave the address. Yes, Quirke said, he knew the house. Then there had been a silence on the line. How much did Sinclair know about Quirke and Mona Delahaye? Sinclair had an uncanny knack of getting wind of things that no one else knew about. Quirke watched until the taxi with Isabel in it was out of sight, then climbed into the next car in the row.

It was Mona who opened the front door to him. 'Oh, hello,' she said, as if his sudden appearance were an unexpected and mildly pleasant surprise.

'I've come for Phoebe,' he said.

'Yes, of course you have.'

She stood there with her hand on the door, looking him slowly up and down, in that way she did, as if measuring him for something, some garment into which he might have to be fitted. She smiled. 'You're the very picture of paternal concern,' she said.

He took a step forward. 'Where is she?' he asked. 'What happened?'

'Oh, she drank too much gin, that's all.' Still she had not taken her hand from the door, and seemed indeed to be considering whether or not to let him come in. Then she shrugged, and stood aside. 'For God's sake keep your voice down,' she said. 'My father-in-law is on the warpath.'

She led him to the drawing room. Phoebe was lying full-length on the white sofa, her head propped on a cushion, and with another cushion under her feet. Her hands were crossed on her breast. In her black dress and white blouse with the white lace collar she looked alarmingly like the corpse of a maiden saint laid out on a bier. He went and lifted her wrist and took her pulse. It was slow. He smelt her breath.

As he leaned over her she suddenly opened wide her

eyes and stared at him in a sort of happy disbelief. 'Daddy,' she said softly, and her eyelids fluttered shut again. She had never called him 'Daddy' before. She must think he was someone else.

He turned to Mona, who was standing in the doorway with her shoulder against the door-jamb and her ankles crossed, smoking a cigarette and watching him with a sardonic smile. 'What happened?' he asked again.

'I told you—she drank too much and passed out.'

'What was she drinking?'

'Gin. I already said. Don't you listen?'

He glanced about the room, saw the empty glasses, the open lid of the radiogram. 'Who was here?'

'I was.'

'Who else?'

'The twins. Honestly, Quirke, you look terribly fierce—you'll have me frightened of you in a minute.'

Quirke made a dismissive gesture, chopping at the air with the side of his hand. 'Why was she here?' he asked. 'What was she doing?'

Mona gave an exasperated sigh, expelling hasty cigarette smoke. '*I* don't know. I arrived and here she was, knocking back gin by the bucketful and dancing. It was quite a party.'

'A party? Were there others?'

'What others?'

'*Any* others.'

'The twins—I told you!'

'And that's all? You and those two and Phoebe? What was going on?'

'Will you stop asking that? You sound like a broken record.'

'My daughter was in your house, comatose, and I was called to come and collect her. You made the call. I think you owe me an explanation.'

She sighed again and was silent for a moment, giving him a level look and shaking her head slightly from side to side. 'I know what it is about you,' she said. 'You think you're living in the movies.' She put on a heavy voice, mimicking him. '*My daughter, in your house, what's going on?* Can't young people have a little party now and then?'

'If they harmed her in any way . . .'

He did not go on, and Mona laughed. 'You mean,' she said, 'if they "dishonoured her"? If they "ruined" her? Now you're playing the Victorian father—you should have moustaches to twirl.'

He shook his head, as if he were being bothered by some flying thing. 'Will you call a taxi for me, please?'

'I could drive you somewhere—anywhere, in fact.'

'A taxi would be best. If you show me the phone I'll call one myself.'

She was smiling at him with a wry expression. 'You're really being a bore,' she said. 'Nothing happened. There were some drinks, we danced, she got dizzy.'

'A taxi,' he said.

She looked to heaven and turned and sauntered out, and a moment later he heard her in the hall, dialling. Then she came back, and stood where she had stood before, with her cigarette.

'Like a drink?' she asked.

On the sofa, Phoebe moaned faintly.

He took her to his flat in Mount Street. It required some effort to get her up the stairs: her legs were not working very well, and kept crossing and threatening to buckle. Once they were in the flat he walked her to the bedroom and put her to lie on his bed and drew the curtains. She spoke some unintelligible words and gave a burbling little laugh and then lapsed back into unconsciousness.

He went out to the kitchen and poured himself a whiskey—he had a bottle hidden at the back of one of the cupboards—and took it into the living room and lit a cigarette and sat down on the window-seat. Late sunlight was bisecting the street into halves of light and shadow. Lines of cars were parked at the kerbs along both pavements, ranked side by side in two neat shoals, their roofs gleaming like the backs of dolphins. He sat there for a long time, thinking, then went to the telephone and called Sinclair.

He had finished his drink and wanted another but instead he filled the coffee percolator and put it on the gas and watched it as it came slowly to the boil. He wondered what it was that Phoebe had taken, apart from the gin. There had been no smell of a drug on her breath. Some barbiturate, he supposed—Luminal? They would have put it in her drink and she would not have noticed. That would be their idea of fun. A nerve began to jump at the corner of his right eye.

He was at the window in the living room again,

drinking a second cup of coffee, when Sinclair arrived. Quirke told of how he had found Phoebe unconscious at the Delahayes'. He said the twins had been there, and then was sorry that he had. Of Mona Delahaye he made no mention.

'What was going on?' Sinclair said, frowning in bafflement.

'I don't know,' Quirke answered.

'What was she doing there, at that house, drinking?'

For a moment Quirke was silent. He was angry with Sinclair, he was not sure why. 'She needs looking after, you know,' he said.

Sinclair considered the toecaps of his shoes. 'She's not a child,' he said mildly.

'In some ways she is.'

'She wouldn't thank you for saying it.'

'I don't ask for thanks.'

There was another silence. Quirke fetched a silver cigarette box from the mantelpiece and they lit up and stood smoking, looking at anything save each other.

'I don't know what I could have done,' Sinclair said. 'The woman on the phone, Mrs Delahaye, seemed to think the whole thing was funny. I didn't realise.'

You could marry her, Quirke thought, surprising himself. Did he want to see Phoebe married? Did he not have doubts about Sinclair? To whose benefit would it be if his daughter were to marry—hers, or his own? Was it not just his own peace of mind he was thinking of? Was it simply that he wanted to be rid of his daughter, rid of the responsibility of being the one nearest to her?

He turned away. In his mind he saw again Mona

Delahaye standing at the door of the drawing room in Northumberland Road, in her green blouse and her little-girl's puffed-out skirt. That recent afternoon, in her shadowed bedroom, he had held her in his arms and she had pressed her mouth against his shoulder to stifle her moans and he had thought himself in love. Now he cursed himself for a fool.

The bedroom door opened and Phoebe appeared, in her stockinged feet, blear-eyed, with a hand to her forehead. 'I heard voices,' she said dazedly. She saw Sinclair and frowned. 'David? Why are you here?'

'I rang him,' Quirke said.

She stood blinking. 'I must have—I must have passed out. I feel really peculiar.'

'I'll make some tea,' Quirke said. 'Tea will be good for you.'

He went into the kitchen and boiled the kettle and set out cups and saucers on a tray. When he returned to the living room Sinclair and Phoebe were sitting close beside each other on the sofa, and Sinclair was holding her right hand in both of his.

Phoebe looked at Quirke as he poured out the tea for her. 'They invited me for a drink,' she said. 'Why did I go?' She looked about her helplessly. 'My head feels as if it's stuffed with wet wool.'

'Do you remember taking anything?' Quirke asked.

'What do you mean?'

'Tablets, pills—anything like that?'

'No.' She frowned, trying to concentrate. She shook her head. 'No, there wasn't anything. We drank gin. I don't know what I was thinking of.' She put her other hand on top of Sinclair's hands. 'I'm sorry,' she said, and suddenly it seemed she might cry. 'I'm so sorry.'

Sinclair looked up at Quirke and said nothing.

'Drink your tea,' Quirke said.

She looked at the cup and saucer balanced on the arm of the sofa beside her. 'He told me I was his alibi,' she said. Both men watched her, waiting. She shook her head again and gave an incredulous laugh. 'He sang it,' she said.

Again the two men exchanged glances.

'Sang what?' Sinclair asked.

'About my being his alibi. He said the guards had questioned him'—she looked to Quirke—'your friend, Inspector Hackett, brought both twins in to ask them about the night when that man died, that Clancy man. So Jonas said. I think he's mad.' She looked from one of them to the other. 'I really think he *is* mad. They both are, both the twins.'

Quirke drew up a chair and set it in front of the sofa and sat down and leaned forward with his hands clasped. 'Which one was it that spoke about an alibi?'

'Jonas.' She turned to Sinclair. 'He was talking about the party at Breen's house, you remember? We saw them there, the twins. Only—'

She stopped.

'Only what?' Quirke said.

'Only I noticed something. You know they have a joke that Jonas wears a ring on his little finger and that's the only way people can tell them apart. But that night, at the party, they were both wearing rings. I saw them. Jonas met us when we arrived—remember, he was with Tanya

Somers? And then, later, we saw James upstairs, talking to that girl in the doorway. But they both had the identical signet ring on the little fingers of their left hands.'

Sinclair was frowning. 'I don't understand,' he said.

Quirke watched Phoebe. 'How were they dressed?' he asked.

'One of them had on a black blazer, the other was wearing—I don't know—something pale, a linen suit, or jacket.'

'And Tanya Somers was there, with one of them?'

'Yes.'

The room had grown very quiet. Distantly in the city an Angelus bell was dully tolling.

'There was only one of them,' Quirke said. 'They pretended they were two, but there was only the one.'

'But why?' Phoebe said. 'They would have had to switch clothes. And Tanya Somers would have had to go along with the pretence.'

Quirke stood up. 'One of them needed to be somewhere else,' he said. 'That was the reason for the trick. That's why you, and whoever else was at the party that knew them, would be their alibi. There was only one twin, masquerading as two.'

He walked to the mantelpiece and took another cigarette from the silver box and lit it, and drew the smoke deep into his lungs. Phoebe and Sinclair sat and watched him.

'I still don't see it,' Sinclair said.

Quirke turned, and stood with his back to the fireplace, wreathed in cigarette smoke that gave him for a moment the look of a magician about to make himself disappear.

'Phoebe said it. That night, the night of the party, was the night Jack Clancy died. The night he was murdered.'

The lights shining down from the big windows on the ground floor seemed to darken the twilight beyond their reach, and in the front garden, behind the railings, shadows congregated among the flowerbeds and under the boughs of the big beech reaching towards the house like tentacles from the road. At the gate Quirke hesitated. What would he say to the twins if they were there? What would he say to Mona Delahaye? Should he not have called Hackett, and told him Phoebe's story of the signet ring?

But he knew that none of this was why he was here, loitering at dusk in front of a dead man's house. He took off his hat and held it in front of him, against his breast, as if it were a shield to ward off something.

She was surprised to see him. 'Back so soon?' she said, with her sly smile. She was wearing a dark green kimono—green again—and her slender pale feet were bare. Without shoes she seemed slighter and more delicate than ever, and the top of her head was barely level with his chin. In the lamp-light her hair had the texture of hammered bronze. 'Come through to the kitchen,' she said. 'I was making myself a nice hot drink.' He walked behind her down the hall. It was plain to see that she was naked under the kimono. 'Maid's night off,' she said over her shoulder. 'I'm all on my little ownsome.' And she laughed.

'What about the twins?'

'Oh, they've gone off,' she said lightly. 'And so has my

father-in-law. He's in the hospital, in fact. He had another stroke this evening. Quite serious, it seems, this time.'

In the kitchen there was the throat-catching bitter-sweet smell of warm chocolate. A small saucepan was simmering on the stove. 'Want some?' she asked. 'I make it with real chocolate, not that awful powdered stuff.' She took up a wooden spoon and stirred the pot, peering into the steam.

'My daughter has recovered, by the way,' Quirke said. 'In case you were wondering.'

'She must have quite a hangover.' She went to a cupboard and took down two white mugs. 'A girl of her age had better steer clear of the gin. I should know.'

'It must have been more than gin.'

She glanced at him, then turned back to concentrate on pouring the hot chocolate into the mugs. 'The boys were just playing, as usual. Your daughter isn't used to that kind of thing, I imagine. Very strait-laced, isn't she? She dresses like a nun. They tell me she has a boyfriend?'

'Yes. My assistant.'

'Hmm. A Jew, isn't he?' She sniffed. 'Anyway, I'm sure she'll always be Daddy's girl. You mustn't let the Hebrews make her one of theirs.' She came and handed him one of the mugs, and clinked hers against it. 'Here's to fun.'

'What kind of drug did they give her?' he asked.

'Did they give her a drug? I told you, I only saw her drinking gin.'

He looked at the steaming umber stuff in the mug. 'She's had a lot of trouble in her life.'

'Yes. I could tell.'

'I have to protect her.'

She smiled. 'Not doing a very good job, by the look of it. Aren't you going to drink your chocolate? It's very soothing. I think you need soothing.' She was standing very close to him. Behind the heavy fragrance of the chocolate he could smell her hair.

'Tell me what was in the note your husband left,' he said.

She sighed irritably. 'Oh, there was no note.' She walked back to the stove and poured herself another go of chocolate and took a drink of it, clasping the mug in both hands. 'I just said that to humour you, since you seemed so pleased with yourself playing the detective.'

'Were you having an affair with Jack Clancy?'

'With Jack? Certainly not.' She chuckled. 'Jack Clancy—my God, what do you think I am? Not Jack, no.'

He caught something in her voice. 'Who, then?'

She gave him a measuring look, thinking. 'Why do you want to know?' He said nothing. She put her mug down on the draining board. 'Give me a cigarette,' she said. 'You know'—she leaned down to the flame of his lighter—'I've been doing a lot of thinking since Victor died. Well, you can imagine. He was such a torment to himself, I wonder if he's not better off gone. Do you think I'm terrible to say such a thing?' She went and leaned against the sink, crossing one arm under her breasts and holding the cigarette level with her mouth. In the opening of the kimono her right leg was bared to the thigh. 'People didn't know him. They took at face value the image he had of him-self—the successful businessman, the expert sailor, the loving husband and responsible father. But really he was a mess. It took me a while to see that. Deep down he disgusted himself. He knew what he was, you see.'

'And what was he?'

She considered. 'Weak. Spineless.'

'He had enough courage to kill himself.'

This seemed to interest her. 'Do you think it takes courage to do that?' she asked. 'I think it was cowardice.' She shook her head sadly. 'Such a mess,' she murmured.

Quirke set the mug down on the table. He had not tasted the chocolate. 'Could I have a drink?' he said.

They passed through to the drawing room. Mona lit lamps, and went to the sideboard and poured whiskey into a tumbler. Quirke looked at the garden's velvet darkness pressing itself against the window.

'Are you an alcoholic?' Mona asked, in a tone of mild enquiry.

'I don't know,' he said. He took the glass and drank off the whiskey in one gulp and gave her back the glass for her to refill. 'Probably.'

She seemed to find his reply amusing. She smiled at him, arching an eyebrow, and turned and picked up the whiskey bottle.

'You slept with me once,' he said.

'Yes, I did. Like you, I'm curious.'

'You were curious, about me?'

'I was. Now I'm not any more.' She moved to the sofa and sat down and crossed her legs. The wings of the kimono fell back on both sides to reveal one bare, glossy knee. 'Remember how I said to you before that people think I'm a dimwit? They do. I mean them to.' She lifted a hand and pushed her bronzen hair back from her face at the side. 'When I was a little girl,' she said, 'I used to lie on the floor and pretend to be asleep, but I'd have my eyes open just the tiniest crack, so I could watch people, my parents, my brothers, my sister that I hated, without them knowing. Now I'm a big girl and I do the same thing, only instead of pretending to be asleep I pretend to be stupid.'

Quirke sipped his whiskey. 'Why have you let me in on your secret?'

'I don't know. I suppose because you're pretending, too.'

'And what am I pretending to be?'

She studied him for a moment, cocking her head to one side, like a blackbird. 'You're pretending to be human, I think. Wouldn't you say?'

He lit a cigarette. The flame of the lighter flickered, he noticed, for his hand was not entirely steady. 'Did you know,' he said, 'that Jack Clancy was planning to take over the business from your husband?'

She nodded. 'Yes. Victor told me.'

'When did he find out?'

'The day before he killed himself.'

He looked at her without speaking. She held his gaze calmly.

'Was that why he killed himself?' he asked.

'Partly.'

He set his glass down slowly on the sideboard, next to the whiskey bottle. He would pour himself another drink, but not just yet.

'What else had he found out?' he asked.

'Oh!' She waved a hand. 'He was impossible. So jealous.'

He waited. She regarded him with a slightly swollen look, as if struggling to keep herself from laughing.

'Who was it?' he said.

'Who was who?'

'Who was he jealous of?'

'Don't you know?' Now she did laugh, giving an odd, sharp little whoop. 'Not *Jack* Clancy,' she said. 'But you were warm.'

He was silent for a long moment, gazing at her. Then he took up the whiskey bottle and half filled the tumbler. He turned back to her. 'The boy, then,' he said. 'What's his name?'

'Davy. And he's not a boy, though he's as pretty as one—don't you think? And so—so *energetic*, with that kind of youthful vigour that gladdens a girl's heart, I can tell you.'

Quirke sipped his whiskey. The glass knocked against one of his front teeth. 'Are you still—seeing him?' he asked, surprised at how steady his voice was.

'For goodness' sake!' she said, and gave another laugh. 'I'm the grieving widow—I can hardly go about sleeping with people.'

'You slept with me.'

'I told you,' she said, with a sulky pout, 'I was curious.'

He felt exhausted suddenly. He shut his eyes and kneaded the flesh at the bridge of his nose between a thumb and two fingers. He had a tearing sensation in his chest, as if there were an animal in there, raking at him with its claws.

He opened his eyes. 'Jack Clancy's death,' he said.

'What about it?' she asked. 'I assume, since his scheme to take over from Victor had been found out, he decided to follow Victor's example. Rivals to the end.'

Quirke shook his head. 'No,' he said, hearing the weariness in his voice. 'Jack Clancy didn't kill himself.' She waited. 'Don't you know?' he said. 'Haven't you figured it out?'

She put a finger to her chin and looked upwards, mimicking a schoolgirl who has been asked a hard question. 'Someone did it for him?' she said.

'Yes. Someone did it for him.'

'Not'—she sat bolt upright and slapped a hand on her bared knee and laughed—'not Maverley? Not that white rabbit? He adored Victor, I know, but I can't imagine him killing someone in revenge for his death.'

'No,' Quirke said, 'not Maverley.'

'Then who?'

He walked to the sofa and stood over her, the whiskey glass clenched in his hand. She leaned back a little, pulling the kimono closed over her knees, and the faintest shadow of alarm crossed her face.

'Are you pretending now?' he said. 'Or are you stupid, after all?' He drank the last of the whiskey in the glass and held it out to her, and she took it, and set it down on the arm of the sofa. 'Where are the twins?' he asked.

'I already said, they've gone.' She was watching him carefully, as if readying herself to forestall whatever move he might make. She was right to be wary. He was very angry. He put a hand into the pocket of his jacket and made a fist of it, digging the nails into his palm.

'Goodbye,' he said, and turned abruptly and walked from the room, and along the silent hall, and opened the front door and stepped out into the fragrance of the night. He felt nothing, only the sensation of something icy melting in his heart.

13

A LIGHT FINE RAIN was falling when they left the city, but it soon lost heart and stopped, and a watery sun came out and put a blinding shine on the road in front of them. They went up by the canal, past lock after lock, the suburbs on their left becoming more tired and shabby with each mile they covered. Then they turned on to the Naas Road, and the trees on either side seemed to hold themselves averted, gazing off elsewhere.

'I wish you wouldn't smoke in the car,' Rose Griffin said. 'I'd much prefer to breathe.'

Quirke opened the window a little way and pushed his half-smoked cigarette out through the crack. They went on for a long way in silence after that, until Rose spoke again, asking if he thought there might be somewhere where they could stop to eat lunch. Quirke stirred himself and said he had not thought about lunch. There was, he said, a hotel in Cashel that might be tolerable. 'Tolerable!' Rose said faintly, and sighed.

They spoke of Malachy Griffin. Rose said she was worried about her husband, about how sedentary he was becoming. 'Couldn't you and he take up golf?' she asked.

Quirke glanced at her sidelong. 'No, I suppose not,' she said. 'Pity,' she added, with wistful regret.

She was puzzled as to the purpose of this journey, and Quirke, it seemed, was not inclined to enlighten her. Although she would not have thought it possible, he was even more taciturn than usual today, shut far off inside himself. She had the impression that he was suffering, gnawing away at some inner hurt.

'The trouble with Malachy,' she said, 'is that he's just not assertive enough.'

Quirke made a noise that might have been laughter. 'Who do you want him to assert himself against?'

'Oh, Quirke, you know what I mean! My Mal has so much to offer, but he holds back. It's an almighty shame.'

Quirke wondered doubtfully what it might be that Mal had so much of, but he said nothing.

The damp green of summer fields rolled past. It was midday and they were almost alone on the long road south. They passed through melancholy villages, ramshackle towns. More than once they were forced to slow to a crawl behind a farmer driving his cows. Outside Kildare town they met in the middle of the road a ram with elaborately curled horns and strings of matted wool hanging down on all sides. Rose sounded the horn impatiently, but the ram just stood there, head lowered, glaring at them, and in the end Quirke had to get out and wave his arms and shout before the beast would move. When he got back into the car Rose was laughing. 'Oh, Quirke, you should have seen yourself!'

The road seemed endless. Fields, trees, then ragged

outskirts, then long streets with pubs and drapers' shops and general stores, then outskirts again, then trees again, then fields again. They crossed a bridge over a river, a broad, slow stretch of stippled silver, with bulrushes at both sides and a single swan afloat in the shallows. The huge sky over the midlands was piled high with luminous wreckage. On a hairpin bend some small creature, rat or squirrel, ran out from the verge and under their wheels, and there was a quick bump, and Rose gave a little scream. 'Oh, Quirke,' she wailed, beating the steering wheel with her palms, 'tell me why we're going down to Cork.'

They stopped in Cashel, at the Cashel Arms Hotel, which even in the lobby smelt of cooked cabbage. With sinking hearts they allowed themselves to be conducted to the dining room, where they were given a table by a window looking down into a cobbled yard. 'Order a bottle of wine, for pity's sake,' Rose said. They ate doubtful fish with mashed potato; the cabbage they had been smelling since they arrived made a soggy appearance. But the wine was good, a lustrous Meursault that in Quirke's mouth tasted of gold coins and melons.

Rose began to feel better. 'Tell me,' she said to Quirke, 'how is that lady-friend of yours, the actress?'

'She's very well,' Quirke said, but would not meet her eye. 'Very well.'

'Is it serious?'

Now he did look at her. 'Is what serious?'

'You and your lady-friend, of course.'

'You make it sound like an illness.'

Rose shook her head. 'Quirke, Quirke, Quirke,' she said, 'what are we to do with you?'

'I wasn't aware that something needed to be done.'

'Well, exactly.'

They went on eating, in an ill-tempered silence. Then Rose tried again. 'This trip, it's to do with those two men who died, yes? Maggie's brother, and then his partner? What was the outcome of all that?'

Half a minute elapsed before Quirke answered. 'An outcome,' he said, 'is still awaited.'

'That's why you want to talk to Maggie?'

'That's why I want to talk to Maggie.'

'You know she's thinking of living permanently down there, in—what's the place?'

'Slievemore.'

'That's it. Fishing town, is it? Sounds like Scituate.' It was in Scituate, south of Boston, that Quirke had first met Rose Crawford, as she was then. 'Why would she want to bury herself away down there?' She chuckled. 'Maybe to get away from her family, especially that Mona Delahaye.'

She stopped. At mention of Mona's name she had felt something from across the table, a tiny tremor, and she looked hard at Quirke. Mona Delahaye. So that was it— Mona had got her talons into him. Well, that would smart, all right. Her gaze softened. Poor Quirke, he would never learn.

Outside, the afternoon had mellowed, and the air, laden with dust and midges, was the same soft gilded colour as the Meursault they had drunk. They did not want to set off and instead strolled for a while in the town's main street. The great grey ruin of the castle loomed above them on its crag against a sky of bird's-egg blue. Rose had an urge to talk seriously to Quirke—it was probably the effect of the wine—to tell him he was frittering away his life on things that were not worthy of him. But somehow Quirke would not be spoken to like that, he would not allow it, and she held her peace, and felt cross. If he had indeed got himself entangled with Mona Delahaye then he was in for a deal of heartache, and serve him right. Rose and Quirke had gone to bed together, just once, many years before. It had not been a success, yet Rose remembered the occasion with a melancholy fondness. Scituate seemed very far away, now.

In Fermoy they stopped again, Quirke having run out of cigarettes, and while he was in the tobacconist's Rose sat in the car and watched in dismay a man belabouring a cart horse with a stick. He was a coarse-looking fellow with a red face and a lantern jaw and a prominent forehead—he might have been modelled on a *Punch* cartoon—and he wore an old coat with a belt of plaited straw. The horse stood between the shafts of the cart, its head hanging, suffering the blows without flinching. *Oh, my Lord*, Rose thought, *this poor benighted country!*

Slievemore was a green hill above a turquoise bay. When they arrived, along the winding road from the north, the early-evening sunlight was tawny, and there was a breeze and the air was hazed with salt, and the blue water was flecked with ragged scraps of white. Ashgrove, the Delahayes' house, was on the far side of the hill, and they had to drive along the harbour front, and climb another stretch of winding road for ten miles. Neither of them had been to the house before, and they had trouble locating it. When at last they pulled in at the gate, the house rose before them, a grey granite mansion with arched windows and a steep roof angled in many planes, and there were even turrets. All that was missing, Quirke thought, was a flag, or pennant, flapping above the chimneys on a tall pole.

The house had a deserted look. No door opened, no face appeared at any window, no voice called a greeting. 'Dear me,' Rose said, 'it seems as if our trip has been in vain. Where can she be?'

They knocked at the front door, waited, knocked again. Then they walked along a gravel path round to the side of the house. French windows there stood open to the evening. They looked at each other, and went in.

Quirke was sensitive to the atmosphere in old houses. It was an instinctive memory, buried deep in his very bones, of Carricklea, the industrial school and reformatory in the west of Ireland where he had passed his childhood. He remembered the sounds, the thud of heels on polished floors, the hollow echoes of distant doors shutting, the whispers in the darkness.

'We should have telephoned,' Rose said. 'Maggie is peculiar, you know. She has peculiar ways.' They went through all the rooms downstairs. Everything was so neat and tidy it seemed no one could be living here. Then they heard it, a sound, from upstairs, as of something being dragged across a wooden floor. They stood and listened. The hall around them seemed somehow to be breathing, slowly, deeply. Above the hall table hung a tall looking-glass in a gilt frame, reflecting the hat-stand opposite and a pair of dusty antlers mounted on a sort of plaque on the wall. Quirke understood they were not welcome here, he and Rose: houses had a way of showing their resentment.

Upstairs all was disorder. Furniture was stacked in the corridors, chairs, dressing-tables, tallboys, a folding screen with painted panels, a full-length looking-glass on a mahogany stand. In many rooms the beds had been stripped and their mattresses raised up and propped against the walls. Curtains, too, had been taken down, and were thrown in untidy heaps on the bare bedsteads. Pictures had been lifted from their hooks and set on the floor against the walls, all facing inwards. A white chamber pot with a shrivelled red rose leaning in it stood on top of a bureau, like a parody of a votive offering.

They found Maggie Delahaye in one of the big bed-rooms at the back of the house. She wore a man's checked shirt and an old pair of baggy corduroy trousers, and a red bandanna was tied around her head. Rose had never noticed before her friend's faint moustache, or the few grey whiskers sprouting on her chin. She looked at them both with a mixture of puzzlement and alarm, as if she did not know what they were. For a moment it seemed she might dive past them and escape through the door and down the stairs and out at those open french windows. She had been pushing, with great effort, a heavy antique wooden chest across the floor, and now she straightened, and brushed her hands.

'I was just rearranging things,' she said. 'I was just . . . tidying.'

In the kitchen she made coffee for them, and put out dry crackers on a plate. There was no butter, it seemed. 'I'm a bit low in provisions,' she said. 'I'd have gone into the village if I'd known you were coming.' She had put Quirke and Rose Griffin to sit at a big wooden table; over the years the surface of it had been scrubbed to furrows and ridges, like sand at the tide-line.

Rose had introduced Quirke, and he had said he was a doctor, without specifying which kind. 'Oh, yes,' Maggie said. 'You were at my brother's funeral. I saw you there.' As she moved about the kitchen she kept shooting quick, sidelong glances at him, in the way that a dog would glance at a stranger it was suspicious of. Quirke wondered if she thought he had come to take her away somewhere, since he was a doctor. In fact, she had not asked them why they had come, unannounced, like this, and she behaved as if they were chance visitors whom she had little desire to see.

'Maggie, dear,' Rose said, 'Dr Quirke wants to talk to you about something.'

Maggie turned quickly to the stove, on which the kettle was coming to the boil. 'Oh, yes?' she said. 'My brother's death, is it?' She looked over her shoulder at Rose. 'Has he found out something?'

'It's not about your brother's death, Miss Delahaye,' Quirke said. 'It's about—it's about Jack Clancy.'

She poured the boiling water into the coffee pot,

moving her lips silently. 'That's what I was doing when
you arrived,' she said. 'I was clearing out the Clancys'
things, getting them ready for the removals men to collect.
I rang up a firm in Cork and asked them to send down
one of those big vans—what do you call them?—pantech-
nicons, is it? Odd word for something so ordinary. They
were very nice on the phone. I spoke to a very polite girl
who took all the details and said I was to let them know
twenty-four hours before I want them to come. I didn't
realise there would be so much heavy work involved. I
think I shall have to call them again and ask them to send
down some men to help me. I don't think I could get all
those things down the stairs by myself, do you? There's
so much—you wouldn't think three people would have
needed so much furniture.' She brought the coffee pot to
the table. 'Do say if it's too strong, won't you, Dr Quirke?
Rose likes hers very strong, I know that.'

'Do you mind if I smoke?' Quirke said.

'No, no, of course not—please, go ahead. I don't,
myself, but Victor used to smoke Balkan Sobranie sometimes and I loved the smell.'

Quirke tasted the liquid in his cup and to his consternation discovered it was not coffee but some kind of beef
broth or powdered gravy. He saw Rose tasting hers. She
grimaced, and looked at him wide-eyed.

'Miss Delahaye,' he said, pushing his cup away from
him with a fingertip, 'on the night Jack Clancy died, did
you see your nephews—the twins, Jonas and James?'

She was standing beside the table, holding the coffee
pot. She had fallen into a daze, and he was not sure the
question had registered, and was about to ask it again

when she stirred herself, and blinked. 'Did I see them?' she asked. 'How do you mean?'

'Were you with them—did you talk to them?'

She went to the cupboard and took down a cup and saucer for herself and filled it from the coffee pot and took a sip, and frowned. 'Oh dear,' she murmured, 'this isn't coffee at all.' She looked at Rose, at Quirke. 'What did I do?' she asked, in helpless bafflement. 'I must have put Bisto in the pot, instead of coffee.' She giggled, and bit her lip.

Rose went and took the cup and saucer from her and poured the contents into the sink, then held her by the arm. 'Come, dear,' she said, 'come and sit down with us. You shouldn't be here on your own, you know. It's not good for you.'

'Oh, but I love it here,' Maggie said. 'This is my home, now. I'm not going back to Dublin.' She let herself be led to the table. 'How elegant you look, Rose. Blue always suited you.' She sat down on the chair that Quirke had placed for her opposite his own. 'I was always happy here,' she said to him, as if explaining something to a child. 'And now I'm going to settle down. I might work the land, you know. There are fifty acres, more. It's good land, rich soil. I could keep cattle, sheep. And bees, I'd like to have bees. There were hives here once, down in the Long Meadow, I remember them. And I could grow crops.' She focused on Quirke. 'Do you know anything about farming, Dr Quirke?'

'No,' Quirke said. 'I'm afraid I don't.'

'It's no matter. I can hire someone in. There are always

farmers' sons, wanting work.' She saw Quirke looking about for an ashtray. 'Do use the saucer,' she said. 'I'll be washing up later. I always do the washing-up last thing. It's very soothing. I listen to the wireless while I'm doing it.' She pointed to the big wooden set on a shelf beside the fridge.

'Isn't there a woman who comes?' Rose said. 'A local woman, who does the housekeeping?'

'Mrs Hartigan, yes. But I've let her go. I intend to keep house myself, from now on.'

'But—but you'll need help. In the winter. There'll be fuel to get in and—' But here Rose's imagination failed her; it was a very long time since she had attended personally to the everyday running of a house.

Quirke finished his cigarette and lit another. 'Which one of the twins was with you that night?' he asked. 'Because one of them was with you, isn't that so?'

She was looking at him in that glazed way again, with her head lowered. He noticed that her mouth was slack at one side, as if she had suffered a slight stroke. The red rag tied around her forehead might be a bandage.

'I always favoured James,' she said, smiling wistfully. 'Jonas was everybody's darling, being so intelligent and charming, but I took to James. I suppose it's because he's not like the others, and neither am I.' She leaned forward suddenly and set both her hands flat on the table before her and looked hard at Quirke. 'Do you think there might be something wrong with my mind, Doctor? I think I haven't been right since Victor died. The strangest things come into my head, all kinds of strange thoughts.

Down here, I sometimes find it hard to know whether I'm awake and having fantasies, or asleep and dreaming. Do you ever have that feeling?' She turned to Rose. 'Do you?'

Rose put a hand over one of Maggie's. 'Yes, dear, of course,' she said. 'We all feel like that at times. Life can be very puzzling.'

'Yes, yes,' Maggie said eagerly, gazing into Rose's eyes. 'That's what I think, too, that life is—is puzzling. That's exactly the word. Puzzling, and so wasteful, don't you feel? Think of Victor, dying. That was a waste.' She turned back to Quirke. 'Wasn't it?—a waste?'

Rose was looking hard at Quirke now, sending him some signal. He supposed she wanted him not to ask any more questions, to leave this poor frantic creature in peace. But he could not do that.

'Tell us,' he said to Maggie, 'tell us what happened, that night.'

She smiled that wistful smile and her eyes slipped out of focus again. 'Dun Laoghaire,' she said. 'James and I had driven out there, to find him, to find Jack Clancy. Such a lovely night. There was a moon, remember? Huge—bigger than I've ever seen the moon. You could have read a newspaper by it.'

She stopped, and took her hands from the table and put them in her lap and sat there smiling to herself.

'Go on,' Quirke said softly.

'What?' She looked at him and frowned, as if she had never seen him before in her life.

'Tell us what happened.'

'What happened,' she said. 'Yes.' Her eyes went vague,

and Quirke was about to prompt her again when she spoke. 'Jonas had got it out of Mona, you see.'

'Got what out of her?' Quirke asked.

She gave him a pitying look. 'Why, about being unfaithful. To Victor.'

'With whom?'

'She wouldn't say, but we knew, of course.'

'You knew?'

'We guessed. It had to be him. You know what he was like, Clancy.' She gave her head a little shake in disgust. 'Jack couldn't keep his hands off any woman. And as for Mona—well.'

Rose was gazing at Maggie as if mesmerised.

'Go on,' Quirke said. 'Go on about that night.'

Maggie sat forward, birdlike, eager now to continue with her story. 'James knew where Jack Clancy was—he had been following him. Clancy had been with another one of his'—she made a sour face—'of his girlfriends, in Sandycove. James had a cricket bat—' She broke off and laughed briefly. 'Trust James, always the sportsman.' She frowned suddenly, bethinking herself, and looked at them both apologetically. 'But I promised you coffee! Oh dear, I'm hopeless. What my mother would have said, I can't think. Mother was a stickler where manners were concerned. She used to keep a ruler in her lap at mealtimes, one of those old-fashioned wooden tubes, and would crack us on the knuckles with it, Victor and I, if we used the wrong knife, or didn't offer things around before helping ourselves. Oh, yes, a real stickler.'

Quirke moved his chair closer to hers. 'Please go on,' he said.

'What?' She blinked.

'You were telling us about that night, in Dun Laoghaire, with the full moon.'

'Oh, yes. We caught up with him at the bandstand'—she turned to Rose—'you know the bandstand, on the front? He was hiding there. I think he must have sensed James was following him. He saw me, coming towards him—I wanted to be there, when it happened. Then I heard it, the blow. It was very loud. He didn't make a sound, though, just fell straight down, like an animal under the pole-axe.'

There was a silence, in which they could hear Maggie breathing, taking rapid, shallow breaths, like a sleeping child. Her eyes shone, and a small, perfectly circular spot of pink had appeared on each cheekbone.

Quirke leaned closer to her. 'And this was because of Mona, yes—Mona and him? That's why you—that's why James—hit him on the head?'

'That, yes. And the other business.'

'What other business, Maggie?'

She looked straight into his face, again with that softly pitying expression, as if he were an idiot child. 'Jack Clancy had been getting ready to take over the firm and push Victor out. Didn't you know? The boys couldn't have that. They were very cross when Mr Maverley told them about it. We had a little conference, the three of us, Jonas, James and I—well, Jonas and I, really. James doesn't think the way Jonas does. He's not clever, like Jonas.'

Quirke had taken his cigarette case from his pocket,

but did not think his hands would be steady enough for him to light a cigarette. He was slightly dizzy, and had a strange sensation; it felt like euphoria. 'And that was when you decided, you and Jonas, what to do about Jack Clancy—yes?'

'Yes,' Maggie said. 'That's when we decided Jack Clancy could not be allowed to go on living, not when Victor was dead.'

'So you and James followed him that night, and James hit him, and then you put him in the boat, and one of you sailed it out, and the other followed, in another boat.'

'Yes, yes,' Maggie said, almost panting now. 'James took him in his own boat—Jack's boat, I mean, the *Rascal*—and I came along with him in one of ours, the *Maggie Dear*. My father named it after me, you know. I was always so proud, sailing in it, with my name on the side. *Maggie Dear*.'

'Was he still alive then?' Quirke asked softly.

'What?'

'Was he alive, Jack Clancy, when you put him in the boat?'

'I don't know. I didn't—I didn't look at him. James did all that. He was always very kind to me, James, very considerate. *You leave it all to me, Auntie Maggie*, he said. He sounded so cheerful, like he used to when he was a little boy.' She paused, remembering. 'I was upset, of course. Jack Clancy was a dreadful man, and deserved all he got, and yet—'

She put a hand up to her forehead and, feeling the

bandanna there, untied it at the back and took it off. 'Oh!' she said, with a wide-eyed smile. 'What a relief! I'd forgotten I had it on.'

'So James scuttled the boat, the *Rascal*,' Quirke said, 'and then the two of you returned in your boat, in the *Maggie Dear*.'

She nodded rapidly. 'Yes, yes, we both came back together.' She looked at her hands on the table in front of her. 'I can still see that moon, shining on the water, a long gold path leading out to the horizon.'

Rose Griffin had lowered her head, and sat motionless, her shoulders hunched. 'Oh, Maggie,' she murmured.

Maggie turned to her. 'Do you think we were very bad, to do what we did?' she asked. She looked to Quirke again. 'Do you?'

'You killed a man,' he said. 'You committed a murder.'

She nodded slowly, considering this. 'Yes, we killed him,' she said. 'But I don't think it was murder, not really. It was more like something in the Bible, you know—my father was fond of quoting the Bible to us when we were little.' She lifted a finger, pointing upwards. 'It was an act of justice.'

'No, Miss Delahaye,' Quirke said. 'It was an act of vengeance.'

'Well,' she retorted quickly, in a petulant tone, 'you can think that, if you like. *Vengeance is mine, saith the Lord*— yet they say, *An eye for an eye, and a tooth for a tooth*.'

'They don't,' Quirke said, shaking his head. 'They say, *Love thy neighbour as thyself*. They say, *Turn the other cheek*.'

Suddenly the woman's eyes narrowed and she drew her lips together into a wrinkled bud. 'You're a fool,' she whispered. 'Jack Clancy tried to take everything my brother had, his business, his wife—'

'No,' Quirke said, 'not his wife.'

She drew her head back and stared at him, her pinched nostrils flaring. 'He was sleeping with that woman. I know he was.'

'No,' Quirke said again. 'Not the father.'

'Not the father? What do you mean?'

'Not the father. The son.'

'What?' She lifted her hands and slapped them down hard on the table once more. 'What are you saying?'

'I'm saying that Jack Clancy wasn't sleeping with Mona Delahaye. His son was.'

'Oh, Lord,' Rose Griffin said, a sort of moan, and stood up with her cup and rinsed it at the sink and filled it with water and drank deep, then stood there with her back turned, staring out of the window into the garden.

Maggie was struggling to take it in. 'Davy?' she said, in a tone of disbelief. 'Davy, and Mona? But Jonas said Mona had told him—'

'Whatever she told him was a lie.'

Maggie was staring at him. 'The boy,' she said softly, 'not the father—the boy . . .'

'Yes. Your brother had found out about him and Mona at the same time he found out that Jack Clancy was scheming to take over the business. That's why he took Davy out in the boat and left him stranded. That was your brother's attempt at vengeance. He meant to kill Davy,

I think, but I suppose couldn't bring himself to do it. Perhaps he thought Davy would die anyway, of exposure, or that he would drown.'

'You're lying.'

'I'm not lying, Miss Delahaye.'

'How do you know—how do you know it wasn't Jack?'

'She told me.'

'Mona?'

'Yes. Mona.'

She looked away. 'That filthy little—! The two of them, filthy animals.'

Abruptly, and as if she did not realise it, she began to cry, big shining tears rolling down beside her nose and dripping from either side of her chin on to the table. She stood up, pressing her fingertips to the worn wood to balance herself. 'I must—' she said. 'I feel—' She shook her head, crossly, it seemed, and turned away, and walked out of the room, stiffly, head erect, her arms rigid at her sides. Quirke looked at the blood-red bandanna on the table. Rose turned from the sink. 'You should have told me,' she said.

He nodded. 'Yes, I should have. I'm sorry.'

'Sometimes, Quirke,' she said, walking slowly towards the table, 'sometimes I don't understand you at all. I don't understand what goes on in your head.'

He lifted his eyes to hers. 'Nor do I,' he said.

From somewhere off at the side of the house came the sound of a car engine starting up. Quirke rose and went to the window, in time to see a station wagon slewing across the gravel and heading off along the drive, towards the front gate. Rose came and stood at his shoulder. 'It's Maggie,' she said. 'Look, she's gone.'

'Yes.'

'Shouldn't we follow?'

Quirke shrugged. 'No, I don't think so.'

The last of daylight was a dense pink-gold sheen on the seemingly unmoving waters of the bay. A lobster boat was coming in past the harbour mouth, and on the quayside two fishermen were gathering up nets that had been drying there all day long. A man was throwing a ball into the water for his dog. The dog would scamper down the stone steps of the jetty and dive in and paddle frantically out and snatch the ball in its jaws and then paddle back again, snorting.

In half an hour the dark would be complete. She wondered if she should wait until then. But, no, the sooner she set out, the better. What she felt most strongly now was a kind of angry impatience—an impatience to be away, to be done with all this.

The rowboat was moored at the far end of the jetty, and she had to untie it and drag it behind her to the steps. The man called his dog, and put it on its lead, and bade her good evening. She did not respond.

She and Victor used to sail in this boat when they were children and staying at Slievemore. Of the two of them she had always been the stronger, and on more than one occasion had fought bigger boys on his behalf. No one was allowed to hit her brother. Strange to think that some trace of Victor would still be here, the memory of his hand on the oar, the mark of his fingers on the tiller, undetectable, but real, something of him, enduring.

When she stepped into the little boat it rocked in giddy fashion from side to side, as if for pleasure, as if it recognised her and was glad of her familiar weight. She sat down on the thwart and took up the oars. She had always loved the moist cool texture of varnished wood; it was the very feel of boats and boating, for her. Amid soft plashings she steered out from the jetty. Each time she lifted the oars from the water thick strings of molten gold cascaded from their lower edges. The man on the quayside was watching her. He wore a flat cap and a sleeveless jerkin made of green felt; a hunter's coat. His dog sat beside him, and it, too, seemed to watch her, one pointed ear standing upright and the other lying flat.

Off to her right a cormorant suddenly surfaced, shaking itself, and so quiet was the evening that she could hear its wetted oily feathers rattling. A sickle moon hung above the hill and, not far off from it, Venus glittered, impossibly bright. The sky low down was a tender shade of greenish blue, and seemed as breakable as the shell of a bird's egg. Everything was impossibly lovely. The cormorant dived again, and the ripples left by its going expanded outwards on all sides, each ripple smoothly flowing, swift as an eel. She pulled harder on the oars and the little boat bounded forward eagerly.

The man and his dog were gone from the quayside, the lobster boat had docked. She could hear faint strains of dance music—the lobster men must have their wireless tuned to some English station. She could see the light of the lamp in the cabin, and the shadows of the men moving about. It seemed to her she had never been so vividly alive to the sights and sounds of this watery world. On she went, and on, into the gathering dark.

14

THEY STROLLED TOGETHER in St Stephen's Green, as so often before. The day was warm and overcast. There was rain coming, Hackett said, he could smell it in the air, and, sure enough, the tip of a cloud as dark as vengeance itself appeared behind the trees to the west.

They stopped to watch a group of children sailing toy boats on the duck pond. Sodden crusts of bread that even the ducks would not eat floated in the brownish water. Hackett was talking about strip lighting. He asked if that was what Quirke had in the dissecting room, and how did he find it. Quirke said it was hard on the eyes. Hackett nodded. 'The wife has me tormented about the bloody lights in the living room,' he said. 'Now she's thinking of strip lighting. Is that, like, neon, those long bulbs with gas in them?' Quirke said he was not sure how they worked, but he supposed it was gas. 'I think there's a kind of filament in them,' Hackett said, 'that makes the gas glow.' He shook his head. 'I'll tell her it's not good for the eyes.'

The children had begun to squabble—someone had capsized someone else's boat, and mothers had to intervene. The two men walked on. They crossed the little humpbacked bridge. The fragrance of flowers, wallflowers, mostly, came to them from the numerous beds round about. A terrier had got into the concrete basin of the fountain and was swimming about in circles, snapping at the water cascading around it and barking madly. In the bandstand the Army Brass Band had finished a recital. The players were packing up their instruments, and the audience was drifting away, scattering in all directions across the grass.

They came to two empty deckchairs beside a bed of asters, and Hackett suggested they might sit. As soon as they did, the park attendant popped up out of nowhere, with his leather purse and his roll of tickets, and took threepence from each of them. 'We'd have been better off on a bench,' Hackett grumbled. He squirmed his bottom against the canvas, making the joints of the chair-legs groan. 'I can never get comfortable in these things.'

The cloud was a quarter way up the sky by now.

Marguerite Delahaye's boat had been found the previous morning adrift in Slievemore Bay. Of the woman herself there was still no trace. Missing, presumed drowned. 'Isn't it a queer thing,' Hackett said, 'the three of them, Delahaye, Clancy and then Delahaye's sister, all of them gone in boats? Do you ever sail, yourself?'

'No,' Quirke said. 'I'm nervous of the sea.'

'As any sensible man would be. I don't much care for it myself, either.' He paused. 'Would you say she jumped?' Quirke did not reply. He was keeping a wary eye on the cloud. They both had their hats in their laps. 'A tragic waste of lives,' Hackett said.

Quirke offered him a cigarette, but Hackett was a Player's man, and preferred his own. They smoked in silence for a while. The smoke would rise a little way and then the breeze would catch it and whip it off at an angle to the side.

'What about the Delahayes?' Quirke asked. 'The twins.'

'Oh, a fine pair of rogues. I should have paid more attention to those boyos from the start. They were thrown out of school, Clongowes College, you know, when they were lads, for tying one of the junior kids to a tree and leaving him all night. The poor little fellow was asthmatic, and had an attack and died. The grandfather got them off that particular hook.'

'How did he do that?'

'The commissioner was a Freemason. No charges were pressed.'

Quirke nodded; such things happened. 'They drugged my daughter.'

'Did they?' Hackett turned in the chair to look at him. 'Why did they do that?'

Quirke shrugged. 'As a warning, maybe, since she was supposed to be their alibi. But more for fun, I think. They're fond of fun.' He squinted at the darkening sky. 'Where are they now?' he asked.

'One of them, the one we're particularly after—James, is it?—skedaddled down to Cork, to his auntie. Too late, though, his auntie being gone. He's still in the house—the boys down there spotted him, and I've asked them to pick him up.'

'And the other one?'

'Not a trace. I imagine he's in England somewhere, or maybe America.' He chuckled. 'I'm thinking of getting Interpol on the job. Wouldn't that be a thing, now?'

'And the girl—what's her name? Somers?'

'Aye—Tanya Somers. I had a word with her. Nothing there.'

'But she had to have been in on it. The night of the party, when there was only one of them but they pretended it was two, she played along with them.'

'She says they told her it was for a bet. She's not the brightest ticket, the same Miss Somers. A grand-looking girl but'—he tapped his forehead—'not much up top.'

'And she doesn't know where Jonas is.'

'If she does, she's not saying.'

'You think she does know?'

Hackett shook his head. 'No. He wouldn't have told her. He would have been planning it—he knew your daughter suspected. He took a load of money out of the bank and had a ticket booked to London. That's the last trace we had of him.' He shifted again awkwardly in the chair, swearing under his breath at the discomfort. 'He'll turn up, sooner or later,' he said. 'Clever as he is, he didn't think far enough ahead. It's no life, being on the run. He'll get careless, and make a mistake, and then we'll have him. Or he'll just get lonely, and come back— you'd be surprised how many do.' He paused, and looked sideways at Quirke, and gave a small cough. 'The widow, Mrs Delahaye, is selling up, I hear.'

Quirke was still looking at the cloud. 'Selling up?' he said.

'Getting rid of the house—the *houses*—and moving to South Africa. I believe it's where she's from, originally.' He paused again, coughed again. 'A cool customer, that lady.'

Quirke said nothing. It was starting to rain; they felt the first stray drops.

'Well,' Hackett said, struggling up from the chair, 'that's three good pennies wasted.' He put on his hat. Quirke remained seated. He steepled his fingers and tapped them against his lips. 'A bad business,' Hackett said.

'Yes,' Quirke answered.

The detective looked down at him, his head tilted. 'Are you all right?' he asked.

Quirke lifted his head. 'I'm all right,' he said. 'I'm fine.'

Hackett nodded, smiled lopsidedly, and touched one finger to the brim of his hat. 'I'll be seeing you, then,' he said, and turned away.

Quirke stood up and walked off in the opposite direction. The rain was falling harder now.

It was a summer deluge. It beat on the roadway and drummed on the roofs of cars, and the gutters raced. By the time he found a phone box he was drenched—the water had even soaked through the shoulder-pads of his jacket, and he could feel the chill damp on his shoulders. He took off his sodden hat, but there was nowhere to set it down so he put it back on. He lifted the receiver off the hook and fumbled in his pockets for change. The park attendant had taken his last coppers. He dialled zero and the operator came on, and he gave her Isabel Galloway's number. 'I'm sorry, caller,' the woman said, not sounding sorry at all, 'please insert three pennies or I can't connect you.' He told her it was an emergency, that he was a doctor and that she must put him through. 'I'm sorry, caller,' she said again, in her singsong voice.

'Look,' Quirke said, thumping his fist softly against the phone's big black metal box, 'please, I'm telling you, it's an emergency—it's life or death.' But it was no good: the operator did not believe him, and broke the connection.

He stood for a long time listening to the pips sounding on the empty line. The rain beat against the small glass panes all around him. He hung up the phone and blundered out into the storm.

My thanks to

Gregory Page and Fiona Ruane

If you enjoyed VENGEANCE you'll love

HOLY ORDERS

the sixth Quirke Mystery from Benjamin Black

She looked at him and smiled sadly. 'You've lived too long among the dead, Quirke,' she said.

He nodded. 'Yes, I suppose I have.' She was not the first one to have told him that, and she would not be the last.

1950s Dublin. When a body is found in the canal, pathologist Quirke and his detective friend, Inspector Hackett, must find the truth behind this brutal murder. But in a world where the police are not trusted, and secrets often remain buried, there is perhaps little hope of bringing the perpetrator to justice.

As spring storms descend on Dublin, Quirke and Hackett's investigation will lead them into the dark heart of the organisation that really runs this troubled city: the church. Meanwhile Quirke's daughter Phoebe realises she is being followed; and when Quirke's terrible childhood in a priest-run orphanage returns to haunt him, he will face his greatest trial yet . . .

The first chapter follows here . . .

1

AT FIRST THEY THOUGHT it was the body of a child. Later, when they got it out of the water and saw the pubic hair and the nicotine stains on the fingers, they realised their mistake. Male, late twenties or early thirties, naked but for one sock, the left one. There were livid bruises on the upper torso and the face was so badly disfigured his mother would have been hard put to recognise him. A courting couple had spotted him, a pale glimmer down between the canal wall and the flank of a moored barge. The girl had telephoned the guards, and the desk sergeant had dialled Inspector Hackett's office, but Hackett was not there at that hour, and instead he got the inspector's assistant, young Jenkins, who was in his cubbyhole behind the cells writing up his week's reports.

'A floater, Sarge,' the desk man said. 'Mespil Road, below Leeson Street Bridge.'

Detective Sergeant Jenkins thought of telephoning his boss but then decided against it. Hackett was fond of his night's sleep and would not take kindly to being disturbed. There were two fellows in the duty room, one, Quinlan, from the motorbike corps and the other in off his beat for a tea break. Jenkins told them he needed their help.

Quinlan had been about to go off duty, and was not pleased at the prospect of staying on. 'He's on a promise from his missus,' the other one, Hendricks, said, and snickered.

Quinlan was big and slow, with slicked-back hair and eyes that bulged. He had his leather gaiters on but had taken off his tunic. He stood with his helmet in his hand and looked at Jenkins stonily out of those gooseberry eyes, and Jenkins could almost hear the cogs of the big man's mind turning laboriously, calculating how much overtime he could screw out of the night's work. Hendricks was not due off until four a.m. 'Fuck it,' Quinlan said at last, and shrugged in vexed resignation, and took his tunic down off the hook. Hendricks laughed again.

'Is there a car in the yard?' Jenkins asked.

'There is,' Hendricks said. 'I saw one there when I came in.'

Jenkins had never noticed before how flat the back of Hendricks's skull was—his neck ran sheer all the way to the crown of his head. It was as if the whole rear part of his cranium had been sliced clean off and his hair had grown back to cover the scar. Must have a brain the size of a lemon; half a lemon.

'Right,' Jenkins said, trying to sound both brisk and bored, as his boss somehow always managed to do. 'Let's get going.'

They had a hard time of it getting the body up. The level in the lock was low, and Hendricks had to be sent to Portobello to rouse the lock-keeper out of his bed. Sergeant Jenkins set Quinlan to examining the scene with a flashlight, while he went and spoke to the couple who had spotted the body. The girl was sitting on a wrought-iron bench under a tree, white-faced in the shadows, clutching a hankie and sniffling. Every few seconds a great shiver would run through her and her shoulders would twitch. Her fellow stood back in the gloom, nervously smoking a cigarette. 'Can we go now, Guard?' he said to Jenkins, in a low, worried voice.

Jenkins peered at him, trying to make out his features, but the moonlight did not penetrate that far under the tree. He seemed a good deal older than the girl, middle-aged, in fact. A married man and she his bit on the side? He turned his attention back to the girl. 'What time was it you found him?'

'Time?' the girl said, as if she did not recognise the word. There was a wobble in her voice.

'It's all right, miss,' Jenkins said gently, not quite know-ing what the words were supposed to mean—it was the kind of thing detectives in the movies said—and then turned businesslike again. 'You phoned straight away, did you, after you found him?' He glanced at the man in the shadows.

'She had to go down nearly to Baggot Street before she could find a phone that worked,' the man said. He had given his name but Jenkins had immediately forgotten it. Wallace? Walsh? Something like that.

'And you stayed here.'

'I thought I'd better keep an eye on the—on the body.'

Right, Jenkins thought—in case it might get up out of the water and walk away. Making sure not to be the one to make the phone call, more like, afraid of being asked who he was and what he had been doing on the canal bank at this hour of the night in the company of a girl half his age.

A car passing by slowed down, the driver craning to see what was going on, his eager face at the window ashy and round like the moon.

The girl had permed hair and wore a tartan skirt with a big ornamental safety pin in it, and flat-heeled shoes. She kept clearing her throat and squeezing the hankie convulsively. She had the man's jacket draped over her shoulders. The man had on a Fair Isle sleeveless jumper. The night was mild, for April, but he would be cold, all the same. A display of chivalry; in that case, he must certainly be her fancy-man.

'Do you live nearby?' Jenkins asked.

'I have a flat over there in Leeson Street, above the chemist's,' the girl said, pointing.

The man said nothing, only sucked on the butt of his cigarette, the tip flaring in the dark and throwing an infernal glow upwards over his face. Small bright anxious eyes, a big nose like a potato. Forty-five if he was a day; the girl was hardly more than twenty-one. 'The guard here will take your details,' Jenkins said.

He turned and called to Quinlan, who was squatting on the canal bank looking down into the water and playing his flashlight over the floating body. He had found nothing round about, no clothes, no belongings, so whoever it was down there must have been brought here from somewhere else. Quinlan straightened and came towards them.

The man stepped quickly from under the tree and put a hand on Jenkins's arm. 'Listen,' he said urgently, 'I'm not supposed to be here. I mean I'll be—I'll be missed at home, this late.' He looked into Jenkins's face meaningfully, attempting a man-to-man smile, but the one he managed was sickly.

'Give your name and address to the guard,' Jenkins said stiffly. 'Then you can go.'

'Is it all right if I give my office address?'

'Just so long as it's somewhere we can contact you.'

'I'm a surveyor,' the man said, as if he expected this to be a significant factor in the night's events. His smile kept flickering on and off, like a faulty light-bulb. 'I'd be grateful if—'

They turned at the sound of heavy steps behind them. Hendricks was coming down the cinder bank from the road, accompanied by a heavy-set man with an enormous head and no hat. The man was wearing a striped pyjama top under his jacket. It was the lock-keeper. 'Jesus Christ,' he said, without preamble, addressing Jenkins, 'do you know what hour it is?'

Jenkins ignored the question. 'We need the water level up,' he said. 'You'll have to do it slowly—there's a body in there.'

As he moved away, the man Walsh or Wallace tried to pluck at his sleeve again to detain him but was ignored. The lock-keeper went to the edge of the canal bank and leaned forward with his hands on his knees and squinted down at the body. 'Jesus,' he said, 'it's only a child.'

They positioned the squad car sideways with its front wheels on the path so the headlights would illuminate the scene. The lock-keeper had used his key and the water was falling in a gleaming rush through the opening in the sluice-gates. Quinlan and Hendricks got on to the barge and found two long wooden poles and braced them against the wall of the canal to keep the barge from swaying in and crushing the body.

The corpse was turned face down, the arms lolling and its backside shining with a phosphorescent glow. Walsh or Wallace and his girl had given their details to Quinlan but still had not departed. It was apparent the girl wanted to be gone, but the man hung on despite his earlier anxieties, eager no doubt to have a look at the corpse when it came up. Quinlan had brought a sheet of tarpaulin from the boot of the squad car and now he spread it on the grass, and the two guards knelt on the granite flagstones and hauled the sodden body from the water and laid it on its back. There was silence for a moment.

'That's no child,' Quinlan said.

Hendricks leaned down quickly and peeled off the man's one sock. It seemed the decent thing to do, somehow, though no one made any comment.

'Look at his face,' the man said in an awed voice. They had not heard him approach, but he was leaning in between them now, staring avidly.

'Kicked the shite out of him, they did,' Quinlan said. Jenkins gave him a look; Quinlan had a foul mouth and no sense of occasion. It was a dead man he was speaking of, after all. Hendricks knelt on one knee and folded in the tarpaulin on either side to cover the lower half of the body.

'Poor bugger,' the lock-keeper said.

No one had thought to send for an ambulance. How were they going to get the body out of here? Jenkins thrust a fist into the pocket of his overcoat and clenched it in anger. He had no one but himself to blame; that, he reflected bitterly, was what it was to be in charge. Hendricks went to the squad car for the walkie-talkie, but it was being temperamental and would produce only a loud crackling noise and now and then a harsh squawk. 'There's no use shaking the fucking thing,' Quinlan said, with amused disdain, but Hendricks pretended not to hear. He kept putting the machine to his ear and talking loudly into the mouthpiece—'Hello, Pearse Street, come in, Pearse Street!'—then holding it away from himself and glaring at it in disgust, as if it were a pet that was refusing to perform a simple trick he had spent time and energy teaching it.

Jenkins turned to the girl sitting on the bench. 'Where was that phone box?'

She was still in a state of shock, and it took her a moment to understand him. 'Away down there,' she said, pointing along Mespil Road. 'Opposite Parson's bookshop. The one on Leeson Street is broken, as usual.'

'Christ,' Jenkins said under his breath. He turned back and spoke to Quinlan. 'Go over there along Wilton Terrace and have a look. There might be one nearer.'

Quinlan scowled. His expression made it clear that he did not relish taking orders.

'I'll go,' Hendricks said. He shook the walkie-talkie again. 'This yoke is useless.'

Jenkins dithered. He had given a direct order to Quinlan; it should have been obeyed, and Hendricks should have kept out of it. He felt giddy for a moment. Getting people to acknowledge your authority was no easy thing, though Inspector Hackett did it seemingly without effort. Was it just a matter of experience, or did you have to be born with the knack?

'Right,' he said to Hendricks gruffly, although Hendricks had already set off. Should he call him back, make him salute, or something? He was pretty sure a fellow on the beat was supposed to salute a detective sergeant. He wished now he had phoned Hackett in the first place and risked the old bugger's wrath.

Walsh or Wallace, who was showing no sign at all now of his earlier eagerness to be gone, went up to Quinlan and began to talk to him about a match that was set for Croke Park on Sunday. How was it that sporting types always recognised each other straight off? They were both smoking, Quinlan cupping the cigarette in his palm—officers were not supposed to smoke on duty, Jenkins was certain of that. Should he reprimand him, tell him to put that fag out at once? He decided to pretend he had not seen him light up. He realised he was sweating, and ran a finger around the inside of his shirt collar.

The girl on the bench called softly to the man—'Alfie, will we go?'—but he ignored her. He was bare-headed as well as being without his jacket, and though he must have been freezing by now, he appeared not to mind.

Jenkins looked at the body lying on the grass beside the towpath. The water had drained from the hair, which seemed to be red, though it was hard to be sure in the stark glow of the street-lamp. Jenkins felt himself shiver. What must it be like, being dead? Like nothing, he supposed, unless there really was a Heaven and a Hell, all that, which he doubted, despite what the priests and everyone else had spent years earnestly assuring him was the case.

At last Hendricks came back. He had found a phone box. The Holy Family was the hospital on duty tonight. The ambulance was out but they would send it as soon as it came in. 'Have they only the one?' Jenkins asked incredulously.

'Seems like it,' Hendricks said.

'A fine player, that lad,' Wallace or Walsh was saying. 'Dirty, though.'

'Oh, a tough bollocks,' Quinlan agreed, and chuckled. He took a drag of his cigarette, throwing a glance of lazy insolence in Jenkins's direction as he did so. 'I seen him in the quarter-final against Kerry,' he said, and laughed again. 'I'm telling you, if that little fucker got his elbow in your ribs you'd know all about it.'

The girl stood up from the bench. 'I'm going,' she said to the man's back. He flapped a hand at her placatingly, and Quinlan said something under his breath and the man gave a loud guffaw. The girl moved irresolutely towards the cinder track that led up to the road. When she reached the gate in the railings she turned back, though it was not the man she looked at this time but Jenkins, and she smiled. For years afterwards, whenever he thought of the case of the body in the canal, it was that sad, wan little smile that he remembered, and he felt, every time, a mysterious pang.

extracts reading groups
competitions books new
discounts extracts events
competitions reading groups
books new extracts discounts
events
reading groups books extracts events
extracts reading groups
new books titles reading groups
interviews extracts
events extracts new
discounts books interviews new
new books events events
events new extracts
discounts extracts discounts
www.panmacmillan.com
extracts events reading groups
competitions books extracts new